2ᴺᴰ EARTH EMPLACEMENT

EDWARD & EUNICE VOUGHT

Text Copyright 2011 Edward & Eunice Vought

All Rights Reserved

Dedication

This book is dedicated to those people

who survive by their ability to adapt

and being prepared for whatever is thrown at them.

PART II

1

It's early fall and we are about as busy as I have ever been around the house. It seems like everything in the garden and in the fields is getting ripe at the same time. The fact that we planted at different intervals to prevent this doesn't seem to matter. With the addition of our new group or family, I think we need to clarify the different groups that all form our extended family. There is our original group, at least mostly, which totals seventy men, women and children at last count. There are three other groups in our extended family. The leader of the next largest group is Ryan, they total thirty-six at last count. Doc McEvoy's group is right at thirty, and Barb's group has sixteen. We consider ourselves one big family even though only a few are actually related by blood.

The one common bond we have is that all of us moved here within the past year from northern cities. As far as we know the population of the Earth we are on has been just about wiped out, except for some scattered groups like ours. We have had radio contact with other groups, only most of them are nowhere near as large or as strong as we are. We all left the cities to get away from the two legged predators, plus the food in the cities would eventually run out, and the groups depending on the scavenging way of life would perish. I know this is going to be difficult to believe, but there are currently five of us who came to this alternate dimension or alternate Earth, whatever it is. Four of us have strong military background, that's myself, Tim, Ken, and Gary. The other one like us is Sara; she was a civilian pilot before coming here. We feel, as do the rest of our families, that we have been sent or brought here for the purpose of helping these good people survive.

All of us read the Bible, and although we are not what you would call religious fanatics, we can't help but wonder if perhaps Heavenly Father is giving us the opportunity to start mankind over again, like he did in the time of Noah. Only this time man almost wiped everyone out with a neutron war. It was more practical than the more damaging nuclear and atom bombs. The neutron bombs killed off most of the population, but did very little damage to the cities and the countryside. The world the others and I came from has neutron technology, but they still choose to kill each other off more systematically, with wars and poverty. I can't complain because I was as efficient at killing as anyone I knew in that world. Tim and I were Navy SEALs, but we were working with a joint military operation with the Air Force Para-Rescue teams. My medical training as a corpsman has helped us tremendously here. So have the ability and the willingness to fight that Tim and I brought with us.

Before we got so busy with harvesting and preparing the food for storage, Tim and I were working with all the men and about half the women from all the families, training them in case we have to fight off a concentrated attack. A majority of our family has already been trained for the most part, but we are still fine tuning and adding to what they know. So far everyone is willing, and is showing that they are more than capable, if what we are seeing is how they will react if attacked. Tim, Ken, Sara, and Gary all feel that it is not if, but when we are attacked. All of us from the other world or dimension, lived lives that didn't exactly make us trusting of our fellow man. We are the most concerned about Barbara's group, because they are the smallest group with the least number of adults. We are all within two to five miles of each other, but a lot can happen in the five to ten minutes waiting for help to arrive.

Barbs group and Doc McEvoys group joined us a little late in the season to get a full crop in, but thanks to Frank, our group and Ryan's group planted enough for all of us to have plenty. Between what we are putting up and the stores that we are able to get from markets in the surrounding cities, we should do fine through the winter. Since we already survived one winter, we have a pretty good idea of what to expect. We are definitely more prepared than we were last year and that was the best winter that all of our family ever had. Prior to coming here, they spent their winters trying to keep from freezing or starving to death. Last year everyone had plenty to eat and was at least warm, that was a very big relief for the mothers in our family. No one wants to see their children freezing or hungry.

Harvesting our crops is a lot of work, but many willing hands make it seem much easier, because we get to know each other better when we work together. One of the topics of conversation is where we should start looking for other settlements like ours, or even individual groups that may want to join our family. We have heard from some groups on the shortwave radio, but it is so intermittent that we are not sure where they are. We know of some groups like ours in Texas and California, but they say they are much smaller than our group. We have decided that when we get the harvesting and the canning done, we will take some trips to see what we can find. We all agree that we will leave most of the fighting men home to protect the family, so only a couple of us men will go at a time along with probably our wives.

Dayna says she would love to go with me, but little Timmy is much too young to be traveling like we will have to. Tim can't go yet because Carrie is expecting most any time now and he should be here with her. We have tentatively agreed that Ryan and Carol will go with Robin and me, at least on the first trip. We have even traced out a route to take, and are marking off several to cover the area in an ever widening circle, beginning here of course. I can't speak for the others, but my life has never been as enjoyable as the past year has been. I don't ever remember working as hard as I have since moving here, nor do I remember ever feeling better about it. I know Ma and Gunny Horton would love to be here with all of us.

The days slip past, and the pantries and shelves in all our basements are getting full of the bounty that we are seeing from our labors. Dan, Don, and Andrew have been joined by another hunting enthusiast named Kyle, who is about the same age as they are. He came with Doc McEvoys group. Those four young men have kept us all in fresh meat, and have also made several large bags of beef and venison jerky, as well as enough smoked sausage and pepperoni to keep all of us happy. They found the recipe for making both types of sausage in one of the file cabinet drawers in the big room where we take care of meat. One very big accomplishment that we have enjoyed tremendously is making cheese. One of the books we brought with us from the city was on the making of different cheeses. We also found several books in the library in town on the subject as well.

Gary actually worked at a place where they made several kinds of cheese. Don't ask me how they do it. But with his help, the girls have made some very good cheese that is very close to Mozzarella. With Tim's and my help we have made some pretty good pizza. Of course the girls made the dough, and we made some really good sauce with some of the tomatoes from the garden. Speaking of sauce, the young men found a recipe for Italian sausage with those other recipes. We got the spices we needed from town and made a large batch of the sausage which came out very good. I remember how Ma Horton made spaghetti sauce, so Dayna and I whipped up about twenty quarts of sauce with Italian sausage and meat balls. Now everyone in all the families loves Italian food.

I love the great breakfast sausage we make with ground pork, and the recipe the kind people left behind. They also left instructions how to dehydrate many of the fruits and vegetables that we grow, to preserve them. We have successfully dehydrated potatoes, carrots, onions, apples, peaches, pears, cherries, and apricots. Those we are able to put in plastic bags, inside of plastic cans, that we found with lids that seal them. The books we have on preserving say that food preserved this way can last for a very long time and still taste good when you rehydrate it for use. To be honest we doubt if the fruits will get a chance to last a long time, because everyone loves to snack on them when we are sitting around reading or just listening to music and talking. There are still a lot of apples, peaches, and pears left in the orchard so we are planning to do more as soon as we can get the time.

While we are busy putting the last of the wheat into bags and sewing them shut, Frank and Dayna's dad, Tom, Rich, and Ryan are getting the fields ready to plant winter wheat again. We have already laid out where we are going to plant our crops this year and what we are going to plant. Ryan and Carol decided that this would not be a good time to be away from their family, so Sara and Gary are going with Robin, me, and Don, who is one of our best hunters. Sara and Gary are now married as she predicted they would be. We still tease her about the way they decided to get married. We were picking peaches during the summer when Sara, who was picking from the same tree as Gary, turned to him and said that it is about time that they got married. Gary said he couldn't think of any reasons not to, so they were married that evening when we finished picking for the day.

Today is Saturday so we figure we will rest on the Sabbath, and leave on Monday. We are taking two vehicles in case we find anybody to bring back with us. We have the CB radios, but we will probably be out of range to use them. We wish there was some way to remain in contact with the family while we are away. We are planning to mainly check the cities and towns, because if people are living like we are, they will probably not want to leave to join us. Robin's children, who are like my own, want to spend as much time with us as they can before we leave. Teddy wishes he could go with us, but I tell him that at twelve he has to be the man of the house while I am gone. That makes him feel better even if Kathy, who is ten, and Karen who is eight, tell him that he is not the boss of them. They will only listen to Dayna and Melissa.

Tammy and Tina the twins tell us we can take Zeus with us to protect us if we would like to. I tell them that he needs them to watch over him, so it will be better if he stays here. At five those two don't go anywhere without that dog. He will not allow them to go away from the house unless they are with one of the adults. If they try, he barks his head off, and does his best to push them back. As big as he is, he can usually push them too. Now that the time is here to leave, Dayna doesn't want me to go. It is only going to be for a few days so it will not be too bad. Billy and Ramona come over on Sunday afternoon to make sure we know what to do in case we get in trouble. I tell them not to worry, I'll have my cell phone, and all I have to do is dial 911. They look at me like I am crazy, but that is nothing new, so I explain what I am talking about and they can laugh at my joke anyway.

When Monday morning comes around, I have to admit I would prefer not to go. Before coming to this world and meeting Dayna I never cared where I went or for how long. The hardest part is going to be not seeing little Timmy every day. He is almost two months old and is a lot more fun to play with. Sara and Gary come over and tell me to get a grip. We will be gone for less than a week. We are taking some of the jerky and dried fruit as well as some canned food to eat while we are gone. We are taking the van and the pickup with several cans of gas just in case. We will probably be able to get gas at some of the stations along the way. Tim comes over and asks if I need to use the credit card, or if I have enough cash for the trip. It's a good thing everyone knows our sense of humor, or they would think we are nuts.

We start out going south, we have been to the closest towns or cities and those are more east and west of our location. There is a city about seventy miles due south of us, plus some that appear to be small towns in between. Having to pick our way through the cars and across broken roads, and other debris that has accumulated, only allows us to make about twenty miles an hour. Around here it is mainly because of the broken roads more than the cars. This is primarily farm land so it wasn't so heavily populated. We see many farms that look like they could easily be put back into use, so we are keeping a log of where we are when we see items of interest. About two hours from home we find a small town that has a gas station, a tavern and a store. The store is pretty good sized and looks like no one has been in it since the war. There are also several houses in a row that looks like they made up the town. This is what Gunny used to refer to as a blink and miss town. If you blink going through it, you will miss it.

We mark on our log sheet to remind us to stop on the way back to check out the store. An hour later we go through another town about the same size as the first one. As with the other one there are no signs of life or even that anyone has been through here in many years. We get to the city about an hour after going through the second small town. There are several stores in this town and all of them show signs that someone has been using them. We stop and go into the first large store we come to and see that the shelves have been just about emptied, and so has the stock room. The only things we find that are of interest to us are the canning jars, lids and rings. We find several cases of each, so we put them in the pickup and go on. The next two stores in town show the same as the first did. Again we find canning supplies that we can use, so we take those. Apparently the people who have been visiting this city or who are living here are not into preserving food.

We see smoke toward what looks like the middle of the city, so we head toward it, being very watchful that we don't wander into some kind of trap. We get close to where the smoke is rising and we see two young children coming out of a store that is close by. They are carrying some canned goods, but when they see us they drop what they are carrying and run. We try to tell them we will not harm them, but they continue running. We follow in the direction that they went and come to an old building that is obviously being used as a home for some of the people here. The people are staying inside and are looking out of windows or doorways at us as we approach the building. We have the ladies along to help anyone we might meet perhaps trust us. Knowing how the people up north had to survive I think we can pretty much rule out trust until they get to know us.

Robin sees two small children standing just inside a doorway so she walks toward them talking softly to them. She gets within twenty feet of them, when a woman comes running out of the building across the street, and starts pleading with us not to hurt her babies. We try to assure her that we have no intentions of hurting anybody. We tell her and anyone else, who is within hearing range, that we are here to help them if they would like us to. The woman asks if we are from the south and we tell her no, actually we have a settlement to the north and are wondering if there are any others, like ourselves, who may want to join us. Two other women come out of the building across the street and walk over to us. They say that we are much cleaner and better dressed than the men who come from the south looking for people to take with them.

The group we are talking to has five women, two older men, and nine children. They tell us that some of the children's parents have been taken by those men from the south. We ask if there are any other groups living around here and they tell us they have seen some others, but were too afraid to try to talk to them, or to even get close. The two children we saw turn out to be a young man and a young lady about nine years old. They were getting food to take back for their family. Robin and I leave Sara and Gary with this group and go looking for others. It doesn't take long. They are living like the others, and are about as scared of everyone else as I have ever seen. Robin is able to win their trust and their story is the same as the other groups. They say they have only seen the one other group, but they have seen smoke coming from a section of the city a short distance away.

You would think it would be difficult to find so few people in a fairly good sized city, but as with all creatures, people need certain things to survive. Food is very high on that list, so even though these people are nomadic, like our groups were, they still have to follow the stores. Because once that source of food is gone, they will probably move to another city or starve, because they know nothing else. From the looks of the stores we are seeing, these people will not have food for more than another year. If it lasts that long, or they don't get taken by these mysterious men from the south. Apparently some of them are able to hide when they come, because there are still people here.

We are checking the area for people when we see smoke rising a short distance away. We ask one of the others if they would come with us, because they will most likely hide if they see us coming. They do, but if we had wanted to get to them, we could have easily. Again there are mostly women and young children. They tell us that the men acted as bait to lead the men from the south off to protect them. The more I hear about these men from the south makes me really want to meet them. We were planning to go further south today, but finding these people makes us change our minds. It is getting late, so we decide to spend the night, and head back in the morning to get these people to safety with our groups. Don seems to have taken a liking to one of the older teenage girls in the groups we found today.

He is showing her how we hook up a gas stove to a propane tank and can cook food indoors that way. We go to the closest store and get more than enough canned goods for the group. We could probably have gotten back tonight, but we are kind of hoping the men from the south come looking in the morning. I am angry at what they are doing, but Sara and Gary are obsessed with catching them, and getting the people back that they have enslaved. At least that's what it sounds like they are doing. Our new friends tell us that they sometimes come in the night, or early in the morning, so we take turns standing guard in two hour shifts.

2

I am the last one on guard duty, or should I say Robin and I are, because she gets up when I do and keeps me company watching the sun come up. We are snuggling to keep warm and talking quietly when we hear the sound of an engine coming toward our location. I am trying to place the direction of the sound when Sara and Gary are beside us, asking if we hear that. They are both carrying guns as are Don, Robin, and me. We determine where the truck is coming from and decide to set a trap for them. From the sounds of the engine, it is a small truck or van, and it has a hole in the exhaust system. Don comes out of the house accompanied by the young lady whose name is Olivia. She says that's the men from the south, she would recognize that noise anywhere. That's another reason they didn't think we were them, because our vehicles don't sound like that. She didn't call it a vehicle; she just said the things we travel in. Sara tells me if that is too technical for me, she can break it down simpler for me.

Robin comes to my rescue though and tells her to quit picking on me. I can't help it if I was given all brawn and very little brain. She tells her I make up for it in other ways though that she will not expand upon, because there are children present. I just keep my mouth shut, I have tried to defend myself and it always gets me picked on more. I am concentrating on defending us from the men from the south. We hear the sound over by the market we got supplies at last evening, and then we don't hear it anymore. Obviously they have turned off the motor because we hear it backfire, probably because of the hole in the exhaust system. As if she can read my mind, Sara looks at me and says the timing is off, she could hear it missing on one cylinder. Gary agrees, but then the traitor always agrees with her, so that doesn't prove a thing.

Olivia and her mother, whose name is Marge, is whispering that now the men will spread out, and look for people to capture. I decide to give them someone to take. I tell Sara to go out there and let them capture her, it would serve them right. I get smacked by Robin, Sara, Olivia, and her mother. Women have no sense of humor. I tell them I will let myself get captured to get close to them, and then the others can turn the tables on them. Marge says that it will not work. She says none of their men are as big or as muscular. They will never believe that I am one of them. Before I can say anything, Don takes off in the direction of the store. We follow at a distance, but we keep him in sight all the time. Olivia asks me to please make sure he doesn't get hurt. I assure her that he is a very tough young man, but we will not let anything happen to our best hunter.

We are in a residential area of two story houses, much like any neighborhood. I kind of wish Tim was here, because I know that he has been trained in urban warfare. I'm not sure what training Gary has had along those lines. We go a couple of blocks and we can now hear distinct voices coming toward us. It sounds like they are arguing about having to get up so early and drive here. They are saying that there are probably not anymore people here anyway. A second voice says that he saw a blonde the last time they were here and he wants to find her. He says he will take his turn before they leave. The other voice says he will as well, because he is tired of the women they have back at the place. This is the worst kind of predator I can think of. They have absolutely no compassion for others, but corner them and they beg not to be hurt. These two are dying today if I have anything to say about it. I'm sure that's Olivia they are talking about.

Don takes the gun out of his waistband when we hear their voices. Something tells me I will have to stand in line to kill these two. We all have our guns out. Sara has a 9mm that is a twin to the one I carry. I am just hoping to find out where these guys come from while they can still talk. We are about a short block away from the two voices when we hear another voice, yelling that he has a couple women trapped in a building. The voice is coming from our left so we all head that way. There must be some women in the city that we didn't find yesterday. We go about a hundred yards, when the other voice yells that they went out the side. I am not expecting to have three teenage girls and an older woman come running straight at me not more than twenty yards away. They haven't seen me yet and almost run into me before they do.

They are obviously frightened and come to a dead stop before they run me over. I put my hand to my mouth signaling for them to be quiet. They start to turn when they see Robin and Sara motioning for them to come to them. Then all heck breaks loose. The guys that are hunting the girls come running around the building. They are yelling, to scare the girls more, and telling them what they are going to do to them. The first one is only about three steps from me when he sees me. I cover that distance and tell him he will have to make other plans; the ladies dance cards are full. I take him square in the face with my forearm and elbow. He goes down like he was hit with an axe handle. The other three, there must have been two in that second group as well, stop short and raise their guns to fire. They never get the chance because the bullets from three guns end the argument before it really ever got started.

  I tell the others to watch the only one left alive while I go see if there are any more. I don't see anyone else, but I hear the vehicle start up and take off, headed out of town. I can see it just before it turns a corner, but I can't get a shot off. I do see that it is what we used to call a panel truck, like the ones they used to use for deliveries, where we came from. I look around a little more, when I don't find anyone I head back to where I left the others. The guy I knocked out is now awake and is obviously scared. He can see the bodies of the guys he came here with. The people we met yesterday are coming to where we are, they heard the gunshots, but weren't sure who won, until they heard the truck heading out of town as fast as it could. When they see the one we captured just about all of them want to hit him, and several ask if they could please shoot him, if we will show them how to use a gun.

  At least this guy isn't like the criminals where I come from. If he was, he would be yelling excessive force, and demanding to speak with his attorney. In this world, he knows he is very close to joining his friends. I ask him where his friends are. He says that he will tell me if I will promise to let him go. I call a meeting of our group and we step off to the side. I tell them I don't like letting this guy go, but it sure would help if we could find out where those guys are. They are already warned that we could be coming after them, but that won't be until we come back, so they may relax by then. We decide to trust him, even if the others don't think we should. Gary asks him where his friends are and what they do with the people they take. He says that they use the people they take to do the work. The women work and are used by the people in charge for pleasure. If they are pretty enough they don't have to work as hard.

This guy is making me sicker by the moment. I am watching his face when Gary asks him where they are located. He starts talking in circles, about how you go down this road then go down another. I see his eyes look toward the roof across the street and a faint smile crosses his face. I take about ten steps to the right, where I am under an overhang, and look up at the building across the street. I see nothing, and then just as I think it was my imagination, I see a face appear over the edge. Then a rifle barrel is being thrust over pointing at the people on the ground. It's a fairly long shot for a hand gun, but that's all I have. At least I can give him something to think about. I fire at the head, and hear the rifle bark death for the guy we were questioning. My second shot must hit the shooter because he stands erect then falls over the edge into the street below. There is no way to know if he was trying to kill the other one, or if that happened as an accident. Neither of them are talking so we will just have to find where they take the people.

We gather up everyone that is going back with us and decide to take a sweep of the city just to make sure. It's a good thing we do, because we find another small group that has three young women, two children, and a man that looks like he is in his forties. We get back to the farm at about four in the afternoon. They are expecting us because we called on the CB when we were about five miles away. The leaders of the other groups are here to meet the new people and to discuss where they should live, at least for now. Later they may have a preference once they get to know everybody. Olivia asks if she can stay here if that is where Don lives. There is room in the house he lives in for her and her mom, but we are all betting that her mom loses her roommate very soon.

Doc McEvoys group takes one of the groups and Barbs group takes the rest. Her group is the smallest and can really use the few men that came back with us. All the people that came back with us are amazed at the way we live. That's not too surprising because we are sometimes amazed at how lucky and blessed we have been. We explained to them before we even came back what will be expected of them if they are going to live with our groups. It's not much really, all we expect is that everyone does their share of the work. We also realize that the people we find have never lived like we do, so it will take them time to learn the different chores we all do. Heck I'm still learning some of the chores that I don't do often or have never done before.

We hold a family council to determine what we should do about the men from the south. Everyone agrees that we should at least try to find them, and free anybody that is being held against their will. We also agree that we should begin cleaning up another farm that is a mile from Barbs family. It is a nice place with four or five houses and some sturdy looking barns. The new people are excited to get started helping with the cleaning and rebuilding. We also decide that we need fighting men along on the next trip we take looking for the others. We also know we can't leave the group without protection while we are gone as well. The gentleman who was with the last group we found in the city volunteers to come along. Oh yes, his name is Ray and although he hasn't had a lot of experience, he is more than willing, so we will use him. Sara and Gary both want to go again. Robin decides to stay home because she missed the children too badly. Ray's wife Carol says she will go because she knows at least some of those who have been taken, and with her along they may not be so frightened of us. Dan, who is Don's brother, decides to come along because Don says he has to make sure Olivia learns her chores properly.

We have an excellent meal and play some music for our new friends. Only a few of them even remember electric lights and eating fresh meat and bread. Tonight for the first time some of them will sleep in a warm bed in a heated home. When they are about to leave to go to their respective homes, Marla, the mother of the children that Robin and I saw first, tells us all how thankful she is that we have brought them here to live. She says that she learned to pray when she was a little girl and she has been praying with all her might for the past few weeks because she was out of options that were under her control. She also asks us if we all lived like they did, how did we ever know to come here, and how have we accomplished so much? We smile and tell her we will explain all that later. Now let's get a good night's rest so we can go after their family and friends tomorrow.

When they leave and we get ready for bed, I get to play with the children for a while, which me and they missed very much. Teddy says he thinks he should be able to go with us because he is almost a man. At twelve he is doing very well with his fighting lessons and can shoot quite well also. I tell him I could really use him on this trip, but I have a dilemma, if both of the men in the family leave, who will take care of the women and children? He thinks for a minute and tells me he will stay home, but those girls better start listening when he tells them something. His sisters Kathy and Karen stick their tongues out at him. Tina and Tammy who are stepsisters tell him that they will do what he says, if mommy says they should. I tell him that if the girls are doing something they shouldn't, or that is dangerous, to tell the moms and they will make sure they don't do it again.

Teddy says he can do that, but he thinks the girls should listen to him the way they do me. Robin and Dayna who are sitting on either side of me whisper, "Since when," so that only I can hear them. Melissa, who is holding Tina, smiles and says, "Yeah right." Don't get the wrong idea about our relationship. If there is an issue of safety, or something important, I have the last word, because that is what I know best. When it comes to raising the children, I bow to the women of the house. Oh, by the way, Dayna asked me if I explained our situation to you. I kind of forgot that you may not know us very well yet. I am married to all three of the women I live with and all the children call me daddy, even though little Timmy is my only biological child. It was the girl's idea, not mine, but I am not complaining either. We started plural marriage because there are so many more women than men in our groups.

So far it is working well, I love Dayna, Robin, and Melissa and I am very proud that the children think of me as their father. Morning comes much too quickly, as it has a tendency to do. This time we are taking more fire power along in case we need it. Roy who is a member of Ryan's family decided to come along. We are glad of that because he has proven to be a very good shot with any weapon and he is his group's best hunter. Dan is bringing along a couple of bows with enough arrows to fight a war with. He is as good with his bow as Roy is with the guns. We are taking two vans and the pickup truck. We saw a couple of dealerships in the city that had some very nice stake body trucks in the lot. There were also two propane trucks and a gasoline tanker in that city. We will have to take a look at getting those, when we have accomplished getting those people freed.

Billy really wishes he could come along, but they may need him here. He is definitely the strongest man in any of the groups, and the biggest. He is over seven feet tall and weighs about 350 pounds. He is also one of the nicest people you could ever meet. We take off about mid-morning. We do not even know where we are going once we get past the city. It takes less time getting there this time because we had to push some vehicles and other obstacles out of the way the first time. We stop by the propane trucks and see that they are both almost full. We will definitely get these either on the way back, or we will come back for them. The gasoline tanker is also almost full, so we will get that as well. We go to where we last saw the guys from the south. The bodies are still here and so is some sign that we didn't expect.

Looking around we find where the truck was parked and not too surprising there is a puddle of oil on the ground. Not a lot, but enough to see they have an oil leak. Now, according to the people we found here, those guys came here fairly often, so there may be a trail of oil leading to where they come from. There is not a lot of traffic on the roads, so it stands to reason that if we find oil on the road it came from their vehicle. Like most small cities there are only a couple of main roads in and out of here. Gary and I decide to walk ahead of the vehicles and look for signs of oil on the road. It doesn't take very long until we find what we are looking for. We don't have to follow the trail closely because there are only so many places they could turn off. We drive a good ten miles before we see more sign that someone has been driving on the road. This is at a cross roads and there are tire tracks on the pavement where someone took the corner too fast, more than once, by the amount of rubber on the road.

We have to be more careful now because we have no idea how far away they are. We are all watching a different direction searching for any sign of life. We go down this road for about six miles then we see the same kind of tracks on the pavement. We are following cautiously, still looking all around, hoping to see them before they see us. We are hoping to see some smoke maybe or something else we can see from a distance then go ahead on foot to see what we are getting into. We are barely crawling, not wanting to tip them off that we are coming. This reminds me of some of the missions that Tim and I have been on. Sara looks at me and asks me if this feels more like home to me. The unit Tim and I were in rescued her when her plane got shot down in a war zone. That was only a little over a year ago, but it seems like such a long time ago. I was going to say worlds ago, but it really was.

I turn to look behind us and when I turn back forward again I am startled by a young woman, who almost runs into the side of the van. She is disheveled like she is running away from something or someone and is about at the end of her endurance. Carol says she knows that girl, who is trying to run around the van, to get away from us. Carol, Ray, and I jump out of the van and Carol calls to her that we are friends. She looks extremely frightened and unsure whether or not to believe us. The next thing I know, I am face to face with a very dirty man carrying a gun, obviously following the young lady. He is as startled as I am, but I am better trained because I strike out with my forearm and elbow knocking him to the ground. He is not out though and is scrambling to get his gun around to bear on me when I hear the whistling sound of an arrow going past my ear, and see an arrow sticking through the dirty man.

My first fear is that they are traveling together and now we have killed her husband, but she finally relaxes and all but falls into Carols arms. She is sobbing almost uncontrollably trying to tell Carol what happened. We give her some water and let her sit in the van, where at least she is comfortable, and can catch her breath. Finally she can tell us what we need to know. She was apparently working in the fields and overheard the dirty guy telling one of the other guards that he was going to take her back to the barn and teach her some manners. We all understand what he meant. She says when he unlocked the leg irons she pushed him down and took off running. She ran for what seemed like a long time, all the while the dirty guy kept yelling for her to stop because he would just hurt her more when he finally catches her. She says she was just about ready to give up, because she couldn't run anymore, when she ran into us. At first she thought that she had run into some of the others, even though she has never seen the vehicles.

She eats the food we give her like she is starving and probably is. We can finally ask her where the others are, how many of them are there, and how many captors are there. She says they brought two more girls in last week, which makes it fifty-three. Thirty-three are women or girls and twenty are men or boys. She says there are ten guards now, there were more, but a couple days ago several didn't come back with the others. Carol and Ray tell her we know. They got killed when we tried to capture them. That news makes her have more hope. Sometimes when you are treated badly by others, you have a tendency to think of them as being invincible. She can see that the one chasing her wasn't. Speaking of that we better get somewhere out of sight before they come looking for their compatriot. We go back the way we came about a mile. There is a place I remembered seeing on the way in where we can get the vehicles out of sight behind some brush.

She can finally tell us approximately where the farm is that we are looking for. She says they keep the prisoners chained wherever they are. In the fields they have chains running down the aisles that they work in and in the barn, where they sleep, they chain them in a stall. She says that they have been very busy picking vegetables and fruit. They aren't allowed to eat any while they are picking. If they get caught they get whipped or worse. Gary, Roy, Dan, and I decide to go in on foot. Ray says he would like to go, but I hesitate to leave the women and the vehicles unguarded. Besides I know all the men with me, I don't know how he will react if he has to kill someone. Actually, in this case it's when, we can't let these animals live to do this to others. Please do not think we enjoy killing, we don't, but we have no organized law, so we have to do what is necessary to survive. Believe me; those men will be trying to kill us as much as we will be them. The young lady whose name is Amy wants to go with us, she says the others won't trust us because they don't know us. It takes a lot of courage to go back into a situation like that one, but we are sure she is correct.

We are waiting until we see the layout before we make any plans. We work our way to the farm, if you want to call it that. It is a group of rundown buildings that was a farm once. These guys probably came upon it, with the fruit trees and vegetables growing wild like at our places, and were too lazy to work it, so they captured slaves to do the work for them. Man's inhumanity toward man never ceases to amaze me. Getting into the barn will not be any trouble, but getting all ten, if Amy is correct, will not be easy. It is getting dark quickly so we make our way down to the back of the barn. There are so many boards missing that we can see pretty much everything going on in there. The nights get cold, and almost none of the people we can see even have coats on.

The back door to the barn is broken and hanging on one hinge, so Roy and I go in that door while Gary and Dan work their way around to the side door. It is so dark inside plus we are in the shadows so no one even sees us come in. We start to take a step toward the first stall when two of the filthiest people I have ever seen come in the side door carrying a lantern. They head to a stall toward the front and we hear a young woman's voice pleading for them not to take her. That is followed by an older woman's voice pleading with them to take her and leave her daughter alone. She tells them she is only twelve and they will hurt her too badly. They just laugh and say that will make it all the more fun.

They unlock the chain and drag the screaming girl out the side door that they came in through. I hand the bolt cutters to Roy and tell him to start freeing these people. I'm going after those two who just left. I back out the door and cut toward the back where I am hoping to cut them off before they can attack that poor girl. I am almost too where I am hoping to meet them when I hear a blood curdling scream that came from a man not the young lady. I keep going and I see Gary and Sara coming toward me with the young lady between them sobbing. The scream brought everyone coming from what is obviously the main house. The man who was screaming is still crying for help. I ask Sara what happened and Gary asks me if I have ever seen a man gelded.

Apparently Sara decided to join us and just happened to walk straight into that pair that had the girl. Gary saw them leave the barn so he followed for the same reason I did. He got to them just in time to see the young girl thrown on the ground and one of the men taking down his pants. The one that was watching lurched suddenly and fell to the ground with his throat cut from ear to ear. He didn't make a sound. The second one wasn't that lucky. Gary says he saw the knife flash and heard something hit the ground then that guy let out the scream that I heard. Sara just says he will never assault another young girl or old girl for that matter. I was going to ask her what she is doing here, but in the mood she is in, I will wait until later.

We can see four men running toward the sound of the dying man so we cut loose with our hand guns and all four drop where they were standing. We stick our head in the barn door to see how Roy and Dan are doing getting all the captives loose. Amy tells us that four of the women were taken up to the house earlier. As angry as I am, I start toward the house with a gun in each hand. Sara and Gary are only a step behind. The people in the barn are now helping our guys get the rest loose. We hear gun fire and the bullets kick up dust around our feet. That reminds me that I have far too much to lose to get myself killed foolishly. I duck behind a car that is parked in the yard. Gary and Sara are behind a small truck that is parked behind the car. I no sooner get behind the car when the window directly above my head is shot out. I look toward Sara and she smiles and tells me it's about time I realized where I am. I definitely have to agree with her.

We are exchanging gunfire with the people in the house. I can count five different guns and that is just about right for what Amy told us. I am looking for a way to get closer to the house or to at least get a decent shot at those inside, but there is just nothing big enough to do that. I am wishing for the .50 I used to use when I was a Navy SEAL when I hear my .307 coming from the loft in the barn. I look back and can see just enough of Roy to know he has the rifle and is obviously putting it to good use. There is another volley from inside the house, only this time I can only count four guns. The .307 roars again and we can hear someone fall out of a second story window and hit the ground hard. He isn't moving so I am pretty confident that they are down to three.

I am getting ready to work my way around the car and maybe get to the house keeping in the deeper shadows. I see movement out of the corner of my eye, I hear the whooshing sound of an arrow and see a figure stand straight up and fall face down in the dirt. Dan is sure pulling his own weight and then some on this trip. I signal for Gary and Sara to draw their attention while I try to get inside and end this thing now. I hear the two guns left firing back so I crawl around the car and into the shadows beyond. When I have only a few steps to go I rush the house in a crouching run. I was going to knock the door in, but it is open. I almost fall down because I was expecting to come in contact with the door. There is one man at the front window firing when I come into the room. He turns quickly, but not quick enough to shoot before I do. He falls out through the window. There was very little glass in it anyway.

The last one must be upstairs, there is no more firing so maybe he is out of ammunition or someone got lucky and hit him. Two of the women that they brought in tonight are lying on the floor, kind of behind a beat up couch. They are scared, but other than that they don't appear to be hurt. Gary and Sara rush the house expecting to be shot at, but no shots are fired. I tell them to cover me, and start to go upstairs, when a man starts coming downstairs holding a young woman in front of him like a shield. He has a hand gun pushed out in front of him. He says that if anybody tries to shoot him, the girl will get killed first. I take a couple of steps back keeping my gun ready to shoot. The man is coming down the stairs slowly and finally we can see his face.

"Bennett, is that you? How did you get here?"

Sara recognizes him as soon as I do, I didn't even know that she knew him. He was a SEAL like Tim and me. I never cared for him, but I would never have guessed that he would be behind something like this. He says he thought he recognized the sound of Sara and my Sig Sauer's. He asks how we came to be here, so we tell him. Ray, Carol, Amy, Dan, and Roy have come into the house. The people who were being held are sitting around outside talking. Ray, Carol, and Amy think that Bennett has lost his mind, believing a story like the one we are telling. When we finish he says it sounds like what happened to him. He was on leave in Atlanta and was on an underground train and fell asleep. When he woke up he was definitely not in the same place or time. He managed to get a car running and finally found the guys he was partnered with here. They found this farm, but none of them wanted to work it so they went looking for women and some men to do the work for them. He says that was about six months ago.

Here is a man who could have helped all these people instead of using them like animals. He says he will leave and we will never see him again if we will let him go. If we don't, he is going to start shooting until one of us finally gets him. I am tired of all the killing so I ask the others what they think. As soon as he thinks he has the upper hand he starts making demands. He says he wants one of our vehicles and four women of his choice to take with him. I tell him that is just not going to happen. When we knew each other in the other world he was always trying to pick a fight with me. I was not afraid to fight him then and I am still not. I ask him if he would like to settle this between him and me. If he wins he goes free without the women unless they wish to go with him. He asks me what happens if I get lucky and win. I tell him he knows the answer to that, only one of us is going to survive this fight. He smiles and says that's more like it.

I hand my gun to Gary, Bennett starts to raise his at me and Sara tells him to try it, he will be dead before he hears her gun go off. He smiles and lowers his gun. He tosses it on the floor and pushes the girl in front of him towards Gary. As he does that he jumps at me from about two steps up. I am expecting it, but his momentum pushes me back against a table. He is trying to knee me in the groin, and he is trying to get his hands on my throat to choke me. I block the knee with my knee and throw a forearm into his face to push him back. That separates us for the moment. He is a vicious fighter who was known for putting his opponents in the hospital. I know of five confirmed kills he had in hand to hand combat, so I know I have my work cut out for me. I am no stranger to hand to hand combat either, I once heard a soldier bragging in the barracks that he was undefeated in hand to hand combat. One of the guys he was trying to impress told him that was obvious. If you lose in hand to hand, you don't get to talk about it.

He is throwing kicks and punches in rapid succession trying to knock me off balance. I have been blocking what he is throwing, but I decide I have to go on the offensive to win. I counter what he throws and start moving in throwing combinations of kicks and punches first high, then low. One of my punches gets through to his face and I can see blood flowing from his nose. Another series of combinations gets a kick into his midsection, knocking him back a step. He is not smiling anymore, nor is he talking, earlier he was telling me how he was going to kill me. He rushes throwing punches and kicks, but I can feel the power has diminished considerably in his hits. I have been working my butt off on the farm while he has been sitting back living a life of self indulgence and debauchery. He is much farther out of shape than he would have guessed about five minutes ago.

I retaliate with combinations that his reflexes are no longer able to block. I am thinking of asking him if he has had enough when he grabs for a gun he has hidden in his boot top. He draws it and starts to aim it at me when I hear the blast of more than one gun and see him jerk erect and fall to the floor. I look toward Gary and Sara, they have their guns raised, but so does the young lady he used as a shield coming downstairs. The second young lady who was upstairs comes down slowly making sure that the danger is over. I look down at Bennett trying to figure out what makes someone who has so much to offer be so selfish. There are too many people outside to stay here for the night, so we decide to go get the vans and take most of them back to the city, at least for the remainder of the night.

We don't have to go get the vans because those who were still with them could hear the shooting and guessed when it was over that everything was safe. With the vehicles they have here we can get everyone in so we all head to the city. By the time we get there it is only a couple of hours until sunup so we decide to go back to the farm. We have to drive slowly in the dark, but not much slower than normal. When we told everybody what we are proposing we gave them their choice of either coming with us or we would leave them in the city. One of the men asked what the difference is of where they were and where we are going. He said it sounds like they are just going from working for one group to working for another. We already proved we are stronger and better prepared to fight than their last captors.

At first I feel like telling him to get out and stay if that's what he wants, but then I realize that I would be thinking the same thing if I was him. Before I can answer him Ray and Carol tell all of them that they have been to our farm.

"We understand how you feel because when we first went with these kind people we were as scared and as nervous as you all are. None of us have ever known anything, but running and scavenging to survive. We didn't even trust each other enough to join forces for strength. Where we are going there are four farms, not one and four different groups living on those farms. We will all have to work, but it will be to build our own homes, where we can raise our families in safety and go to a warm bed at night with a full stomach. We know it sounds too good to be true, but we have seen it with our own eyes. A year ago they were all just like us, living in small groups, being hunted by predators and hoping to find enough food to feed our families. What have we got to lose going with them even if we didn't know what was in store. Can it be any worse than what you have already been through?"

One of the women in the van we are in asks me if all that is true. I tell her all except the part about having four farms. Some start to ask them why they lied, but I cut them off and tell them that there will be five farms either by the time we get back or soon afterward. The fifth one is for them if they want it. We will help them get settled in and show them how we do everything and they can take it from there. We are getting close to home and it is still only mid-morning, but the people in all the vehicles are getting excited. Every time we see a deserted farm they ask if that's where we are going. When we finally get to our farm and they see the newly painted buildings, the windmills spinning, and several people out in the yards doing different chores they are very much impressed. Everyone is expecting us, we were able to call on the CB and let them know. Tim, Ken, Billy, and Ryan come to meet us when we park in the area we have laid out for that. The people we brought back are very self conscious because their clothing is very dirty and worn out. They don't look any different than our groups did when we first got together.

We have some quick introductions, mostly introducing some of our people to them. There will be plenty of time to get to know each other later. I don't know about anyone else but I smell bacon and fresh breakfast sausage cooking and I won't be surprised if there are some pancakes and eggs to go with the meat. Dayna comes running out of the big meeting house and yells at me for not inviting our new friends to breakfast. This breakfast is for the new people and for those of us returning. Many of our family come over to meet the new people and to welcome them to the family. While we are eating, one of the ladies that was riding in the vehicle with us turns to the gentleman who was nervous earlier.

"Paul, did our last hosts welcome us this way? If we are going to be this warm and fed this well they can hold me prisoner for the rest of my life."

The others laugh and agree with her. For all, but a few this is the first time they have eaten fresh meat and had milk to drink. The fresh bread and toast is a big hit as well. Many of the people ask us if we think they can learn to grow and make the great things they are eating. We smile and tell them if we can do it, they sure can. Someone must have sent a signal because just about the time they are all through eating, our friends arrive from the other farms. We all go outside to introduce everybody and we can see that many of our new friends are cold, because although not exactly winter, the temperature is probably only in the high forties, low fifties right now. Our friends and our people come to the rescue with heavy sweaters and jackets to give to our new friends.

The younger boys and girls are met by our contingent of young people and are getting a tour of the farm. We are showing the older people around as well, but not quite at the pace of the younger people. Most of what we are showing them is totally new to them. They are not sure that they can do everything we have, but we assure them we will help them and they will have no trouble at all. When we get the tour completed most of our people are acting pretty antsy. Finally I tell them they may as well say what they want to before they bust. Dayna and Robin ask our new friends if they are ready to see their own farm now. They are careful to tell them that it isn't as finished as ours are, but they will be able to get it in shape pretty quickly.

We load the vehicles and all head to the new farm. Even I am surprised at the amount of work that has been done on the new farm. There are six houses and three barns on this farm. The windmills have already been serviced and are working fine, so all the houses have electricity. The electric baseboards have been installed so they have plenty of heat, plus each house has a fireplace and a woodstove with plenty of wood cut and stacked at each house. Each house also has a good supply of canned goods from the stores we have visited and a good supply of the fruits and vegetables we canned. The houses are in good shape, except for needing a good coat of paint, and some minor repair work. Most of the people have tears in their eyes as they walk around seeing their new home.

Doc McEvoy and Barb tell them that some of their people as well as some of ours have volunteered to move in here with these people to help them get settled in. That way if some of these people would like to stay with one of our groups to learn by helping us, they are welcome to do that. Most of the people in the new group don't really know each other very well, but they are all willing to live as they have seen us living. They are not quite sure how to get started, so we help them divide the people into the six different groups that will live in the houses. As we already said, some will come back with us, and stay with us for a while, and others will go with the other groups who will send people to help them. All in all we know it will work out fine.

After we returned to our home last evening, we finally had a chance to sit down and discuss the things we saw in the city that we can use. Sara and Gary made a list, as did Roy and Robin on the first trip. Dan and Roy made a list on the second trip. I also made a list so we sit down to relax and discuss our plan to get the items and supplies. There were three main things that caught my attention. There was a very large gun shop in town, it may be empty after Bennett and his men got through, but I didn't see anything special in the guns they were using against us. It won't hurt to check it out. The second thing is a lumber yard, it appeared to have large stacks of lumber which may not be any good, but then again it may be. There may be many tools and other supplies there that we can use as well. The third thing I saw is a company that had a sign that said Flour Mill on the outside.

Everyone saw pretty much the same large things and there is a long list of smaller just as important items. Some of those are the gas tankers that we already talked about. We counted at least five between the two cities. That's gasoline and propane, but we can use both. We discuss whether we should get everything we need from the cities before looking for more people. Look for more people and get the items after, or send one group to look for people and the other to bring back the items. Some of the people we freed told us about another small city about twenty miles east of the larger city we found most of the people in. We decide to get the stuff we can and investigate the other items while a group goes to that other city to see if anyone still lives there. In all the excitement I forgot that it is Sunday, so we are going to rest, the women are planning to show off a little for our new friends and invite them over for a huge roast beef dinner with potatoes and carrots. They even made more ice cream than I have ever seen at one time for dessert.

The dinner is a huge success, at least if you go by the amount of food that is consumed. We hold a meeting afterward and make our plans for the next adventure. Personally I wanted to stay home this time and let the others go on this trip. We decide to do this project in a couple of stages. First we are going to get the trucks and anything else we can use from the small town before going back to the city. We are doing that right now, we are on our way to the first town to get the trucks we want and will definitely need. Sara and Ken are our best mechanics with Gary and Tim second. I can sometimes figure out how to get a motor running, but the others are very good. We get to the first truck and drop Sara and Gary off there with Don to act as a guard. We don't expect any trouble, but you never know, so it is better to be careful.

Ken and I go to the second truck, which is a propane truck that we saw earlier. We have a tank that holds air to fill the tires with. At least it gives us enough air to get the truck to the gas station where we can start the compressor and fill them correctly. Ken has it running in no time while I put air in the tires to see if they will hold it. Luckily for us they do, and we are able to get the truck back to where Gary and Sara are working on the first truck. We were able to refill our air tanks at the garage, so between us we have enough air to tell us that we may get lucky enough to make it home with both trucks. I know I have made this sound like it only took a few minutes, but by the time we get the trucks back to the farm, it is almost dark.

We did take about an hour looking through the other small store in town and the bank. We also found a house that says Guns on the outside, so we just naturally have to check it out. This happens to be one of those that doesn't have any hidden compartments or an area for special guns. We do find some really nice guns though and quite a bit of ammunition. Don found several dozen arrows which is a real treasure for him, Dan, Ray, and Andrew. On Tuesday we set out for the city knowing we will probably not get back in less than two or three days. We take the same group plus Ryan, Carol, Doc McEvoy, Marge, Amy, and Paul one of the men we brought back. They are going to go to that smaller city to see if there are any people living there.

We get to the city before lunch and get right to work on the trucks we want to take back. There are three of them here and there may actually be more. We haven't really gone over the entire city yet. Maybe we are getting better at it, or maybe these trucks are just in better shape, because we have all three of them ready to travel by late afternoon. We have time so we decide to go to the gun shop I saw last time and are not too surprised to see that there is very little left in the store. This is another gun shop that doesn't have a hidden stash somewhere. From the gun store we go to the lumber yard to see if there is anything we can use. There are piles of all kinds of lumber here. There are also hundreds of pallet loads of bricks and cinderblocks. There are three flatbed trucks in the yard that look like they were used to deliver the materials. There are also some very large fork trucks that must have been used to load the flatbeds.

It is getting dark when our other team gets back. They have five frightened young women and three men who appear to be in their twenties. We decide to spend the night here and head back in the morning. We get to know our new friends better while we eat dinner and after until we fall asleep. Morning comes early and we decide to see if we can get the flatbed trucks running and at least one of the fork trucks. There is a large compressor right in the yard, so while Gary and Sara work on the trucks, Ken and I go to look at the other building that caught my eye. This was apparently a wheat mill and processing plant. What interests us is the large stone wheels they have to grind the wheat in large quantities, instead of spending half a day grinding enough wheat to make a dozen loaves of bread. Ken and I estimate from the size of the hoppers that feed the big wheels, we could get at least two bushels of wheat at a time in them.

There are actually three sets of the big stone wheels in the building along with several pallets of fifty pound plastic bags full of wheat. There are also several pallets of bags that have been ground. We study how we might be able to get at least one set of the grindstones out of the building and reassemble them back at our farm. Gary and Sara come looking for us and agree that we could really use these wheels. Gary has apparently done quite a bit of maintenance work in factories, because he sees right away how to disconnect the controls and the wheels. He has a note pad and a pencil so he draws the controls and makes a sketch of how the wheels come apart. He says he wishes we had a camera to take pictures because he might and probably will miss something. Sara is looking through the offices, she is interested because as she points out, these are prefab offices that can be taken apart and moved. They could come in pretty handy if we want to put a room in the barns.

I start to ask them a question when Sara tells me that yes, they got the trucks running and the largest fork lift. She also comes out of one of the offices carrying a fairly large book that contains the prints of the equipment as well as the electric schematics. She also found the operation manual for the grindstones and the instructions for grinding wheat as well as other types of grain. We decide we have to go for now, but we are definitely coming back for building supplies and these grindstones. When we get back to the lumber yard, Ken and I can see that they not only got the trucks running, but they got air into the tires and loaded one of the trucks with eight pallets of cinderblocks and two pallets of concrete mix. The truck has two fifty gallon tanks for fuel so we fill them both, as well as our vehicles, from the gas storage tank in the yard.

Gary and Sara want to drive the loaded truck back so we all load into the other vehicles, with the items we are taking back, and we head out. We go about four blocks when one of the young ladies from the other city says she is sure she saw a girl looking out a window as we went past. We stop and she jumps out to investigate. She comes back in only a couple of minutes with a very frightened young lady who looks to be about fourteen. We tell her she is safe now and ask how she came to be alone. She tells us that she used to live in the city where the others were found, with her parents. They were taken by men a while ago. She hid so they wouldn't take her. After they didn't come back she started walking and wound up here yesterday. She says she saw the vans going and coming back, but was too afraid to let them see her, so she hid. She was afraid to talk to us when she got here, but she was also afraid to stay here alone. She was so relieved when the lady named Mary came to ask her to join us.

Doc McEvoy says he thinks this is the young lady that one of the couples we took back already asked him to look for. The young lady gets excited and asks if he knows their names. He smiles and says his memory isn't quite what it used to be, but he still remembers where he keeps the notebook he writes things he wants to remember is. He takes out his little book and asks the girl if the names Andrew and Caroline mean anything to her. She is so happy she hugs him and asks if she can ride in the van he is in. That is not a problem for us. We just want to make sure we don't leave anybody that would like to come with us. On the way back we get to know our new friends quite a bit better. We get to tell them about the things we have done, we are not sure that they believe us or not, but they will get to see for themselves soon.

When we pull into the yard and everyone sees the truck load of building supplies, they all want to know what our next project is. When they see our new friends, they forget the supplies for at least a few minutes. The young girl's parents are here, it is a very emotional reunion for them, as it is for several of the new people with those we brought back last time. Once everyone is taken care of, and has a place to live, we can finally relax for a little while and discuss what we can do with the wheat grindstones we found. Billy, Tim, Rod, Tom, Frank, and the others are all excited to hear about our good fortune. We are discussing how much electricity the grinding wheels are going to take when the children come over and show us a picture of a wheat mill being driven by the current of a river.

We decide to take a walk to the river a short distance away and see if that is feasible. The river has a slow, but steady current and none of us can see why we couldn't make a paddle wheel to turn the large stones. The women are excited to hear that they may be able to grind a large quantity of wheat at a time, instead of having to spend most of a day grinding the wheat before they can make bread or rolls. We take the prints and instructions we have and start to formulate a plan to build a wheat mill. We decide to at least get part of the building up before we bring the stones back. Ken and Gary have had some drafting experience, so they volunteer to draw up the plans for our mill. While they are doing that we measure the barns to see if we can fit any of the offices we found at the mill.

Several of the young single men in each family have built a rough barracks kind of room in the lofts of a couple of the barns. With the weather turning colder we decide we should probably insulate and make the rooms more comfortable for them. With the number of people we are finding to join our groups we are starting to run out of housing within a distance that we can defend. It may be that I am thinking about this problem when I go to bed, or it may be some sort of revelation, but I dream that we have a solution to my concerns. We already have a sketch of the layout of each of the groups in our family. At breakfast I explain to Dayna, Robin, and Melissa, along with all the children what my half formed plan is. In my dream we built several houses mostly out of cinderblock and brick, but they did not exactly look like the average house.

The houses we built were one story with the doors in the middle of the building. The buildings were straight and big enough to house several families if need be. Inside they had a large living room, dining room and kitchen that was an open area. Off of that, there were bedrooms going both directions. I recall seeing at least four rooms on each side of the main area with bathrooms in the middle between the rooms. Each house also had a tower that was approximately thirty feet high that could only be accessed from inside the house. That would be for defense purposes, plus could be used as a lookout post and could be fitted with a radio to keep in contact with the other houses. The best thing about them is that they were along the road we live on heading toward Ryan's group, and some the other direction toward Doc McEvoys group.

After listening to what I have to say Dayna says she had the same dream, Robin and Melissa say that they have all discussed the fact that we are becoming too spread out to defend each other. We decide it is worth telling the others to see what they think. We do that and they agree that it would be a good idea to at least start to do something like that. While we are talking Gary sketches the house I describe. It looks just like it did in my dream. We discuss what the dimensions of the houses should be, at least approximately. Tim who worked as a mason's helper a couple summers when he was younger calculates how many cinderblocks it will take to build each house. It will take a lot of cinderblocks to accomplish what we want to do. Billy says that he remembers seeing a very large yard full of blocks, just like the ones on the truck we brought back. A couple of us go into town and sure enough there are dozens of pallets of blocks. We can only guess that we didn't notice them before because we weren't planning to build anything.

We decide to put up a building for the mill first. We get the base dug and poured. The instructions we have, explain in detail how to prepare the area for the stone to be set in place. We also found enough insulation and other building materials to finish off the dorms the young men built in the barns. They work on that while we older guys work on the mill. We make it large enough to accommodate at least two of the sets of stones. When we get to the point where we need the stones, we make a trip over to the city to get them. It takes us a couple of days and several pinched fingers and hands to get them dismantled. We mark everything with a number and mark corresponding pieces of the puzzle to make putting it together back home at least possible. Since we can't all work on this project at the same time, a couple of us load the large flatbed truck we got from here with building materials, and make runs back to the farm with them.

Our family has a very simple rule about doing our jobs or chores. Once someone has been asked to do something, or has volunteered to take on a project, the rest of us leave them alone as far as telling them how to do it, unless of course we are asked for our input. Sara, Ken, and Gary have volunteered to do this project, so the rest of us are letting them handle the technical aspects of this move. Naturally we are all supporting them in any way we can. We prepared the building that will house the mill, based on the prints that we found. Ken and Gary drew the plans for a paddle wheel to drive the grindstone and using the tools in the barns we have been able to build a pretty fair paddle wheel. The group that has been at home working on this end has done a remarkable job as far as I'm concerned. They set the wheel in place and it turns perfectly so far. Of course there are no grind stones in yet, but we are certain it will work fine. The big day is finally here to set the bottom stone and then install the grinding stone.

We use a big fork truck, that we brought from the city closer to us, to carry the big base stone into place. It slides in perfectly and looks just like it did in the mill where we found it. The top moving stone will not be quite as easy. Our team is more than up to the challenge though. They have every detail worked out, even though there are some minor surprises along the way. It takes them a couple of days to get everything hooked up and installed, but when we release the paddle wheel the stone turns perfectly to grind our wheat. The wheel is even adjustable so that they can vary the coarseness of the flour. When everything is in place, we finish off the end of the building that we left open to make moving the large items in easier. We put a two car garage door and a walk in door so that we still have access for large items and can open the door in the summer when it will probably get too hot in here.

Our new friends are proving to be more than willing to do their share of the work. It has been warm for this time of year. They have painted all six of the houses in their group. They have had some help from the other groups, but they are all hard workers. They all say that if someone would have told them even a month ago that they could live like this they would have thought they were crazy. Jessica, Jenny, Samantha, and several other teenage girls have been helping the other groups build their flocks of chickens. They show them how they were able to catch our chickens when we first came here, and so far it has worked well for them too. Don, Dan, and Andrew have more than enough willing students to teach how to hunt. Like we did with them, they always stress not hunting close to home so that we don't frighten the game away. They have even started butchering most of our meat and have shown most of our friends how they do it.

Tim and I have been studying the layout of the groups and we are concerned that we are leaving ourselves open to attack. Dayna told her sister Charity about the dream and she told Tim. Tim told me that he had a very similar dream about building houses. The trouble with that is no one wants to leave the farms that they have worked so hard to get to where they now are. We were thinking more of building the houses between the groups, to eventually combine the groups into a community. We are planning to start building a road across the fields and through the woods. There is already a rough road which is actually more of a trail, but we want to grade it and perhaps even put gravel down to smooth it out. The last time Billy and Tom went into town to get more building supplies they decided to check out an area that said it was the Department of Transportation. From the front it looked just like any other building, but when they drove behind it they found huge piles of gravel and more building supplies than we did at the lumber yard. They also found some dump trucks that we are going to see if we can get them running soon now.

The women love the new wheat grinder. They can do several bushels in the time it used to take to do enough for a few loaves of bread. They do have to go farther to get it, but there is no shortage of helpers at least for now. The children love to watch the big stone go around while it is grinding the wheat. Some of the older boys were swimming in the river and decided to take a ride on the paddle wheel. They would hold on as it comes out of the water on the one side and ride it as far as they could before falling off into the water of course. We know it's a lot of fun, but repairing or replacing that wheel won't be, so we asked them to refrain from that practice. Besides the younger children wanted to try it and it is just too dangerous for them. We are into November now and the weather is starting to turn colder, but is still not what I would call cold. We are continuing our trips to see if we can find anyone else before winter gets here.

Tim went out with Billy and some of the others while I stayed home this time. They have been gone for two days, but we expect them to be gone for most of a week, unless they find something early. They are traveling east toward the coast, but they don't expect to get that far at least on this trip. Yesterday we received a call from our new neighbors. They were concerned because they heard a very large something out in their yard during the night and had no idea what it could be. Andrew, Don, and I went over, accompanied by Dons new bride Olivia, to see if we could figure out what was running around their yards at night. Don is anxious to impress Olivia, he really doesn't have to, she thinks he's the greatest husband ever. Anyway when we got there we started looking for prints in the dirt and sure enough we found out what it was.

Actually we didn't need the tracks, because while we were looking we heard one of the young ladies, who was sprinkling chicken feed out towards the woods to draw in more chickens, screaming that she is being chased by a wild animal. It wasn't really chasing her but she was being watched by a hog about the same size as the ones we have been finding for meat. This one is big enough that if he had openings on his sides we would think he is a compact car. I ask Ray, who is one of the leaders of this group, if he is ready to learn how to smoke meat and make lots of sausage. Before he can answer, the pig decides he has seen enough and charges toward us. Don has a .307 that he found in one of the gun shops. He takes a step toward the charging pig and fires as coolly as anyone I have ever seen. It took three shots into that huge head to stop it cold about thirty feet away from us.

Several of the young men in this group who idolize Don, Dan, and Andrew were more than ready to help dress and butcher the hog. Tom and Frank have already fixed the freezer in the barn on this farm, so they have a place to keep the meat fresh. They also have a smoke house, which we get ready while the young men are manhandling that huge beast into the barn. They are loading the sections of the pig, as they quarter it, onto the plastic tarp in the back of the pickup, then take it into the barn and unload it. Even quartered, it takes a couple strong men to get it onto the table. Don and Olivia spent most of the day helping them with that hog. On the way home I got a call from Robin wanting to know if we would like fresh fish for dinner. The girls went to the mill shortly after we left and the children decided to take their fishing gear to have something to do while they wait.

The short version, which I did not get by the way, is that the children caught enough fish for the entire group. Some of the older young people decided to try their luck and caught enough to share with our friends. Since most of the people in the new group have never had fish, they are happy to have some. The deep fried fish and the deep fried corn meal balls were a big hit for supper last night. Today I am thinking about starting on the road between the groups. We have a backhoe with a bucket on the front to level the ground with. I am getting the backhoe when Dayna comes running and says that she just got a call on the CB that Barbs group has some guys on motorcycles riding around their houses, trying to get them to come out. Around here you can't have a conversation outside without having several people hear it. Don, Andrew, Dan, Rod, and I grab our motorcycles and guns and head cross country to get to that group.

We get there just in time to see the bikers speeding off. Barb comes out of her house and tells us they heard us coming and took off. Luckily they were not able to get to any of the women or young girls in this group. This is the one I fear the most for, because it is the smallest. The men in the group have guns, but they say they didn't want to shoot anyone unless they tried to get into the houses. As long as they just drove around the yard they didn't want to shoot. Andrew and Dan decide to stay here for a couple of days, to make sure they have help, in case those guys come back. What scares me is what brought them to our area in the first place, and will they leave now knowing that there are women here, plus food and other comforts. Rod and I decide we better get going on that road to make the time getting to each other as short as possible.

The next three days go by very quickly. Rod and I have finished the road to the newest neighbors and to Barbs group. We put gravel down so that in the rainy times the road doesn't turn into mud. It is just a rough road, but we can make much better time than we could before. Ryan's and Doc McEvoys are only a couple miles away and we have paved road to get to those. On the fourth day we get a call on the CB from Ken. He, Tim, and Billy along with their wives are only a few miles away headed toward home. They say they have seven more new friends to join our groups. It must make the new people happy to hear all the groups answer him saying that we all have room for them.

The new people are two couples, and three children, who are just about the same ages as Teddy, Kathy, and Karen. They are all very shy and nervous. We understand fully and just try to make them feel welcome. I take Tim, Ken, and Billy aside and tell them about the attack the other day. They say they thought they heard motorcycles in the distance about four nights ago, but couldn't be sure. I show them the roads that we built while they were gone and we all feel better that those are in. Ryan's group takes the new people, a few of the single men from his group are going to join Barbs group for a while, just in case. When that is all settled, the guys tell me they have a surprise for me. I was so preoccupied with those motorcycles that I never even noticed the tarp covering something quite large in the back of the truck.

While they are uncovering the surprise Billy says he has been dreaming about finding one of these since he saw one in a book. Ramona smacks him lightly and tells him she thought that he only dreamed about her. He smiles and tells her that now she will be the only thing, because now we have this one. He climbs up onto the back of the truck to be the one to actually take the tarp off this treasure. When he pulls the tarp free it really is a treasure. They found a very large saw for cutting rough cut lumber into finished boards. The blade must be five feet in diameter. They were only able to get about half the table, but are sure we can build one. The part they weren't able to get is the table up to the saw and the table going away from it. We can always go back if we have trouble duplicating the ones that were with it, but they don't have to be exact. The saw has a power feed that drags the wood into the blade as it is being cut.

We start to look for a likely place to set this great find up. We all agree that it should be close to the woods, or at least where we can take logs off the truck and set them on the bed of the saw. We decide to build a three sided addition to the barn that is closest to the woods and has a driveway that runs right up behind it. Most of the wood we found in town and in the city is still good and solid. We don't waste any time getting started. We all enjoy building and this is a project that will be worth its weight in gold very soon. All we get done today though is marking off the ground in the dimensions we feel we will need. The barn is sixty-five feet long, but there is a large door at the one end that gives us a straight wall of fifty feet. We are intending to use all that space to allow us room to bring large logs into the saw area and set them on the table with a fork truck. We have to have an equal distance on the other end to give the logs room to cut completely off.

After we knock off for the evening, Tim and Ken come over to talk about our next trip. They want to go to the coast where there is a Marine base. At least there was one in the world we all come from. They are in a hurry to get the next trip started, they have no idea why, but they feel strongly that we should go there soon. I assumed that they wanted to go, but before they leave they ask me when Sara, Gary, and I can leave. Dayna says she wants to go along this time, Robin and Melissa say that they can watch little Timmy for us. We have no idea what we will run into so we have no idea how long we will be gone. We don't anticipate it taking more than a week, but we can't be sure of that. Dan asks if he can go on the trip as well, in case we need to fight. We are always happy to have the younger men along. They are becoming very confident and always helpful.

Dayna and I both have a dream that something very important to us is going to happen at that Marine base. Neither of us ever saw what, but we both felt strongly that we need to get there as soon as possible. We decide to prepare today and leave in the morning. We have everything prepared by midday so we decide to get started. We have only been east about thirty miles, so what lies beyond that we can't be sure. The road is fairly clear so we can make pretty good time. By the time the sun is going down we are sixty miles from home. We are in a city that looks like it has been deserted since the war. The stores here are full of canned goods, clothing, and canning supplies, and pretty much anything people need to survive. We watch for smoke before sunset and there is not a sign of life anywhere.

We decide to push on and stop on the way back to load up the trucks with supplies, if we have any room. We get to the base around midday and the city outside the base is as deserted as the one we were at last night. The buildings here seem to be in rougher shape than where we are, but that could easily be because of the storms that come in off the ocean that don't get inland as far as we are. It feels strange to drive onto a military base without having to stop at the guard on duty. We are not sure what we are supposed to be looking for so we decide to drive around the base and see if anything catches our eye. I see a sign that catches my eye and apparently Gary and Sara see the same building, because they call us on the radio and tell me to turn in at the armory.

We go up to the door and it is still locked. We carry tools for situations such as this. A pry bar works nicely to break the lock although it doesn't really feel like it has deteriorated any. There are rooms in the building so we start checking them to see what we can find. There are plenty of great military weapons and ammunition.

We find rocket launchers, cases of grenades, pretty much any kind of weapon we could ever want. Well almost, I am looking for one of the fifty caliber rifles like I used to use in the SEALs. Dayna finds a door marked experimental weapons so we head that way. This is where the guns like the ones we were using are located. That makes sense because this time is way before we were in the military. I find a whole case of the fifty caliber rifles with infrared scopes on them and several dozen cases of ammunition for them. These are going out to the truck right now.

As much as we would like to we can't take everything that we want, at least on this trip. We discuss it and load one of the trucks with guns and ammunition to take back. We also take several cases of plastic explosives as well as hand grenades and grenade launchers. We lock back up as best we can and head for a warehouse that looks promising. We find cases of camouflage clothing, military blankets, and enough supplies to outfit several thousand soldiers. We could really use some of this stuff, but we only have so much room, so what do we take first? We are contemplating that when Dayna, who is checking out the offices, comes running back to us and says she saw a couple coming our way.

We run for the door to see who she is talking about. When we get to the doorway, we see a very nice looking young couple, looking very confused staring at us. The young man asks us if we are supposed to be in that warehouse without permission. Sara tells them she got permission from the C.O., but he died in 1969, so there is no way she can prove it. The couple looks even more surprised and asks what we are talking about, it's 2010. I am staring at the uniforms they are wearing. Dayna smacks me and tells me to stop staring at the young lady, even if she does look very good in that uniform. I explain that I notice that they are in the Air Force and ask them what they are doing on a Marine base. The young man has been doing all the talking up to this point, but the young lady says they are stationed here on a joint venture with the Marine Corp and the Navy. She introduces them to all of us. Their names are Jenna and James. They are married and have just returned from a camping trip.

Sara asks them if they were flying when they came back. She answers that they were, but how does she know. Sara goes on to tell them that she bets she can tell them exactly what happened. She doesn't wait for an answer, but continues.

"You were on your way back to the base when you ran into fog thicker than you have ever seen before. You managed to land using instruments, when you couldn't raise anyone in the tower. The fog was so thick you decided to sleep in the plane because you had no idea where to go to get to the buildings. When you woke up the fog was lifted, but nothing looked familiar anymore. You decided to look around to see if you are indeed where you think you are. My guess is, that happened last night."

They are both astonished that Sara knows so much about them. They ask what is going on, everything seems like it is unreal except us. Sara asks them if they would show us the place that they landed their plane, and then we will explain everything to them. They say they will be happy to, but for us not to be too surprised if they decide to leave when we get back to the plane. They are shocked when we get to the runway and there is no plane like theirs anywhere. The runway is destroyed, there's no way anyone could land a plane on it during the day, much less in the dark, in a heavy fog. The young lady Jenna has to sit down she is so shocked, she asks us what is going on. We explain about ourselves and how we came to be here. Something told me to bring a newspaper with me, but there are several in the building that acted as a terminal for the base.

When they read about the neutron technology, James and Jenna become very interested and start asking us questions faster than we can answer. That is if we knew the answers to the questions. Finally they say they have to go to their quarters to get their clothes and some other belongings. Then they will be ready to come back with us. We go to the location they direct us to and there is nothing there, it is a field at the edge of the base. Jenna is the practical one of the two. She says in that case lets go to the Base Exchange so she can get some civilian clothes and other necessities. We were going to go there anyway, so we all go there to see what we can find. There is a very large selection of tee shirts and jeans as well as other clothes and other items. I find a display of knives and see that they have the K-Bar knives, which were the soldier's best friend for generations. Between Gary and me we take all of the knives in the display and go into the stock room where we find several more cases of them.

There is way too much stuff here that we can use not to at least try to get another truck or two running. We go to the motor pool and find some very nice trucks, but the weather here on the coast has not been good for them. Jenna says she knows where we can find some trucks in decent shape. She leads the way back to where the airplane hangars are and we find a couple really nice twenty-six foot covered trucks. There is a compressor in the hanger that Sara and Gary have running in no time and luckily the tires hold air. While they were working on the tires Jenna and James were working on the motors getting them to turn over. Finally we have them running and head back to the Base Exchange, where we proceed to load one of the trucks. We leave enough room to go back to the armory and gather up as much ammunition and guns as we can get into the truck. It is almost dark when we leave the base, but we want to get at least part way back before we camp for the night.

We decide to take a different route back, but still going through the deserted city we came through on our way here. It's a good thing we do, because we find two women and three children, in a small town that isn't even on the map. They were getting desperate because their food was running out and they had no idea how to get more. The children all appear to be under five and remind me how much I miss our children. One of the women, Marla, has been without her husband for two winters and the other one, Carol, says that her husband died of a fever last winter. Since then they have been doing the best they could, but were very close to giving up. They say they don't know if what we are telling them is the truth or not, but they don't have any other options. We assure them they will be part of a very large family that works to help each other. Jenna and James can't wait to see what we have done. I am getting a little worried that they will think what we have done is very primitive and criticize our efforts.

We load the last truck with supplies from the city then head for home. Dayna calls me on the CB, because we are all driving some vehicle, and tells me she has a very strong urge to turn right at the next cross roads. Everyone comes back on the CB that we should turn right at the next crossroads then. We do and within a couple of miles we are pretty sure we have found what we are supposed to. There is a large collection of pre-manufactured homes, on what was once an outdoor showroom for homes. We stop to look at them and Jenna, who is some kind of engineer, says if she had some equipment she could tell if the wood that these homes are made of is safe. I tell her I can do that without any special equipment. We walk into one of the homes and I jump up and down on the floor. I don't fall through so I assume it is safe to live in.

James, who is a nuclear physicist or something like that, has been studying everything we go near. He says what we have guessed, but coming from him it means more because he knows what he is talking about. Ever since we found them he has been asking us questions about the homes we found here and about the buildings where we came from. He has also noticed the same thing we did about the cars and trucks. There is almost no rust on any of them, even though they have been out in the weather for almost thirty years. We are going through some of the houses to see if we think we can get them back to our settlement. There are three tractors for eighteen wheel trucks on the lot with the twenty houses here. As far as we can see they are solid enough to move them, we will just have to figure out how to accomplish that.

We are only about fifteen miles from home, so we make sure we know how to get back and finish our journey. As soon as we are close enough to raise the base stations at home we let them know we are on our way and that we have six trucks full of supplies and seven new family members. The twins must be with Tim because we hear their little voices asking if any of the new family members are their age. Dayna tells them that there are three young people within a year or two of being the same age, so they will have some new playmates. Tina and Tammy are excited about that, especially when they hear that one of the little girls is the same age, and is named Tina also.

We spend the rest of the journey telling Tim and the others about our adventures.

When we pull into the yard the twins, accompanied by Zeus and a couple of his brothers and sisters, are right here to welcome us back. It feels so good to have the girls jump into my arms and tell me how much they missed me. Our new friends are not sure how to take the dogs, but they are so friendly that the children wind up playing with them in no time. As I said, I am afraid that what we have accomplished will seem pretty primitive to James and Jenna. They come walking up kind of sheepishly because of the crowd that is beginning to form around us. I can see they are looking around and talking to each other. I can even see them pointing out different things so I work my way over to them with Robin, Melissa, Tim, Ken, and Billy. I introduce everyone then tell them we will be happy to give them a tour, but we would like to get at least some of the supplies put away.

As we do with all the supplies we bring back we take them into the large meeting building we have and lay everything out so we can see what kind of treasures we have. By the time the first two trucks are unloaded the rest of our family is getting here. Much of what is on the first two trucks is food and clothing along with a lot of canning supplies. The new group needs more than the rest of us so they get first pick and then everything is divided amongst those who need the clothing or coats or whatever it is. That includes the newest members who have been invited to stay with Tim and Charity at least until they know everyone better and can decide where they may wish to live.

The canning supplies will be kept with the others to be used when we need them. We all get together when it is canning time and split whatever it is we are canning. When we open the two trucks that are loaded with guns and ammunition the young men and just about all of the not so young men say they could use a new gun or five. When I show everyone the case of fifty's I brought back, Tim says that Zeus has risen from the dead. We have to explain that to many of our family members. Each of our basements, as well as most of the other groups basements, have been fitted with a small room that can be locked where we store the extra guns and ammunition. Like everything else we divide the guns up and each group takes their share. The men that would like one of the new guns for their homes can have them as well as an ample supply of ammunition. We make sure that guns and ammunition are kept out of reach of little hands.

Most of the grenades and plastic explosive will be stored in the barn farthest from the homes. We found a large root cellar that was dug right into the hill that the barn was built up against. We found the door totally by accident when we were cleaning the barn one day last spring. The K-Bar knives are a huge hit, all of the men and most of the women in our group's carry some kind of knife with them at all times. We brought back enough for everyone who wants one and some extras. I can see that Teddy wants one about as badly as he has ever wanted anything. I ask Robin if she would mind if I give him one. She tells me he is my son too, but if he gets hurt she will kick my butt and not his. Jenna overhears our conversation and asks me just how long have I been in this world. The girls laugh and explain our marriage arrangements. Jenna must like to tease James because she asks the girls if that works both ways. She thinks two husbands could work out nicely sometimes. She is going to fit right in here with our wives.

6

When we can finally show James and Jenna around properly, I am a little nervous, because these people are experts in their fields and what we have done here may appear somewhat primitive to them. Ken is along for the tour and explains why we are using the windmills the way we are and how we have tried to make our homes as electric as possible, because that is a renewable resource as long as we have wind. From the way Ken is explaining everything I think he is as nervous as I am. We show them the fields of winter wheat we have planted and the other fields that are waiting to be used in the spring. We even walk over to the river and show them our mill with the paddle wheel.

During the tour both Jenna and James keep shaking their heads like they are agreeing with what is being shown and what is said. Finally I can't take it any longer and I tell them we realize that what we have done is pretty primitive compared to what they are used to, but if they would like to make some suggestions to improve our systems, to please let us know. James looks at Jenna and says he doesn't know about her, but he is very disappointed. She nods her head in the affirmative and says so is she. Ken starts to get a little defensive, and Jenna holds up her hand, asking him to let her finish.

"I'm disappointed alright. I figured we would come back here with you all and find some rundown farm buildings, with antique windmills, barely cranking out enough voltage to light the houses. What we find is a magnificent settlement that looks like you have lived here all your lives, and have done as good a job as I could have done with the windmills. I'm even more jealous about the mill, you people are amazing. I'm sure James and I will be able to help you some, but you definitely don't need us."

We are all happy to hear that, we are proud of what we have accomplished, but we also realize we still have a long way to go. Now that we know we are doing things right, we begin planning how we are going to get those pre-fabricated homes back here. The general consensus is that we try to bring one back, and if we are successful we will get the rest of them. This is one area that Jenna and James say they can help us. Jenna's dad was a mason before he passed away, and Jenna worked with him building basements and even houses out of cinderblock and bricks. James worked for him to put himself through college, that's where he and Jenna met. We discuss our idea about building homes to join the groups, rather than spread out any farther than we already are. Everyone agrees it's a good plan, but will take a lot of houses to fill in the gaps.

Billy, who usually doesn't say much at meetings like this has been acting like he really wants to say something, so I ask him if he has a question or a comment. He asks if when we get some of the new houses ready to live in, could some of us who have been with the group from the beginning and already live in a house, possibly move into one of the new houses. It takes a minute for what he asked to sink in, I tell him I am hoping some of the solid working and fighting men in the groups will want to move into the new homes. He explains that he is not complaining about the living arrangements now, it's just that if we have enough houses, maybe some of the families can live separately.

Ken who is married to Dayna's sister Carrie and lives in the house next to Billy and Ramona tells him he will help him move. Maybe then he can get some sleep. Billy asks him why his moving will let him get more sleep. Ken tells him that he snores so loud he can hear it through the walls. Billy who is moving when he says it, tells him that is not him snoring, that's Ramona. She is much too fast for him and hits him before he can go a step. We all tease each other like a real family, actually the only family I ever had was Gunny and Ma Horton. They were always teasing each other and me so I really enjoy our big family here. It's decided that since we have nothing better to do anyway we may as well start the project of getting one of those houses home. Billy, Tim, Rod, and Ken will go to see if they can get the trucks started and get one of the homes ready to bring here.

I will not go into great detail of how they accomplished this task. I will say however, that every day as they recounted their adventure, it was becoming more obvious that they are having way too much fun with this project. They started the project on Monday and by Friday afternoon they have two of the trucks running and the tires at a point where they will hold air. The first move is scheduled to take place tomorrow. James has been going with them every day and is still fascinated with the effects of the neutron bomb radioactivity on the metal objects and even much of the wood. He has been studying everything he can get his hands on and comparing it to what he knows from the world we came from.

While the guys have been working at the homes, some of us have been working on the sawmill getting that ready to start cutting wood. The blade we have is large enough to cut a twenty-four inch in diameter log into boards for building. In our mill building we also put a large radial arm saw that will cut up to a four foot wide board. It hangs and pivots allowing it to be drawn across the boards. We are going to start cutting timber for making wood for building. Jenna has fallen totally in love with Tammy and Tina. She loves all the children, but they are so much fun and you never know what they are going to come up with next. Zeus, their dog, is their constant companion, at least when they are outside. He is so friendly and watches those children like a hawk. If they try to go anywhere they shouldn't, he barks and gets between them and where they want to go. He watches all the children the same way, along with his brothers and sisters of which there are now seven more. Prince and Princess are proud parents again. With as many families as there are in our extended family, all the puppies found good homes as soon as they were weaned.

On Saturday morning we go to the yard where the houses are and get ready to bring the first one back. They are in two pieces and it is easier than we thought it would be to move them. They already have axles and wheels under them so all we have to do is hook up to them and tow them to the farm. The guys have been clearing the road between there and home, as well as getting the trucks ready. At least we can make the move before rush hour, which will cut down on the traffic. That's okay, no one here laughed either. No traffic is one of the benefits of being the only living people within sixty miles. We are still deciding whether or not we want a full basement with a foundation under the homes, or if we want to put a temporary foundation under them. First things first, let's get a complete home here before we worry about the foundation.

Tim and Gary are going to drive the big trucks that are towing the two halves of the house. They have both driven eighteen wheelers before and know what they are doing. We were able to fill the trucks from a tank on the home site that has diesel fuel. When we are getting into the vehicles to leave, Sara asks if we think we need an escort vehicle to keep traffic back. Sure, everyone laughs at her, I tell almost the same joke and all I get is people rolling their eyes at me. The trip is very anticlimactic, the guys drive the two halves of the house right to the farm and park them approximately where we want them permanently. We decide to go ahead and put in a basement at least in the first couple. Teddy and I take James and Jenna into town to show them the kinds of gravel, sand and other supplies that we found at the department of public works facility.

We are walking around looking at what we can use for our project when Teddy notices some conduit that looks like it was used to carry water under roads and possibly through hills. It is in sections that are approximately twelve feet long and it must be six feet in diameter. There is also some that is around two feet in diameter, but Teddy tells me the large conduit would make great tunnels between the houses. That way we could get to each other without having to go outside. I am about to tell him that he has a good idea, but that it is not very practical when I stop, because I can't think of any reason we couldn't do that. Jenna and James who have been hearing stories about our adventures since coming here, both say that it sounds like a great idea to them. They say that we may even be able to find some larger conduit if we look around. Now we are getting excited about the possibilities.

All the way home we are formulating a plan to put a series of tunnels underground, leading from basement to basement and maybe even out to the barns. We would have to be very careful to disguise the entrances in the barns, and even in the homes, in case someone got into one of the other homes. By the time we get home we are getting carried away thinking about running a tunnel between the groups, but that would take several miles of conduit and probably a couple of years to accomplish. When we get home I tell Robin and all the others what a great idea Teddy has. We let him present it to the others, which he does very well. By the time he gets through telling them pretty much everything we talked about on the way home, everyone is in agreement. Ryan and Doc McEvoy are visiting and they think it is a great idea as well. With most of the farm work on hold until spring, we have plenty of willing men and women to help on the project.

We decide the best way to do this project is to dig a trench large enough and deep enough to drop the conduit and the concrete box like connectors into and fasten them together. Naturally we will have to cut a hole in the basement wall making sure not to weaken the foundation any. We decided that the six foot conduit is plenty big enough, even though most of us will have to duck to walk through it. We decide to start with the house that is the farthest away from the others and join it to the next farthest one. We have two backhoes going, digging the large trench that is required. We also have two crews working on the basement walls, to get them ready. We decide to set the tunnel slightly lower than the floor level in the basements so that the conduit will be totally covered by at least a couple feet of dirt on the surface.

Jenna and James are proving to be very valuable on this project and on the other building project we are doing at the same time. The basement is being dug for the home we brought over, and the first trench is just about dug, when we realize that it is Thanksgiving. I have been so busy that I totally forgot about it. I should have noticed from the weather, but to be honest, I have been wearing some of the uniforms we got from the Marine base and haven't even noticed that it is getting colder. For Thanksgiving we have a huge feast of turkey, compliments of Don, Dan, Andrew, and Teddy, who is now learning how to be one of our hunters. He is learning very fast according to his teachers. We also have a couple of great hams to go with the turkey. All of our friends from the different groups come to our place, to share a meal and great company. They are all sharing the work that is going on, so we may as well all eat together on special occasions like this.

All of the new members of our family get up and say how thankful they are that we found them, and how grateful they are that there are people willing to share with others. They all say they feel bad about receiving so much and giving so little at this time, but they are looking forward to being able to do their share when the time comes. When the day is just about over Tim decides to see if he can raise any of our friends from around the country on the short wave radio. He talks to the group from Texas who say they are doing much better than they were and that they are growing in numbers. There is a group in California that is doing well also, but we hear from a group we have never talked to before. It is a woman's voice, saying that they just found the radio and were wondering if there is anyone else out there.

They ask where we are calling from and to be careful we are vague about our exact location. The lady says she understands, but she is just trying to figure out if there is any way that they might be able to join us or if we would be willing to help them. She says there are twenty people in their group and they are running out of food. This lady doesn't sound like the survivors we have found. We ask how many men, women, and children they have. The lady says three older men, eight women, and nine young people in their teens and younger, five young ladies and four boys. She says she overheard our conversation with the other groups and it sounds like we have a pretty good settlement going.

I have to know where they are calling from. I know that the women have already decided we are going after these people. Tim asks and they say that they are in a city that according to the map we have is about a hundred miles to the southwest of us. After we hang up we discuss the possibility that it could be a trap. Dayna, Robin, and Melissa all say that we can't just leave those people to starve to death, just because it might be a trap. Charity tells Tim that he is always telling her about ambushes and close calls we had when we were with the teams. She says she understands that we have to be careful, but the bad guys we have seen so far are very tame compared to the fighting men we faced in our own world. We have no doubt we are going, we just want to know who is going with us. We decide that Tim and I will go, along with Billy, Sara, Gary, Don, and Olivia. We want the women along so that the people there don't think we are predators. I get to take my new fifty caliber with the infra red scope, so I don't care who else goes.

We spend the next day getting ready for the trip. In the world we came from, a hundred miles would be a short trip, but we have no idea what we are going to run into. Besides, according to the map, there are some cities between here and where they say they are and we want to take a look around. There may be more people than just those we talked to. That goes for bad people as well as good people. Tim is able to raise them on the radio again on Friday evening and we tell them we will be coming tomorrow to get them, and that if they know of anyone else who would like to join us they are welcome, as long as they are willing to abide by the rules. The lady we spoke with last night is the same one talking this time. Dayna and I both get the distinct impression that she doesn't talk like a survivor. She sounds too educated, and is very tuned in to detail. She gives us excellent directions once we get to the city they are in. We caution her to be careful. We may not be the only ones listening.

We get an early start and are carrying plenty of gas for any eventuality. We are taking enough vehicles to carry more than the twenty people we are looking for, just in case. Plus we have a truck in case we find something worth bringing back. So far we always have. The road to the southwest is in pretty good shape and we are making better time than we anticipated when we get about three quarters of the way and find a fairly good sized city. We take a quick look around and can see no signs of life. The stores are still well stocked and it seems odd to me that someone would stay where they might starve rather than walk to the next town or city. Of course they may not even know that this city is here or may be too afraid to attempt walking that far. We should know in about another hour.

We get to the city where the new people said they are and we start going to where we were directed. The directions are excellent, maybe too excellent. We stop about a quarter mile from where they are supposed to meet us and I jump out with the fifty and head toward the rendezvous point. We have our walkie-talkies so we can stay in touch. They are waiting for me to find a place where I can see them hopefully without being seen. It only takes a few minutes for me to find them and a place where I can have high ground and see quite a distance around them. All I see is exactly what they said we would find. There are some pretty run down looking people, mostly kids looking hopefully toward the direction we should be coming. I take a look around and feel secure to call the others in.

The people who are waiting get pretty excited when they hear the vehicles approaching. An attractive lady, who is dressed in fatigues, tells them they should hide until they know for sure that we are what we say we are. This lady is definitely not a survivor. She gets everyone but herself hidden then stands there waiting to see if we are friends or enemies. I have to hand it to this lady; she is taking care of those people. I see the vehicles round the corner and I tell Tim in the front vehicle that the lady is standing on the steps of the fourth building on the right. She sees the vans first and I can see her stiffen slightly, like she is afraid, but she stands her ground waiting. The vehicles pull up in front of the building and I can see the people inside sneaking peeks to see what we look like. As soon as they stop, Olivia and Sara jump out and run over to meet the lady on the steps. She relaxes perceptibly and turns to call the others out for everyone to meet.

One of the men is limping badly when they come out to meet everyone. I am thinking about heading down when I catch movement out of the corner of my eye. It's a group of motorcycle riders, about six or eight blocks away, heading in this direction. I call Tim and have him ask the people if they are expecting company. The lady, who appears to be in charge, says she was hoping to get away before those people came back. I am thinking about shooting them, but as far as I know they have not done anything threatening at least to us. I tell Tim that if these guys are not part of this group we may want to get loaded and get out of here. The other option is to get the women and children clear of this area and have a welcoming committee to see what their intentions are. We decide on the first option.

The people here have very little to take with them, so they jump into the vans and they high tail it out of there. I watch the guys on the motorcycles for a few more minutes, and then meet Billy who is driving the big truck behind the others, who are putting distance between themselves and this place. I call Tim to let him know that Billy and I are going to hang back to make sure they are not followed. Besides there are a couple of places we would like to check out before we leave this city. We go to the bank and find that this bank kept a lot of silver money on hand as well as a large amount of the paper kind. We have been gathering the silver and gold coins when we find them, just in case money is ever worth anything again. We just finish putting the money in the cab of the truck when the six motorcycles come around the corner and pull up near the truck.

Billy and I are standing outside the truck with military issue Thompson .45 caliber machine guns in our hands. We have them pointed at the ground, but I think our visitors get the idea that we know how to use them. The one in the front asks us where we came from. I smile and tell him we came south for the winter, it gets pretty cold up north. He smiles and says that he knows what we mean. I ask him if there are any other people around here. I point to the store a few doors up the street and say that it looks like someone cleaned the place out. He says if there is anyone else they wouldn't know, because they are new to the area as well. He goes on to say that they are just passing through on their way south. They're tired of the cold as well.

I can see that they have not taken their eyes off the guns we are holding. The one who is obviously in charge asks us where we found those. I make a gesture like I am looking at it and tell them we found them up in Fort Bragg, in Kentucky. They all look confused and ask where Kentucky is. I tell them about three days drive north east of here. I only know where it was because of the road signs in the area. They seem to buy that. Billy must think that they are trying to decide if the six of them can take us. I can only assume, because that's what I am thinking. As if to prove to them that they can't, Billy picks out a truck sitting in the road about twenty-five yards away and shoots about ten rounds on full auto. That gets their attention. The leader says they are definitely going to have to look for another military base on their travels. They start their bikes and ride off heading back the way they came. Something tells me we haven't seen the last of them.

We catch up with the others in the large city we came through on the way here. This is the first time any of them have seen me. The lady in charge comes over and introduces herself, her name is Betty Samuels. Sara introduces me to her as Zeus. She picks up on the name immediately.

"So you are the Greek God that is always ready to rain down retribution on all who would oppose him. Did you meet our motorcycle riding friends in town?"

I tell her that as a matter of fact Billy and I did meet them and they told us to wish them all the best of luck, and they hope you have a great Christmas holiday. She asks if we are talking about the same people. The ones she is talking about have been trying to find them for the past several weeks. Last week they caught George, who is the man with the limp, and tried to make him tell where the women were hiding. Kyle has a gun and ammunition that he found in one of the homes. He went out and fired a couple of shots to get them to let George go. We have been expecting them, but we were hoping that you would come to rescue us before they did. Kyle is almost out of ammunition for the gun.

Sara and Olivia are supervising the loading of the big truck with food supplies from the supermarket we saw on the way up. Betty says if they had known there was this much food this close they would have tried to walk here. I see a sign in a store window that tells me I should be able to get Kyle some ammunition for his gun. He was carrying cases of canned goods, but stops to come across the street to the gun shop with Tim and me. Betty comes with us as does Sara. Betty walks in and takes a 9mm out of the display case and reaches under the counter bringing out several boxes of ammunition for it. Kyle has one of the bullets in his hand trying to match it with the ones on the shelf behind the counter. There are rows of shelves containing guns and ammunition throughout the store.

Tim stops next to a stack of boxes of ammunition and tells Kyle he may want to get the hand truck over by the door and take this entire stack. Gary comes over and asks how much room we want to leave open for guns and ammo. Don comes in and heads directly to the bow and arrow section. He has his arms full in short order heading for the truck to stow away his treasures. We spend almost a half hour picking out what we feel are the best guns in the place and as much ammunition as we can load along with the food. It is dark before we get home, but seeing the lights shining in the houses, and the welcoming committee, makes the new members of our family feel comfortable for the first time in a long time. The hot meal doesn't hurt either.

    The newcomers are absorbed into the households at least for the time being. George, Kyle and Thomas, the men of the group, are invited to join the single men in the large dormitory they built in the loft of the big barn. Two of the boys are about the same age as Teddy so he asks if they can bunk in with him for a while. The other boys find friends in another house. Kathy who is ten and Karen who is eight both find friends in the new group. They along with their mother are invited to stay with us. There is no shortage of invitations for the others as well. For most of them tonight is the first time they were able to take a bath and sleep in a warm bed, without having to worry who might find you. The two young girls wake up crying during the night, so Dayna goes and takes them to their mom, who is just sleeping in the next room. They spend the rest of the night with her. It takes a while to get used to being comfortable.

7

In the morning at breakfast we finally hear the story about how Betty came to be here. She tells us between bites of French toast and bacon.

"I'm a doctor. I was working in a hospital not far from where you found us. One night, about a month ago, I was on duty for twenty-four hours. That is not uncommon when you work at a large hospital, but that day and night I was so busy I couldn't even catnap between cases. When I left it was only a short time before sunup, but I could barely find my car the fog was so heavy. I have never seen fog that heavy before and hope to never again. I sat in my car trying to decide whether or not I should try to find my way home, or go back inside to catch a little sleep in the doctor's lounge, and wait for the sun to burn off the fog. Anyway while I was trying to decide the fog got so heavy I didn't think I could even find my way back into the hospital, so I locked the doors and fell asleep right there."

Sara and Gary come in about then. Sara is getting a plate of food and says, "That damn fog will get you every time." She is looking for a chair, of which there are no empty ones this morning, so she comes over and starts to sit down. I get up and tell her all she had to do was ask and I would have gotten up. She laughs, and tells me that she knows how much I like it when she sits on my lap. Dayna and everybody else laugh. She tells me she will get up, and let me sit in her chair, and then she can sit on my lap. The young ladies of the family roll their eyes and say "Mommy". They say that whenever one of the moms says something like that. They only do it to make me blush, one of these days it's not going to work. Betty can finally continue with her story.

"When I woke up the fog was almost all gone, but nothing looked the same as it did when I parked my car there. For one thing it was a ramp garage and now I was parked in a lot, and all the other cars were at least thirty years old. I got out of the car and went back to the hospital, or at least what was where the hospital had been. It was still a hospital, but was less than half the size it was and was much older and run down. There was no one there, so I went back out to try to find my apartment, but my car was no longer there. I went looking for something familiar until I found the group of people you have met. I have been trying to figure out what happened since then."

We explain about how those of us who came here under similar conditions all got here. We also explain how we all came together to be here and about how we are trying to form a community where we can all be safe and prosper. She says she can't wait to see everything we have done and be able to help us as well. Tim comes in when we are getting ready to go out and tells the young men in the house that he has a job for them to start earning their keep. They say they are willing to do anything we ask, as long as we show them how to do it. Tim says that Teddy, Don, Dan, and Andrew will show them what they need to know. Teddy already knows what Tim wants. He asks me if he can take his knife with them. The twins want to know if they can go hunting with Teddy today, and Melissa has to tell them for about the fiftieth time that they are too young to go hunting.

They tell her they are older now than they were the last time they asked. Melissa tells them they are correct, they are three days older than they were the last time. They remind her that Zeus and Gramma and Grampa Horton won't let anything bad happen to them. Zeus even stops eating French toast that happened to get dropped on the floor when he hears his name mentioned. The new children have never seen a dog before, but he is so friendly they have adopted each other as family already. Teddy comes back displaying his k-bar proudly. When he doesn't need it for hunting he keeps it locked in a gun cabinet in the living room, so that little hands don't get hurt on it. The other young men are impressed to say the least. Teddy takes them outside after making sure they have coats, gloves and hats. It's not like New York in December, but it isn't warm either.

The guys remember it's Sunday, so they don't get to go hunting today, but are definitely going tomorrow. We spend the day showing our new family members around all the groups. They feel bad that they weren't here to help with the planting and harvesting, but promise to do their share of the work from now on. We assure them that we can ask no more than that of anyone. Betty and Doc

McEvoy hit it off right from the start. We are all glad that we now have a doctor that knows about more up to date medicine. Doc is great, but even he is happy to have someone like Betty join us. She gets put to work the very first day with us. One of the women in Barbs group has a beautiful baby girl about three o'clock in the afternoon. Betty jokes about it saying that even the babies are more cooperative here, back home they always seemed to come during the night.

The days are going by as usual, but we are all excited about the headway we are making with the new houses. We now have three of them here and approximately where they will be placed when we get to that point. Jenna and James are doing a great job of teaching our people how to put in a basement and they are more than happy to learn. We hope to have the first house set on the foundation by mid January. The weather doesn't allow us to work every day, and since we are not really in any great hurry, it doesn't matter. We have made a couple of trips to the farther away cities to get more supplies. The one that we stopped at on the way home from picking up Betty's group showed signs that someone else was getting supplies there, so we didn't take anywhere near as much as we would have otherwise.

We checked a bunch of the houses around the city and more than made up for what we didn't take from the store. We did some exploring and found another supply of the large conduit that we are trying to use for an underground tunnel. We expect to have the first two houses connected by a tunnel in just a couple of days. Again Jenna and James have done a great job cutting a hole large enough for the doorway in the basements of the first two homes. They built a very nice frame out of block and we were able to make a door that blends right into the wall with some of the lumber we found. We have tried our sawmill and that works pretty well if we say so ourselves. The wheat mill is working fantastic. Jenna suggested we make a couple of minor changes so we did. We had originally made the paddle wheel paddles out of wood, knowing that they would not last forever, but we were hoping to get a year or so out of them.

Jenna had a pretty good idea where we could find some large sheets of fiberglass that we were able to cut and replace the wooden slats with that. We even went to an auto parts place and got some of the fiberglass bonding material to seal the joints. The wheel is now much lighter and turns easier than it did before. Teddy has two admirers in his new friends Jerry and Steve. They have had the opportunity to go hunting with Andrew, Don, and Dan. They have all been practicing with the bow and arrows that we found and they are not doing badly at all. The first time they went hunting Teddy got a very large buck with a single shot. It was probably more luck than skill because the arrow severed the spinal column and the deer dropped where he was standing. Jerry and Steve have each gotten a deer since then, and Don dropped another large steer. That one was more in self defense than hunting. He and Olivia were out walking in the woods when the bull decided he didn't like them trespassing on his turf.

Luckily he was carrying a .45 automatic with him. Most of us have carried a handgun since we started living here. This time it probably saved Olivia and him from some very serious injuries. When Jerry and Steve got their deer, they asked Teddy to see if they might be able to have one of the k-bar knives. I was expecting that from the first time they saw Teddy's, so I asked their moms if it would be okay. Steve's mom is living in the house with Tim and Charity, but Steve stays at our house most of the time. Jerry's mom Becky, and two sisters are living with us. It is working out well because they are all the same ages as Teddy, Kathy and Karen. Becky and Tara were happy that their sons have found such a good friend and are being able to contribute to the whole group as hunters at such a young age.

We remind them that in the old west, many young men were working like men when they were twelve years old. The fact that they have no idea what we are talking about reminds us that we may have been a little lax in the children's lessons, and in making sure the new people learn to read and write as well. Anyway the young men are now the proud owners of a k-bar knife that they are only allowed to carry when they are hunting. They do however; have pocket knives that they can keep all the time, as long as they treat it with respect. The first tunnel is complete except for covering it over and planting the grass over it. If you aren't looking for a tunnel opening, you cannot find it. The door was made with a counter balance, to allow even a smaller person to open and close the doors from either side. Our team on this project took it a step farther than any of us imagined. Where they put one of the large concrete connectors, they dug a good sized root cellar for want of a better description, to store supplies in just in case someone has to stay hidden for a period of time.

They also put battery powered lights, as well as candles, and lanterns that use propane cylinders in the tunnels. The project went so well that the other groups are going to start linking their homes, and we are going to continue with ours. We also all agree that it would be great to have a tunnel from each group into the woods just in case. December is going by quickly and in just three days it will be Christmas. Many of us want to make another trip over to the Marine base to pick up more clothing and guns as well as other supplies. We have taken everyone into the towns close to us so they can look through the stores and even the houses to find Christmas presents for each other. Some of them remember Christmas, but have not celebrated it for as long as they can remember. Everyone is excited about it this year, like we all were last year.

The trip over to the base is uneventful, as is the loading of the trucks we brought along to bring our treasures back. James and Jenna came along just to make sure they aren't imagining this whole adventure. They both say that they hope it is not a dream, because they are enjoying life more now than they ever did before. Robin is watching little Tim so Dayna could come with me on this trip. It's a good thing she did because she sees two things that none of us see. The first one is dozens of cases of chocolate candy in tin containers in the Base Exchange. The second she sees as we are getting ready to leave. I am making sure the trucks are loaded to the brim when Dayna comes over and tells me not to look to the right, but there is a young girl watching us from behind one of the barracks buildings.

I can see the young lady by looking into the mirror on one of the trucks and she sure looks scared. I tell Dayna I will go through the warehouse we are at and come up behind the girl. Before she can say anything I head through the warehouse and work my way behind the place where the young lady is watching us. When I sneak a peek around the corner, I see Dayna walking back toward the truck, with the young lady and two others about the same age. When I get back to the truck Dayna introduces me to the young people. Jenna, who is every bit as bad as Sara when it comes to picking on me, tells me that I did a great job stalking those dangerous teenage girls. She starts to say she will sleep better tonight knowing I am on the job, but she is laughing too much.

We get acquainted on the ride home. The three young ladies are living with their mother, after their father passed away a while ago. Their mother got sick about ten days ago and hasn't been able to even go anywhere since then. They heard someone at the base, which is us and they came to see if we looked friendly, or if we were the type to steal the girls away. Naturally we stop and pick up the mother, who sounds like she has bronchitis or possibly pneumonia, but I don't have a stethoscope with me and it's hard to tell anyway without a chest x-ray. We make her as comfortable as we can for the ride home. They say that wherever we are going it has to be better than where they are living.

We get home after dark and Doc Betty comes over to check out the lady that is ill. We have several books on natural medicines and Betty knows more than anyone I ever met about using natural herbs to heal people. She brews up a tea, using something that smells bad enough to be great for whoever takes it. We have enough teenaged young ladies to welcome the newcomers. They are about as happy as I have ever seen anyone after eating a hot meal and meeting Jenny, Samantha, Rachel, Emily, and Ellie. I'm sure I left out some, but I can't keep up with everyone around here. Betty is living with Billy and Ramona now, and they have an extra room, so they take Angie, the mom, and the three girls, Meghan, Mickie and Nickie, over there with them. That way Betty can keep an eye on her.

Today is Christmas Eve and everyone is excited, even if they have never celebrated Christmas before. It is even cold enough today to snow. Jenna is in rare form this morning, she, Dayna, and Robin started picking on me early. All I did was tell them that I think it is going to snow this evening so the children can have a white Christmas. Jenna told me we could find out easy enough. All we have to do is go on the weather channel on the TV, or check the weather web site on the computer. I made the mistake of telling her my mind is like a computer, and she has been harassing me ever since. That's okay, nothing could bother me today, I think I am as excited as the children are. The day passes quickly with the preparations we are making for tomorrows celebration. Each of the groups are going to get together in their individual meeting houses and read the story of the birth of Christ from the Bible. Then everyone will get presents and of course we will eat a nice breakfast.

We are planning to show a couple of movies that we have, that are appropriate for this time of year. As the day winds down we are all in our homes relaxing. Kathy and Karen have been quiet all day and even the twins have managed not to get into any mischief. I haven't seen the boys much today and Lisa and Christy have not been around much either. I ask the moms if they have any idea what I may have done to get all the children upset. Robin and Melissa tell me they are afraid the girls overheard a conversation that we had the other night and misunderstand what we were talking about. I know which conversation they are talking about and I can see how they may be confused. I figure it's time we explain what we were talking about, so no one gets the wrong idea.

I call the children, who seem to be in their rooms at the moment. Our children come, but the others don't, so we are sure they misunderstood what was said. I ask them to go and get the rest of the family so I can tell them all at once. That brightens their mood up a little. They run and come back with our new family members. Usually it's a mad scramble to see who is going to sit on my lap, but tonight Tammy and Tina ask me politely if they can. Now I know something is wrong. When all the children are present, as well as Becky their mom, I start to tell them I would like to explain what they think they heard the other evening. Kathy starts telling me that they will be better and not argue so much anymore. Karen says she will not yell at Teddy, Jerry, and Steve anymore if they can stay with us. Tina and Tammy tell me they will share Zeus with everybody if they can stay.

I tell them I wasn't aware that Becky wanted to move. Is this something that has come up recently? Teddy says that they overheard us saying that they would have to move soon. He starts to continue but, I raise my hand signaling him that I would like to say something.

"I know what you all think you heard, but what that conversation was about is the new homes we are bringing in. We adults were just explaining to Becky that if she would like to move into one of the new homes, when it is ready for that, we will be more than willing to help her. We don't anticipate the first house being ready to live in until spring and the ones after that will be when they are. So even if Becky wants to move, which by the way she doesn't, as long as we don't mind them living here, it will be at least next summer before that will happen. I guess we should take a vote to see if we want to make Becky, Lisa, Christy, Jerry, and Steve a permanent part of our family. All those in favor say aye."

Even Zeus barks in the affirmative, so it is as official as it can get. It takes all of about ten minutes before the bickering starts again. Nobody's really angry, and nobody really means it, so we figure we can let the children be children for a while longer anyway. Little Timmy agrees with me by smiling. Even Robin saying he must have gas doesn't bother me tonight.

8

Christmas morning comes just like it did when I was a young boy. The children are all waiting on the stairs when we come out of our rooms in the morning. Then they all rush down and check out the presents under the tree. There are presents in the meeting house for everyone, but we all got each other, and the children a bunch of small stuff to make it more exciting for them. We are having a common breakfast, so the women and the older children leave to help get everything ready. The women cooked what they were asked to at home, and are bringing it to the meeting house. Dayna, Becky, and I have the job of getting the younger children ready, and bringing them over when the bell sounds.

The breakfast and the reading of the birth of Christ are a complete success. Everyone gets a couple of presents, which for the adults are mostly clothes. Everyone loves the uniforms we got at the base so we got all of them we could carry and gave them to everyone as presents. The chocolate in the tin boxes is a huge hit, we found enough for everyone in all the groups to have a couple, and still have several cases left. We also found some hard candy in sealed tins like the chocolate, and that is very popular as well.

Unfortunately even on Christmas, we who live on farms have chores that must be done. Eggs need collecting and chickens fed. Cows need fed and milked, and the milk needs to be pasteurized, and stored properly in the freezers. Last, but definitely not least, the horses need fed. They spend most of their time in the pastures like the cows, but since it's Christmas we want to give them some oats that we found in town. Fortunately no one shirks their duty, and many hands make the work lighter. We are relaxing after the common meal we all shared for an early supper or late lunch, when Teddy comes in and tells me that he, Steve, and Jerry were outside setting up some targets for when they get to shoot the rifles we gave them for Christmas. We told them they can only shoot the guns when they are with us, or when they are hunting with the older young men. Back to Teddy coming in, he is out of breath from running and so are Steve and Jerry. They tell me that they saw some men sneaking around the woods. It looked like they were watching the people who are outside.

I grab my gun, and have Robin call Tim and the others, and tell them what Teddy told us. I ask where they saw the men and head out the door. I am afraid it is the men we ran into when we found Betty and the others. I don't go directly where they saw them, but I circle around trying to get behind them. I get to the woods behind the barn without being seen, at least no one shot at me yet. I can hear voices whispering, but I can't make out what they are saying. I work my way around until I can come up behind three of them. If this is the same group, there are three more, and these guys do look familiar. I hear an owl hoot, and look to my right to see Tim working his way around to where I am. Apparently he saw me before I saw him.

The three we can see don't seem to be carrying guns, or any other weapons that we can see. We decide to ask them what they are doing here. We step out of from behind the trees, and they spin around surprised to see us. They see our guns and tell us they don't want any trouble, they just saw our settlement, and wondered how many people live here. They explain that they have never seen lights, and the houses are in much better shape than any they have ever seen. They say what drew them here, is the smell of food that is like nothing they have ever tasted. I recognize the one doing the talking as the leader of the group in that city. I ask him where the rest of their friends are. We hear a voice behind us saying that they are about twenty feet away. The one talking tells us we have nothing to worry about. They were just looking and wishing they had somewhere like this to live.

They all come up and join their friends. They say they parked their bikes down the road, and walked back to see how big this settlement is. By now, the rest of our guys find us, and ask if there is any trouble. Tim and I tell them that for once, we didn't have to go looking for new friends, they came to us. George and Kyle are two of the men that came to see if they would be needed. The new men recognize them and tell them how sorry they are that George got hurt that time. They say they were looking for people to join up with, but now realize they went about it the wrong way. They say that after meeting us, and the way we kept our guns on them, they realized that maybe they were scaring everyone else the way we scared them.

George and Kyle both tell them there are no hard feelings, but if they are lying they will definitely regret it. We invite them into the meeting house, and call the council together to decide whether or not we let them prove that they are serious. While they are being asked questions, they get to taste the ham, sweet potatoes, and home baked pie that they must have smelled as they were riding past. I don't blame them; I think it smells great too. We have a decision before they are through with dinner. We decide to give them a chance to show us that they are serious about wanting to be part of our family. They will stay in the dormitory, which has been losing occupants fairly regularly to matrimony. We make sure the new people realize that sex is frowned upon unless the people are married, and forcing someone to have sex with you will get you sent packing. So far we have had no incidents like that, and we would like to keep it that way.

It is very nice to have a situation like the one today end peaceably, and with no bloodshed. The men who joined us today seem like nice enough people, but only time will tell. Tonight we are sitting here enjoying the twins, who are reading us a story for a change. They do okay, but the book they chose is not quite at their level of reading, although the story is very interesting. Betty stops over to tell us that Angie is doing much better, her cough seems to have broken, and she is able to eat more solid food now. She tells us that she hopes she was mistaken about the men we took in today. She even says that when she thinks about it, there may well have been a big misunderstanding. At least here, they will have a chance to either prove they belong, or prove that they don't belong. I know we are all hoping that they are serious.

The day after Christmas is Sunday, so we rest from our labors, or at least we only do the same ones we did yesterday. Our six new family members are up bright and early to help with the chores. They have to be shown how to do everything, but so did we all. We gave them all new fatigue jackets, and fatigue pants and shirts to wear when they are working. They seem to be as excited as kids with their new clothes, and the tins of chocolate they received confused them for a moment, but once they tasted it, they decided that they could learn to like that a lot. The days go by and we turn the calendar to start another new year. The work is going well with the help of our new friends. This is the first time they have done anything like the work we do, but they are definitely willing and prove to be hard workers. I had an opportunity to cut firewood with two of them this week, and they both said that all they want out of life is what they see us having here. They both said that they knew their lives were empty, and had no meaning until they just happened to be riding by on Christmas. Now they know they can do something more constructive than ride from place to place.

The weather is cold but the work on the basement and the tunnels is going forward. The basement in this first house is deeper than most, because Billy would like to live here when it is completed. Since he is over seven feet tall, we wanted the basement to be deep enough that he doesn't have to walk all hunched over, all the time. We chose the house that we are putting in here, with him in mind as well. The ceilings are higher than most and we have the option of making the doorways high enough for him to walk through without having to stoop. It's just some of the things, which most of us who are average height, take for granted, but that make his life more difficult. We have managed to get three more of the homes to where they will probably be placed. We have been discussing whether or not we need a basement under every home, or if we can just add a large shed type building. We can also put the tunnel system under those homes by putting a trap door leading down into the tunnel.

I know we sound a bit paranoid, but if you have been some of the places we have been, and seen man's inhumanity toward other men, then you may see security the way we do. Not one member of our groups doubts that we will need the ability to escape without detection some time. We have also read in the history of this area, that hurricanes have come this far inland before and most likely will again. There are even reports of tornadoes hitting this area, and our tunnels will be excellent storm shelters, as well as a way to get back and forth in severe weather. We have found plenty of the large pipes that I have been referring to as conduit, so we might just as well use it. Our biggest problem is that Jenna and James are our only masons at this time, and they can only be in one place at a time. We are taking care of that though, because we have several men that want to learn to do what they are doing, and are working very hard right alongside them.

Josh, who was kind of the leader of the group that joined us on Christmas, and Isaac, who is another of that group, are working like mad men learning all they can. They are already able to work on one area while James and Jenna work on another. We expect that we will be able to break into two or three crews soon, and really get to work on the projects at the other groups as well. We have decided to look for more of the pre-fabricated homes, and if we can find more, we would like to start at the other groups and work toward each other, forming like a big square of homes with a roughly 20 square miles of land in the middle. It will take quite a while to accomplish our goals, but what else have we got to do, besides make sure we have enough food to eat and see if we can find any others who need a place to live.

The days go by, and every day we see that we are getting closer to our objectives and growing closer as a family. We are now through January, and the basement and foundation is almost ready to have the house put into place. I am still not sure how we are going to accomplish that, but the others assure me they know what they are doing. I hope so, with my luck I will probably be standing in the worse possible place if something does go wrong. I have been spending most of my time at the mill, where we are cutting lumber to be used for building and other projects. We have been going out into the woods and finding the hardwood trees that are already down that are still solid. That's like maple, walnut, oak, locust, and ash. We have found that some woods cut better than others, and some dull the blade up pretty badly when you cut them. We are getting a pretty good supply of lumber cut and stacked to season before using it.

Teddy, Jerry, and Steve have become very good hunters. They have another friend about their age who is learning also. His name is Trey. He is from Ryan's group, but seems to spend more time at our house now than he does at home. We have had some weddings that really didn't surprise anyone. The dormitory for the single guys is losing many of its occupants, but we have more young men that will be old enough to stay there soon. There always seems to be a time in a young man's life when he just wants to be on his own, even if it is only a hundred yards from his parents. Tomorrow is the day we are going to put Billy's house on the foundation, and get it ready to live in. It will take more than one day to get it ready, but at least we will be able to work indoors to finish it.

The morning is finally here, and we have everyone from all the groups here to watch us set the first house. No one seems to doubt that we will accomplish this task, and their confidence makes me more confident. James and Jenna say they have done this before and it is no big deal. I know we have to remove the axles and the tires from the two sides, then slide them onto the foundation and connect the two halves. Naturally we have the usual jokes, about not realizing we wanted to put that house on this foundation. They really know what they are doing, because it takes less than an hour to get the two halves pushed as close together as we can push them. Now James gets this device that looks like a come-a-long, that he fastens to the two sides of the house. He has a second device for the other end, and then they draw the two sides tight up against each other.

The rest of the day is spent anchoring the two halves to the foundation and bolting the two halves together. Tomorrow we will tie the siding in, and begin working on the inside to get it ready to be lived in. Of course we will have to connect the basement stairs, and finish off the basement with shelving units, and maybe even an extra room down there. The houses that are going to be put on a slab instead of a basement will be easier and take less time. This house already has the tunnel in connecting it to the house we live in, and the tunnel goes out the other side to the slab where the other house will be put. Crews are also working on joining all the houses that already exist in the group. Josh, Isaac, Jake, and Adam seem to be everywhere today, helping with the house. They along with Ben and Hank have proven to be some of our best workers, and in this group that's saying something. Everyone helps no matter what the job is.

When the day is finally over and we can relax a little or at least I could, if Robin and Dayna would let me. They want to know what I am going to do to help Josh win over Betty, who they claim he is in love with. I saw him trying to talk to her today, I say trying, because every time he got close she walked away. Something tells me she still holds a grudge about when George got hurt. Now George has been spending a lot of time with Marge. He is a little older than she is, but they make a nice looking couple. Dayna, Robin, Charity, Carrie, Cassie, and Melissa think it's their duty to play match maker for our group. In this case they want me to talk to Betty and see why she doesn't like Josh. They don't like my attitude when I tell them that if Betty doesn't like him that only leaves about thirty other single women in the groups that would jump at the chance to marry Josh. All the other guys seem to have met girls that at least talk to them regularly. My loving wives tell me that if I don't try to help, that's more than we will be doing so I figure what the heck. I can at least talk to Betty.

My daughters love me, I get to read them stories, plus they tell me how much they love me all the time. In the morning the crew starts working on the house we set yesterday, and another crew gets started moving the next house into place. I do manage to get a few minutes to talk to Betty, and she says that she just doesn't trust Josh and the others yet. She thinks he's a nice enough guy, but she is no hurry to get married, or even get serious with anyone. At lunch I tell the women and they say they will just have to think of a way to get them together. Naturally I wish them good luck, hoping that I will not be involved in the next plot to get them together. The next house is set to be put into place tomorrow. It will go in much the same as the other one, except there will not be a basement, but there will be a crawl space to get at the wiring and duct work that is below floor level.

9

The morning starts out kind of cold and gray. Definitely not an ideal day to be working outside, but we want to get that second house set in place. I have a feeling of foreboding that just won't go away, and I can't figure out what could be wrong. We have the wheels and the axles off the one side of the house when Robin comes running and says that Barb's group is under attack. All the men with me take off for their homes to get their rifles, and head for there to help. Robin brought my fifty with her, and like the others I am wearing a sidearm, so I run to the barn to get one of our motorcycles to head cross country. Barb's group is between five and seven minutes away across the fields and woods, since we made a trail and graveled it. Josh, Isaac, and Ben are already on their motorcycles with rifles hung over their shoulders. They take off about twenty seconds before I do.

We are tearing across the gravel path, going as fast as we dare without losing control and crashing into a tree or flipping the bikes. When we are a few hundred yards away, we can hear gunfire coming from that direction. Josh is riding right next to me, when he leans toward me and says that Doc Betty came over here this morning. He says if anybody hurts her he will personally kill them. I know that Isaac and Ben like girls that live over here as well. I think of everyone in all the groups as my family, and will kill anyone that tries to hurt them, or does hurt them. We pull up just before we get to the yards of the homes here. We don't want to blunder in and get ourselves killed either. We can hear sporadic gunfire, so we know that the group has not been taken over yet. I tell Josh and Isaac to go around one way, while Ben and I go the other way. We can hear more motorcycles coming the way we came.

We can hear motorcycles in the front of the houses as well, and it sounds like they are firing as they ride past because we hear glass breaking. I can hear children crying, and I am really starting to get ticked off. I have no idea where these guys came from, but I am pretty sure I know where they are going today. We get to the edge of the porch on the house where Barb lives. I know for a fact there are a couple of mothers who share this house, and at least six children, and these animals are shooting into the windows. I am getting ready to look around the porch when I hear a man's voice, demanding that they send out girls for them to take with them, or they will set fire to the houses. I am close enough to hear what he says afterward to his buddies. He laughs and says they are going to set fire to the houses anyway, but why waste good women.

I step around the porch and find myself facing three of the attackers. I am holding my fifty at arm's length, so I just point at the closest one and pull the trigger. That gun makes more noise than most people have heard from a gun, plus it picks the guy up and throws him back about ten feet. The others dive behind the other end of the porch. Josh and Isaac come around the corner and get driven back by gunfire from those two, plus some guns across the way that we can't quite place. I don't know where he learned to do it, but Josh dives out from behind the building firing his handgun toward the two at the end of the porch. He must hit at least one, because we see him start to rise up, then fall face down in the dirt.

The bullets are hitting all around him from the other side of the road where one of the other houses is. We still can't see them, but we send some lead of our own in that direction, which at least makes them move. We now have reinforcements, who are spreading out to surround the enemy and end this battle. The biggest problem is that we don't know how many there are. We know for sure they are down two men, but that's as much as we know for sure. We hear some shooting coming from behind the house where the other bad guys were shooting from, then we hear Dons voice saying that these three won't be hurting anyone else. Our guys come out from behind the house, and start walking toward us. They are saying we better get the backhoe out and bury these guys. For some reason I don't feel like it is all over yet. I am looking around to see if we missed anyone when one of the moms, Caroline, comes running from one of the other houses, and her son and daughter, who are like five and six, come running out of the house we are standing in front of.

Josh is smiling, watching Caroline and the children meet right next to him. He turns to look my way when he yells "NO", and wraps his arms around them turning them away from us. Just then one of the guys we thought was dead, raises up and fires at them with a semi-automatic handgun, hitting Josh at least two times, before we can shoot the guy with the gun and put him down for good. I run to Josh, because I have had some training, and I have to lift him off Caroline and the children, who are unharmed, because he took all the lead meant for them. He is still alive, and it doesn't look like the bullets hit the heart or lungs, but there is still a lot in there to be torn up. Doc Betty is beside me before I can even assess the damage, telling two of us to carry him into the house.

Barb has the table cleared, and tells us to lay him on it, so that Betty can see what she is doing. Josh is coherent anyway, and asks me if Caroline and the children are okay. I tell him they didn't get a scratch. He asks how many times he got shot. Betty comes over and smiles telling him he didn't get shot, he just got the worse brush burn she has ever seen when he fell on the dirt. We have some drugs that we found at the hospitals we have visited, but we are not sure they will do any good now. Betty asks him if he would like to drink some whiskey to help kill the pain, and he tells her he will put up with the pain. He tried whiskey once, and that was enough for him. One of the bullets went straight through, and the other one we can see bulging against his side. Betty cuts the skin where we see the bulging, and the bullet falls out.

Betty checks the wounds closely and says that it looks like the bullets missed all the vital organs, but she does have to operate to make sure. Apparently some of the medication we found works, because she is able to knock him out, and operate on his shoulder and his side, where the wounds are. She has him all stitched up, and is washing her hands when he wakes up. He smiles, which is more than I think I could do, if I was just hurt as badly as he was. He tells Betty that this has to be the most painful brush burn he ever got. Caroline has been standing close by ever since we brought Josh in. She asks if she can thank him for saving her life and the lives of her children. Betty smiles and tells her that depends on how she wants to thank him. She goes over and gives him a hug and a kiss on the forehead. The two children come over and climb on a chair to see him, and then kiss him, but they lean against his side to get close.

He just smiles and says it was worth it to get good kisses like that. Betty comes back over and is running her fingers through his hair when she tells him he will have to rest for a while before he can go back to work. She also tells him that he won't be able to climb that ladder up to the bachelor's dorm in the barn. She says she has two beds in her room, or at least she will have when I put a second one in there, so he can be where she can keep an eye on him, at least until he can get around on his own. Betty asks if we have a gurney to take him back to our group on, and Isaac, Jake, Hank, Ben, and Adam come in with one of the gurneys we confiscated from the hospital in town. They load it into the van and ask us if we can take care of him when we get home. They don't want to go back tonight just in case there are more attackers around. If there was ever any doubt about Josh and his group's intentions, there are no more.

When we get back to our homes, we have to tell everyone all the details, after we carry Josh in to the house and into Betty's room, so she can keep an eye on him. Tim and I tease her saying that we know he is too weak to attack her, but what if she attacks him, the poor guy is defenseless. Josh smiles and says he is willing to take his chances, Betty smacks me and Tim, and then our wives smack us for teasing her. I pick up little Timmy so that no one else will smack me. It's all in fun, and when I say we get smacked, it really doesn't hurt. Josh is up walking around the next morning. We make sure he knows enough to take it easy until he is back to full strength. Our biggest fear is infection, because we do not know how good the medications we have found are. Betty is very knowledgeable about herbs and plants that are good for healing, so he should be fine in a few weeks.

Our chores, and the projects we are working on, continue through the winter. There are days when all we can do is the chores, like making sure everyone has firewood for their woodstoves. The chickens need tended and fed every day. The same goes for the cows, they have to be milked in the morning and again in the evening. The milk has to be pasteurized and the cream skimmed off. That's what we use for ice cream and butter. We also have to grind the wheat into flour at the mill. We have been doing that once a week even if we don't need the flour right away. With all five groups making bread, and other things with it, we do use quite a bit though. The young people love to ride the horses, so they get plenty of exercise. The hunters will often take the horses, so they can go a mile or so from home and not have to go back for the meat.

We are still planning to make trips farther out than we have previously gone, looking for people who may wish to join our groups. We have made a couple, where we went out about a hundred miles, but so far we have not tried any long trips. Tim, Ken, Gary, Sara, and I, all know of other military bases in North and South Carolina. We are planning a trip over that way soon for two reasons. To see if there are any people, and to see if there is anything we can use on those bases. Teddy, Jerry, and Steve have been asking if they can go on one of the trips when we go to those bases. I told them to ask their moms, and they were a big help. Their mom's told them to ask me. I don't have a problem with them coming along. I just hope we don't run into any real trouble. If any of them get hurt, I will never forgive myself and neither will their moms.

We decide to go on Monday morning, figuring we will easily be home by Friday or Saturday. Isaac, Adam, and Jake are going with Jenna, James, Gary, Sara, and me. Of course the boys are coming along as well. Don't tell their moms, but I have been teaching them to drive. It's not like there are a lot of other drivers on the road, plus if they hit something, there is no one to sue you over it. Whenever I think about car accidents, I think of Ma Horton. She got in more accidents than anyone I ever knew, and none of them were ever her fault. I'll never forget the time she was parking the car in the BX parking lot, after dropping Gunny off at the door. This PFC tried to beat her to the parking place, and hit her car just behind the driver's side door. He proceeded to yell at her, but several people saw the accident and told Gunny, who had already gone into the store. He came out and got to the car at about the same time I did. Not that she needed any help. That young kid was trying to brow beat her into admitting it was her fault, and she wasn't about to.

Ma never took any guff from Gunny, she wasn't about to take any disrespect from that kid. When she got through reading him the riot act, she even had his mothers phone number and called her to tell her how rude her son was. Ma wasn't going to press the issue by calling insurance companies, because Gunny and I always enjoyed working on the cars and we got pretty good at body work, but his attitude was so nasty, she let his insurance pay for the damages. Every time I tell the girls about Ma, they all say they would have loved to have known her. They have all said that they met her in dreams and enjoyed those dreams very much. The children all say that Ma and Gunny visit them in dreams all the time.

The trip to North Carolina takes us most of a day. It's not that far, but the roads are not good at all, and there are a lot of cars parked all over the place. The damage is much worse here than where we live, because of the weather that hits the coast. James and Jenna want to study the structures at the base, and check out some of the cars, and other things that are made from steel. The rest of us are checking the base for whatever we feel we can use. The weather has ruined a lot of goods we could have used, but we do find a large supply of uniforms, tee shirts, weapons, and some of the military rations that are still good. Of course that topic can get an argument started as to whether or not they were ever good. The young people love them almost as much as they love the military knives they find for sale in the Base Exchange. They empty the entire warehouse of every knife, every tee shirt, and every uniform they can find. There are numerous items that I will not go into, but we leave there with one full truck.

We find that we can fill our gas tanks from the supplies at the base. They were prepared for power outages, because the gas pumps can be worked by hand. We have to prime the pump, but after that we can fill all of our vehicles and replace any gas that we used from our cans of gas. We find no signs of life anywhere, but that doesn't surprise us much, because of the harsh storms this part of the country gets. We visit two bases in North Carolina, and do well at each of them. There is more than one military base in South Carolina as well, and we visit two of them. One of them is almost to Florida, and in our world was a training base for the Marine Corp. The weather seems to have hit that one the hardest of all. We fill our last truck from this base, but we don't leave much behind that is good either.

We decide to go back to the west, and then head north. There are some fairly large cities going this way, and we find some very large food stores that have barely been touched. We also find a great outdoor store that we all decide we can't leave without seeing what they have. We all also agree that we would love to have this building back at the farm. They also have several trucks similar to the ones we already have. We spend about four hours getting one to where we can drive it. We hope it will get all the way back home. The boys have it loaded with supplies while we are working on it. We find some great cold weather gear, not that we need it where we live, but you never know, so we throw in a couple dozen sets of the under clothes and at least that many one piece suits and parkas.

There is a great gun department, where we pick up some very nice guns and thousands of rounds of ammunition. The boys find a large supply of bows and arrows of all styles and sizes. They also find room for a large supply of fishing equipment to take back. This store has a large supply of dehydrated foods packed in aluminum foil so they should still be good. Naturally we can't get everything we want in the truck, but we do get a lot, plus we are planning a return trip in the near future. While we are working on the truck, Jenna nudges my arm, and tells me not to look to the left, there is someone next to a building over there. I pretend to be reaching for a wrench and glance that way. There are two young children watching us from behind a dumpster. The only reason we can see them is because we are standing on the loading dock of the store.

Sara and Jenna decide to go back into the store and work their way around behind the children. We definitely don't want to frighten them away, and we want to know how many more people are here. I continue working with James glancing that way, but at least trying to look like I am looking beyond where the children are. In a few minutes we hear a ruckus coming from that direction, and turn in time to see those two children trying to get away from Sara and Jenna. It only takes a few seconds for a woman to come to where they are, and ask us not to hurt her children. She assures us they won't bother us, it's just that it's been so long since they have seen another living soul. Sara and Jenna assure her that we are not going to hurt anyone. In fact if they would like to join us, they are more than welcome, and if there is anyone else around they are welcome too.

The lady says that she is not sure if there are others around or not, but she has smelled smoke coming from north of where we are. We have loaded everything we can fit in the trucks so we are ready to leave. The lady's name is Carla, her children are named Beth, who is nine and Sandra who is eight. They decide to come with us, so they gather up their belongings and join Jenna and Sara in the van. We go north looking for any other people who might want to join us. We spot the smoke rising from a fifty gallon drum before we see any people. When they see us they run for cover. We stop and show them that we mean them no harm. They finally decide to at least half believe us, because they do come out, but not close enough if we wanted to grab them.

This is a group of eight. They say they came here a while back, because where they were living was just about out of food. We tell them what we are offering, but I think it's the young men who actually convince them. Half of the group looks to be about the same age as Teddy, Jerry, and Steve, plus they are girls, so that makes our young men even more interested. The other half of the group is two couples that appear to be in their late twenties. They say that even if just half of what we are saying is true, they can't afford not to come with us. They say they have seen no one else since they have been here, but we watch carefully as we drive through the city and back home. It is almost ten when we finally get home. Our new people are surprised to see lights that are not candles or lanterns, and the hot meal they are given when we introduce them to everyone, makes them very happy that they came with us.

We will wait until tomorrow to unload the trucks. The other groups come over in the morning to meet our new friends, and to see what we brought back. As usual everyone gets something, plus we put a supply away for any new people that we may find. The new people we brought back with us all say that they have no idea how to do any of the things they see us doing, but they are more than willing to learn and to help. The teenage girls become instant friends of Jenny, Samantha, and the other young teens that take care of the chickens and help with the cows as well. The boys found some really nice, really big hunting knives, that they are trying to keep from their moms but, their little sisters see them and just like that old expression, "time will tell". Well so will little sisters, if you give them something to tell about. The boys don't get into any trouble, but they do have to keep the knives locked up when they are not going hunting.

They are big heroes anyway, when the other young men and even some of the young women see all the archery equipment they brought back. They brought back what looks like several hundred arrows made of aluminum or fiberglass, along with several different types of hunting arrow heads. Those are as sharp as a razor, so we insist that those get stored with the guns and ammunition, away from little fingers and hands. Today is Saturday, and the boys are hoping to go hunting, but Don, Dan, and Andrew have been hunting and have filled all the groups' meat coolers and the smoke house. Actually that's a good thing, because the weather turns nasty later in the day and doesn't let up until Tuesday. I for one do not mind the time off to just do our chores and spend some time reading and playing with the children.

I forgot to mention that Billy is now living in his new house, and loves it. His mom and Dayna's dad Tom, live with him and Ramona, as do Frank and Connie. Tom and Frank have been great friends since Frank and his family joined our family. Frank is our resident farmer and has forgotten more than I will ever know about farming. It's a good thing Rod, Tim, Ken, and several of our other men are so interested in learning all they can. I am learning, but nowhere near as fast as they are. Josh is getting around pretty good for a gimp, that's what I told him when I saw him this morning, and I got smacked by Betty for calling him that. He thought it was funny, I got to talk to him alone for a few minutes, and he was smiling from ear to ear. I asked him if he ever regretted taking those bullets. He said what I thought he would.

"Jon, if I had known that getting shot like that would help Betty fall in love with me, I would have asked that guy to shoot me. Caroline and the children stop by to see me every time they come over. It feels so good to have those special spirits hug me and tell me how much they love me. They even asked if they can call me daddy. Betty says that she doesn't think she can have children so she told me it would be okay with her if Caroline, Samantha, and Samuel live with us as part of our family. I will be forever grateful that you let us have a chance to prove that we wanted nothing more than to be part of a family. I know the other guys all feel the same way."

I have to tell him that we had our doubts, but they have proven themselves many times over. We are into the second half of February, and the weather is worse than it was last year at this time. We have had more snow, but still very little compared to what they get up north. That combined with the cold is slowing down the progress we were hoping to make on putting in the tunnels and the new homes. Tim is still in contact with other groups around the country, and one evening he even got through to a group that said they are in England. They sure sounded English to us. They told us that they have been in contact with groups in France and Germany, and it sounds like conditions are the same everywhere. We kind of figured that because if other countries were untouched, or had much less devastation, they would have been here to see how this country fared.

It was during one such evening, when Tim was talking to the different groups, that we learned of a group up north that is in serious trouble, and is asking if anyone could possibly help them. The only reason they are able to send out a message, is because they have a man with their group that was into short wave radio before the war. They came across the radio they are using by accident, and were hoping desperately that someone would hear them. They say they are in Rochester, New York, and if they don't freeze to death this winter, they will probably starve before spring. We talked to them about different things we have done to find food, but they tell us that may work in the south, but when the temperatures are below zero, canned foods whether in metal cans or jars freeze and are no good. We tell them we will try to get there as soon as possible, but that we can't promise anything.

The general consensus is that we have to at least try to save them. They said there are twenty people in their group, so we will need to take at least two vans and the bus. We will also have to take a pickup truck to carry gas, in case we don't find any along the way. We will have to travel back almost the same way we came down, so we know what kind of shape the roads are in. We are thinking three days to get there, and that long coming back. We ask for volunteers and the first two hands raised are Sara and Gary. Josh raises his hand, but Betty tells him he is not strong enough for something like this yet. Isaac, Ben, and Hank raise their hands and right after them Teddy, Jerry, and Steve raise theirs. Tara, Steve's mom, looks at me and shakes her head no, then Becky, who is Jerry's mom, says that we shouldn't let three of our best hunters go all at once. Steve and Jerry say in that case they will stay home this time, and Teddy can stay home next time.

I was hoping that I would not have to go, but I would worry all the while they are gone; wondering if this is a set-up or some kind of trap. Little Timmy is almost six months old and is so much fun to play with. We hold a meeting to decide when would be the best time to leave. Tomorrow is Sunday, but since lives may be at stake here, we decide to leave tomorrow anyway. We spend the remainder of the evening getting things ready for the trip. We are very grateful that we found all that cold weather gear on the last trip. At the last minute James, Jenna, and Tim decide to come along. Tim laughs and says he can't let daddy Zeus go and have all the fun. That's his way of saying that he is well aware that this could easily be an ambush. I have to admit that I will feel better having him along. I try to talk Teddy out of coming, but he will not listen to any of the arguments I bring up. She's not here saying it, but I can hear Ma Horton telling me that he takes after me. She was always telling me how stubborn I was when I made up my mind.

10

We leave in the morning, after we have a family prayer. For some reason this trip seems to have a cloud hanging over it. Tim and I were commenting on that earlier, saying that we both remember missions that were like that. It doesn't necessarily mean that anything is going to go wrong. It's just that we have this hollow feeling in the pit of our stomach. It may just be that this could easily be the longest trip we have made so far, and that we don't want to be away from our families for however long this will be.

We head north the way we came down, but then we go a little farther west than we did when we came here. We figure we may as well check the area in between, just in case there are more people that may need our help. The roads are not in bad shape at all, so we are able to make better time than we ever expected. Tim brought a shortwave radio along in case we can find an antenna, but we feel it is important to let the family know when we find those people, and when we are on our way home. We make good enough time that we have a good chance of being there tomorrow. Teddy is having the time of his life, we rode together all day in the pickup, and I don't think he quit talking for more than five minutes all day. I don't mind at all, I would much rather listen to him than have him think I am not interested in what he is thinking about.

The weather is much colder already and we are still in Pennsylvania. We are definitely farther west than when we came down, but there is still no sign of life anywhere. We stop for the night at a motel that is deserted, but at least we can get out of the night air. There is a gas station next door to it that we are able to get the generator started to run the pumps. We have a generator with us that we can patch into the electrical controls anyway, but this way we don't have to. We are able to fill all the vehicles before we turn in for the night. The next morning dawns, with at least six inches of snow, and the thermometer telling us it is only ten degrees above zero out here. I can't ever remember being so happy to have a good heater in our vehicles.

The going is a little slower in the snow because we can't see the pot holes, and the places where the pavement has moved and caused some pretty hefty bumps in the road. Tim radios all of us that he is going to write to his congressman for the shameful lack of snow plows on this road. Some members of our team have no idea what a snow plow is, so we have to explain it to them. They think it's funny when they know what he is talking about. Teddy is not talking quite so much today. I think he is starting to worry, because the snow is not showing any signs of stopping, and it looks like we are heading right into the worst of it. By the time we get to the outskirts of Rochester it is getting dark, and we are pushing snow with our bumpers. Tim has been trying to raise the group of people we are here to rescue, but has not had any luck yet.

We figure we will be better off looking for them in the daylight, so we find another motel and gas station, and settle in for the night. With the snow continuing to fall, we discuss our options, and decide we need to find some snow chains for our tires, just in case. We cannot see anywhere in the dark where we might find something like that, so we decide to wait until morning, but we definitely have to do something, or we may get snowed in until spring. In the morning we are able to raise the people that we are here for. They tell us where they are in the city, but this is a large city, and we are not sure how accurate our maps are. Behind the desk on the way out, we find several maps of Rochester, and the surrounding area. One of the maps we find shows us that we are not more than maybe ten miles from them. We head out again pushing snow with the bumpers of our vehicles. We come to an intersection where there is a large plaza that has two auto parts stores in it. We turn in and check out the stores for chains and anything else we may need.

We find what we are looking for, and some shovels that will come in very handy as well. We decide not to take the time to put the chains on until we need them, but that is starting to look like it will be pretty soon. The closer we get to the people we are here to pick up, the more wary we become. Everyone is watching all around to make sure we don't drive into an ambush. It doesn't take long to find the folks we have been talking to. They are extremely happy to see us. Their leader is a man who looks to be in his mid forties. His wife and two children are here as well, along with ten more women and girls, and six other men and boys. We checked a couple of super markets on our way through the city, and what they are telling us is apparently the truth. They have a pretty good place to live, but I am sure it is terribly cold all winter here. They are heating just like our group did before Tim and I came along. They stand around a fire barrel, and at night try to have enough covers to keep you warm.

The snow is continuing to fall, I remember where we came from, this part of the country was always getting storms that would drop snow by the foot, not the inch. Tim reminds me that one year Buffalo, not far from here, got eighty inches of snow in a weekend. They had snowplows, and a population to drive them, and it still took several days to dig out. Across the street from where we find our new friends, there is a large garage, where we can pull our vehicles in and put the snow chains on them. We have been sliding all over the road for the past two days. Thinking about those snow plows gives me a crazy idea. I talk to Tim, Sara, Gary, Jenna, and James and they think it's a good idea, if we can find one and get it running. Isaac, Ben, and Hank have no idea what we are talking about, and our new friends don't either, but if we think it's a good idea they are all for it.

We think about looking in a phone book to find the nearest place where we might find one, but when we ask if our new friends know where we may find a phone book, they tell us anything like that would have been burned already. Teddy, who is scrounging through the buildings around us, comes running back and asks if this is what we are looking for. He says he found it in a pile of junk in the building a couple doors down. It's a phone book alright, and we are able to find the city garage, and it is only about ten blocks away. At least the closest one, this city is large enough, or at least it was once large enough, to need several garages located strategically around the city. Gary, Sara, and I take the pickup, with the chains on the tires, and go looking to see if we can find that place.

Actually luck is shining down on us because we find it, and there are several large trucks parked in a row in the back of the parking lot. There are more plows than trucks, lined up neatly, waiting to be picked up by the trucks. We try to get one of the trucks running in this cold, and we are freezing, so we use the pickup to tow the truck to the huge garage doors they have, apparently to service these vehicles when this place was functioning. We would never have made it without the chains, it's a struggle as it is, but we manage to get the truck in out of the wind anyway. Our team is getting very good at this sort of thing. I head for the generator, while Gary checks out the compressor, and Sara is already checking the tires over for cracks and splits from sitting for so long. The engine is diesel, so it is less complicated than a gasoline engine. Sara has the engine running in less than an hour, after we get the generator going and the compressor.

The tires will hold air so our luck is holding so far. We drag one of the huge plows inside using the pickup, and have it mounted in place, and the hydraulics working in about another hour. Since we have heat in this building, with the generator running, we decide that I will go back to get the others and we will spend the night, since it is starting to get dark anyway. There is a store a short distance away, so Gary and Sara are going to check it out and see if they can find enough food for all of us, at least for tonight. That will help our supplies last if they can. I get back to the group, and I no sooner get the truck parked and start to get out, when a bullet slams into the side of the truck near my head. I look toward the building with our friends in it and they are motioning me to get down. That's a waste of effort. What do they think I'm going to do when someone is shooting at me?

I am armed, but only with my 9mm pistol, so I pull that and return fire, while I am working my way to the building where everyone else is. I manage to get inside, but not without a couple of very close calls from our attackers. Tim meets me as soon as I get in the door, and tells me he tried to warn me, but there was no way to tell me, without getting shot himself. I tell him what we have accomplished, and what we are planning. Actually, now that's what we were planning. My SEAL training is kicking in, I'm studying the surrounding buildings to see if I can get an advantage by getting above or behind our enemy. The leader of our new friends comes over and apologizes for everything. He says that they were hoping to get away before those guys out there realized they were leaving.

He explains that those men and women out there leave them alone as long as they find food or other things that those people want. He says that's why they are in danger of starving and freezing to death, because those predators take everything that they find. I call them predators, he called them guys. So far they have left the women alone, but they have been making some references about the young girls keeping them warm this winter. He tells us he wouldn't blame us if we left them here, they shouldn't have gotten us involved in their problems. I tell him and the entire group that we wish they would have told us up front, we would have been better prepared for this, but that's all water under the bridge. Now we have to figure out how to get out of here.

Tim shows me my fifty caliber rifle with the heat sensing scope. I was hoping he got that out of the van before they were attacked. I can see a four story office building that should give me a pretty good range of vision, and help me spot our enemies. Teddy asks if he can come with me. I tell him that our new friends need him here, besides if anything happens to him, his mom will skin me alive. I slip out the back door and make my way to the building I saw. Tim, James, and Jenna estimate the enemy as being about ten or twelve strong. They are basing that on what our friends have told them, and what they were able to see from the windows. These people are much better at military tactics than any we have met so far. I am impressed with the composure that Isaac, Ben, and Hank are showing. They have been taught by us, but have no real formal military experience. They are good men to have on our side. I have to quit thinking about anything except what I have to do right now. It's been a long time since I have needed these skills.

It sure is cold out here, all I want to do is get our group together, and head for home first thing in the morning. I am at the building now, I get inside and work my way up to the fourth floor without being seen. At least there have been no shots in my direction. They are continuing to shoot at my friends in the building I just left. I have a walkie-talkie that I can stay in touch with Tim on. I am telling him my progress as I make my way up to the fourth floor. I get there and find out I can't see what I wanted to, so I decide to go up to the roof. I am worried about that, because there are places where the snow is coming right in through small holes in the roof, where it has obviously rotted away. Just how rotten it is I won't know until I am up there. I get to the roof and I can feel the roof giving under my feet, but not all the way, so I keep going as close to the edge as I can get.

There is a raised edge on this roof, about three feet high. I am crouching, to keep from being seen from below, until I get to where I expect to be able to see our attackers, or at least some of them. I am right in that respect, from where I am now I can see into the buildings that they are holed up in. I am continuing to talk to Tim telling him what I see. I ask him if I should kill or just warn those people, after all they haven't killed any of us. He tells me I'm getting soft in my old age, the Daddy Zeus he used to know would never think about giving them a second chance. I tell them what the people I see look like and Sam, the leader of the group, tells me the guy I am looking at assaulted one of the teenage girls last summer. He doesn't finish saying it when that fifty speaks loudly, and we have one less attacker.

I am spotted by at least three of them, so I have no choice anymore. I take aim one at a time and take out all three of them firing at me. I can see two women sneaking out the back of the building where I shot a man just a minute or so ago. They look like all the fight is gone from them. It's always easier to attack people who can't fight back. I am looking for more targets, or at least proof that they are calling it quits, when I hear a sound that scares me instantly. I can hear the roof creaking under me, and then I hear the report of a large caliber gun directly below me. I feel the bullet tear into my leg and go out the other side, just before I crash through the roof into the room below. I try desperately to hold onto the gun, but the hole I am falling through is jagged, and rips it out of my hands.

I land hard and awkward, I feel the bone in my leg break, and my arm is broken where I landed against a desk, or something down here. I must also have some broken or badly bruised ribs, because I can hardly breathe. I am more worried about the guy, or whoever it was that fired that shot. They must still be down here, or hopefully I got lucky and fell on them. There is not that much luck in the world.

I can see the fifty about ten feet away, but I am not sure I can move that far to get to it, even if I don't get shot again before I can. I try to move toward it and the pain in my leg, arm and side is pure agony. I can't recall ever being hurt this badly before. I hear a very nasty laugh coming from my left side, and it's all I can do to turn my head in that direction. I see a man holding an M16 military rifle, casually pointing it at me.

He is smiling, and obviously since he has the upper hand, is in no hurry to finish me off. In fact he tells me he is debating whether to shoot me, and put me out of my misery, or to just let me die of exposure. He figures in this cold, and with my injuries, I may even last until morning. He is wearing a Special Forces uniform from the army. He also lights a cigarette, which is the first that I have seen since I have been in this world. He actually looks old enough to have been in the army when the war started. That would explain the military tactics being used in this attack. He smiles again; he asks me what I am thinking about. He says that he will take a guess.

"You are wondering where I got my training from. I am wondering the same thing about you. You are not old enough to have been in the military before the war, so where did you learn urban war tactics? We have heard on the short wave radio that there are some people that claim to have come from a different dimension, or maybe even a different world. Are you and your friends downstairs some of those people? It is a shame to have to kill such a worthy opponent, but I have plans for those young ladies, and I know you won't just drive away and leave them for me. Besides I can use those vehicles that you so thoughtfully brought to me. I tell you what, I will give you to the count of ten to get to your gun and try to kill me. If you don't, I will put another bullet in your other leg, and let the cold kill you. Sound fair to you? Okay, it's a deal."

I am under no delusions, there is no way I can get to that gun, but I am going to try anyway. I try, but I can't even move enough to get turned toward the gun. He is laughing again when he says that it is too bad, but he is just going to have to shoot me. I look toward him, and then I hear a voice tell him that they don't think he ought to do that. I see the look of surprise on his face as he turns toward the voice, and then I see the large red stain spreading across his chest. I don't even hear the report of the rifle until the attacker is falling backward. My rescuer fires again, knocking our attacker down for good. I can hear Tim's voice coming over the radio yelling, asking if I am alright. Everything that just transpired couldn't have taken more than a minute or two. I can't reach the walkie-talkie mouth piece, so Teddy brings it to me still carrying his rifle. Tim asks me again if I am okay, and I tell him I will be thanks to my son. Tim tells me that Teddy snuck out when no one was watching. He thinks he is coming after me.

    I tell Tim that Ted is now with me, and I couldn't be happier or prouder than I am right now. Tim says that the attackers seem to have disappeared since I killed those three. I tell him that at least one stayed behind, and I think he was their leader. I stress the word was, I tell them that I am going to need some help very soon, or Dayna, Robin, and Melissa are going to be very angry with him. They have a little trouble finding me, but Teddy cleared a path large enough for them to get through, to put me on a stretcher and carry me out. The pain is terrible, and I think I am starting to get hypothermia, because I am shivering uncontrollably. I manage to tell them how to find the garage where Sara and Gary are before I pass out, from the pain I guess. I wake up with Teddy sitting beside me. I tell him he better get some sleep, because we are getting out of this place first thing in the morning. I also tell him how proud I am of him. Not for killing another man, I'm proud that he did not panic, or do something foolish. He conducted himself as well as any seasoned soldier that I have ever served with.

    He turns red from embarrassment, and tells me that he learned from the best, his dad. He asks if I will be upset if he asks if he can snuggle up close to me tonight to sleep. Even with the heat on it is still very cold in here. Every time he moves it hurts like heck, but I still remember the first man I killed. Even though it was in self defense, I still wondered if there wasn't maybe something else I could have done. When I am asleep, or at least I think I am asleep, Ma and Gunny come to see me. Gunny tells me what a fine job I am doing with Teddy and the other children, but that I better learn to keep my mind on business when I am in a fire fight like that one last evening. The way I feel, I ask them if it is my time to join them. They tell me not yet, they have talked with the head man, and he says that I still have a lot of work to do in this world. There is another couple standing with them, but before I can meet them I am jarred awake by being put into the back of one of the vans.

Teddy yells at whoever almost dropped me, I try to tell them I will be okay in a little while, but I pass out as fast as I woke up. The next thing I know I am lying in my bed at home and Dayna, Robin, and Melissa, along with the children, are standing around the bed watching me I guess. It sure feels good not to be cold again. I try to move, but I still have that terrible pain in my side, arm, and leg, actually both legs. Doc McEvoy and Doc Betty are standing just behind the family. I can barely speak, but I do manage to ask how long we have been home, after Dayna holds a straw up to my mouth so I can drink. Robin says that we have been back for three days, but that it took four days to get back from Rochester, so it has been a week since I got hurt.

Doc Betty tells me that they had a heck of a time setting my broken leg and my arm. She asked me if I knew that I was hit twice by bullets, once through the leg that I know about, and once in the side. That one I didn't know about. She says it glanced off the ribs and made a terrible gash along my side. She says that also broke several ribs, but without any x-ray equipment it is almost impossible to tell how many. She says they were afraid that they were going to lose me a couple of times, because of the fever and what sounded like pneumonia in my lungs. They ask me how I got injured so badly, no one saw it, so there is only speculation how it happened. I recount the incidents of that day that seems so long ago. Robin tells me that Teddy wouldn't tell her exactly what happened. He just told her that he did what he had to do, to make sure the other guy didn't kill me. Apparently I kept slipping in and out of consciousness on the trip home. I don't remember anything about it.

Tim, Charity, Sara, and Gary come into the room. Tim tells me that if it weren't for my idea to get a snow plow, we may still be up north. He says he is from New York and never saw snow like that before. With the plow they could push enough snow off the road to get the other vehicles through. I tell him that I remember it as being a family decision. Tim laughs and says he tried to take credit for it, but the others reminded him that it was my idea. It's not important who has the idea. It took the whole team to make it happen. Sara asks me how I'm feeling. I tell her about as well as can be expected, if you don't expect too much. Everyone laughs then she tells me we're even. I must look confused because she laughs and says that she finally got to see me naked like I did her when she got injured in the other world.

Melissa tells her to watch what she's saying with the children around. Sara says she's sorry, but the twins are already on their way to tell their friends that their daddy and Aunt Sara saw each other naked. Even Melissa laughs about it, we are one big family, and there are very few secrets anyway. Dayna asks if I would like something to eat besides broth. Apparently I have been waking up enough to get a couple mouthfuls of broth down, but that is all. The children must be satisfied that I am not going to die just yet anyway, because they find somewhere else to be to play with their friends.

Between sips of soup, I tell them all I can remember about the attack and the fighting. The last thing I remember is Teddy wanting to be close that evening after the fight. Tim surmised what must have happened when he came up and found us in that room. He says they were all afraid that I was not going to make the trip home. It was a brutal trip that they all hope to never have to go through again. I am getting very tired, but I am curious if all twenty people came back with us. I am also curious what the difference is between soup and broth. Dayna smiles and tells me that the soup has meat and vegetables in it. She didn't let me have any of those yet. I must have heard him wrong, because I could swear that Tim tells me they brought back forty-five people. I don't get the chance to ask again because I am out like a light.

When I wake up again, it must be night because Dayna is lying on a cot next to the bed I am in. Little Timmy is sleeping with her, it sounds so soothing to hear the people you love sleeping soundly. I feel like I need to go to the bathroom, so I start to swing my leg over the edge of the bed, but my arm won't move so I can throw the covers back, and when I even think about moving my leg, the pain is excruciating. I have definitely never been hurt this badly before. I must let out a groan or something somewhat louder because Dayna is now awake and so is Timmy. She is up as quickly as I have ever seen anyone go from a sound sleep to being awake. She sets Timmy on the bed next to me and asks if I'm okay. She is rubbing my forehead while she is asking. I try to talk, but my mouth is too dry, she gives me a drink using the straw again. The water is nice and cool, it feels really good going down my throat.

Betty comes into the room without even knocking. I ask her what if we were messing around, then she would be embarrassed. She laughs and tells me she would be amazed if we were messing around in my shape. I tell her I really need to go to the bathroom, so if they wouldn't mind helping me to the bathroom, I will be forever grateful. Betty tells me I don't really have to go; it just feels like I do. She lifts the blanket and shows me that I have a catheter in to drain my bladder. She says she will take it out when I start waking up regularly. Then I can use one of those bottle things like they did where I came from. I am still too weak to hold Timmy, and my ribs hurt too much for him to sit on my chest, like he always did before we went north. He can still talk to his daddy though and he does just that. The fact that we can't understand a word of what he is saying doesn't mean anything. We carry on a very interesting conversation anyway.

This time I am able to stay awake a little longer, and I even get a couple of small pieces of vegetable in my soup this time. The days go by and my wounds and injuries heal. I am able to get out of bed long before I can do anything. I am not the type to spend my time in bed or even sitting around. It has been colder than last winter even here, and we think we may have a little more snow this year as well. Dayna confirms that they did indeed bring back forty-five people from Rochester. Not all of them were from Rochester, but forty were. There was another group of fifteen living a few miles from the first group, and five of our attackers, who were women, asked if they could come with us. They never wanted to get involved with those other guys, who were not quite so fortunate when they attacked us. Everyone says they are hard workers, and there has been no trouble, so they are welcome. The last five came running out of a building in one of the towns we were going through on the way home.

Since our group is the strongest, all the groups had a meeting and decided to put most of the new houses up at the smaller groups, rather than wait until the groups maybe join up, somewhere in the future. That makes great sense to me, which also explains why I haven't seen the crews working on the houses in that direction. Many things are happening around our community. Since each group has a meeting house now, everyone decided to have school for the children in the meeting houses, instead of in each individual home. The classes are not necessarily broken up by age, but by how well the children can read and write. Since only a few of the people who have come here could read before they came, there is no criticism or people picking on others because they are perhaps a teenager and in a class with a six year old.

Teddy has taken it upon himself to help the twelve and thirteen year old girls learn how to read. He is so much more confident than he used to be. The day I could finally get out of bed, and get out to the front porch, he pulled up in front of the house with the largest buck I have ever seen. Jerry and Steve told me that he dropped it with a single arrow. We had a very good talk while I was stuck in bed. He told me he has nightmares sometimes, but they are always that he wasn't there to help me. I assure him that I will be forever grateful that he was. I also told him how proud I am of him for the way he has handled the situation. Everyone knows what he did saving my life, but not one person heard it from him.

The new people are happy to be here, and to be able to learn how to be self sufficient. Well as self sufficient as you can be in a large family like ours. Frank, his son Eric, and Dayna's dad Tom, have been refiguring how many acres of each crop we will need to feed the much larger family than we had last year. They are getting ready to plant some of the crops already. I should know better than to open my big mouth, but I have never learned how to think before I speak sometimes. I ask them if it isn't still a little early to be planting. Last year we waited until the middle of March to plant the beans and the potatoes. Robin tells me I'm a great husband and father, but I have a lousy sense of what time of year it is. She shows me the calendar that we made at the beginning of the year, and it is actually the third week in March. I guess I just didn't realize that the time has been ticking away since I was injured.

There is plenty of help to make up for my inability to do much of anything yet. I have been helping teach the adults how to read and write. Since most of the new people are women Dayna, Robin, Melissa, and now Becky, don't want me teaching them unless they are with me. Many of the women who have been with the family since we started have been practicing their handwriting. I asked Dayna about that and she said that she thought she had already explained that to me. I assure her if she did, I do not remember what she told me. This time she tells me that she has heard that the memory is the second thing to go. Then she laughs along with Robin, Melissa, and Becky. Those women spend way too much time around Betty, Sara, and Jenna. I finally find out by accident. I am pretending to be taking a nap on the sofa while the women are practicing their writing in the kitchen. Sara and Jenna come by and ask them how it is going and they tell them that they should be ready to start writing in the new Bibles soon.

Naturally I have to ask what Bibles they are talking about. Sara and Jenna come into the living room and tell me how sorry they are to hear that I have lost my memory now as well.

"Look at the bright side Jon, now you won't remember what the first thing that you lost was."

I tell them that I have not lost my memory or anything else, at least not permanently. Dayna, Robin, and Melissa all say that I couldn't prove that by asking them. All of the women laugh, even

Timmy laughs, but that's only because his mommy is laughing. Dayna comes over and tells me she is only kidding, she has always wondered what it would be like to be a nun since she started reading about them. She says she will never survive if she has to live like this much longer. Now that I am bright red from embarrassment, they are all happy. I change the topic and ask which Bibles they are talking about. Sara finally tells me about it.

"Oh, that's right Jon, you were not yourself when you came back to the garage that night in Rochester. Well Gary and I got nervous about what might be taking you guys so long, so we decided to look around the neighborhood we were in. We found a church that was really beautiful, so we went in to see what it looked like on the inside. There were several rooms, so we checked those out to see if anyone might be living there. In one of the rooms we found several cases of Bibles that were still in the boxes. They all had pages in the front for people to put their family tree in. We also found cases of large Bibles that have room in the front for a very large family to keep their records in. We thought it would be a good idea, and the others agreed, that we should bring some of them back with us to keep a record of our family here. Even if it does look like your family isn't going to get any bigger anytime soon."

I think that's a great idea, many of our family members still remember their families even though it has been quite a while for many since they have seen them. Some of the younger ones like Josh, Isaac, Ben, and Hank had their moms tell them about their families before the war. Those that can write are going to work with those who can't, at least until they can. There are enough of the smaller Bibles for each family to have one and enough large Bibles for each group to have one. One evening in early April, I am sitting with the children in the living room while the moms are busy putting names in their Bibles. Dayna has been busy all day getting all the information that she could squeeze out of her father. She has been putting all that information in the Bible tonight.

Robin is doing the same except she doesn't have a father to ask so she has to rely on what her mother told her. Teddy and Kathy, her two oldest children ask her why she doesn't put their last name in the Bible too. They continue to say that their name is Gorman, just like daddies. She looks at me like she is asking me to help with an answer. I tell her if she would like to put Gorman in the Bible, I would be honored for everyone to know that they are my children. Tammy and Tina tell Melissa that they are my children too. They look at each other and nod their heads in the affirmative. Jerry, Lisa, and Christy go out to the kitchen to watch their mom working on their family Bible. Becky says she is just planning to put her last name in for the children. She says she never did know the children's fathers last name. It just didn't seem important at the time. Most of the time you couldn't be sure that you would even see the sun rise tomorrow. Karen tells them that they are my 'dopted children, just like her, Kathy, Teddy, Tammy, and Tina so they should just use the same name. That way they would all be sisters and brothers. Becky smiles and says that makes perfect sense to her, if the rest of us don't mind.

I am back in the living room when Dayna calls in to me asking what my real mothers name was. I am trying to remember when Tina runs in and tells her that their grammas' name is Diane, and Tammy says grandpas' name is Jon, just like daddies. Melissa asks them how they know that. They laugh and say they told them their name when they come and play with them. They point to the older children and say that they have seen them too. The older children all admit to seeing them and talking to them, but they think it was in dreams. Tina and Tammy say they weren't dreaming, we can ask Zeus, he was there every time. Zeus agrees by wagging his tail and barking. Of course, he does that whenever his name is mentioned.

I tell Dayna that makes it unanimous, their names are Jon and Diane Gorman. I also tell her that now that I heard them, I remember that is their names. Dayna is laughing as she writes them down, she asks if I remember the Horton's names, or should she just call them Gunny and Ma. Again before I can answer, Tina says that is Gramma Anne, Tammy says Grampa Francis, but he doesn't like gramma to call him that. Dayna is laughing when she writes the names in the Bible. She puts the given names, then in parentheses puts Ma and Gunny. She tells the others what he told me he would do if I ever called him Francis again. Robin, Melissa, and Becky all look up and say it was Dayna who called him Francis, not them. At least the women are having a good time keeping our family trees.

When we go to bed for the night I dream about Gunny and Ma again. This time that other couple who was with them before, is here again. This time they come forward to where I can see them and it is my mom and dad. I am able to hug them and tell them how much I have missed them. They tell me how proud they are of all my children. Gunny tells me I finally did something right, then laughs and tells me how much he enjoys getting to see the children. He and my dad seem to get along well, they argue about nearly everything, but wind up agreeing on just about everything as well. My ma's just roll their eyes and tell them they will never grow up. They just laugh and ask them what's wrong with that. When I dream like this I never want to wake up, but I am always glad that I do.

When I get up everyone else is already up, the women are hard at work filling in more of the family trees. Dayna says she had a dream last night where my moms came to her and told her all about our ancestors. She is trying to write it all down before she forgets it. The others had the same dream and are doing the same thing. They keep reminding each other of small things that one or another forgets. It's a nice spring day so I decide to go out and limp around seeing what kind of mischief I can get into. Everyone I see is working hard. They are pleased to see me walking without the crutch. I couldn't use two crutches because of the broken arm. I walk to the wheat mill and see that the people working here are from the group we picked up in Rochester. They tell me how much they enjoy living here and how grateful they are to be here. Naturally we are happy to have them living here.

When I get back to the yard, Tim, Gary, Ken, and Billy are watching me come toward them. They tell me it's about time I get off my butt and do something. We are bantering insults back and forth when Charity comes up with baby Jon, who is one month younger than little Timmy. Tim and Charity refuse to call him Little Jon because of the Robin Hood books. He has a big smile for his uncles and manages to be held by each of us in turn. Charity asks

Tim if he mentioned the idea they discussed the other night. Gary and Ken tell her that if it has anything to do with sex, Carrie and Sara have enough ideas of their own. Charity tells them she heard all about that. It's just a shame that their husbands don't have any imaginations. Ken and Gary take out a handkerchief and wave it telling her they surrender. Charity takes Jon and heads to our house to visit with Dayna and the other women. She tells Tim to mention the idea they had.

Now we are expecting something bigger than life. Tim says that they were discussing the fact that our families are growing much faster and much larger than anyone expected. So far it is not big news, but none of us can argue with the logic.

"How many houses do you think there are in town where we get most of our supplies, and in the towns and cities that are within say sixty miles of here? I'm not looking for an answer, but we all agree there are probably several thousand, if we count all the towns and cities right? Of course you all remember how much food and other supplies we found in some of the homes we have gone into. Charity and I were talking and we figure there is a whole lot of food sitting in pantries and basements that is only going to go to waste, because no one is using it and eventually it will all spoil. Of course there is probably already a large percentage that is spoiled, but if it is in jars we could use them as well."

We are not saying anything, so Tim throws up his arms and asks us what is wrong with us. Even a bunch of dumb military types should be able to figure out that we could use that food and other things. Billy says he resents that, he has never been in the military. We tell Tim that we think it is a great idea, and that we will thank Charity when we see her, because he is nowhere near smart enough to think of that by himself. We decide to call a family council meeting with the representatives of each group present, and decide how we will accomplish this task. We all agree it should be done and we all agree that we could put our teens to work helping with this project. When we present it to them they are all happy to do it. Naturally there will be adult supervision. We decide to start with the town closest to us and then do the others working outward.

When we brought the last group of forty-five back we didn't have room for everyone so we went to the next closest farm and cleaned that up for people to live in. There were many volunteers to move there and let the new people live in the more established groups. This all happened when I was out of it, but it's nice to see our people are willing to help others. We are still in good shape for food supplies, but why let good food go bad when we can use it, especially as we continue growing. The people from up north say that up there this would be a waste of time, because everything froze during the winters unless it was in a well insulated room. We are lucky that is not the case here. It gets cold, but it doesn't bottom out the thermometer and stay there for weeks at a time.

We start the project on Friday morning. The teens are all upset about having to miss their school time for this project. Yeah right, for some reason when they were all studying at home they loved it, but when we started holding classes in the meeting house, they look for excuses to get out of it. Not all of them, but some, I guess some things will never change. We decide to start on the far side of town and work our way toward home. We are driving through town when Teddy points and tells me there are people at two o'clock. I know he means that he sees them off to our right, but I have to be a smart aleck and tell him that's impossible, it's only 8:30. The people are trying to hide, but they are not able to avoid us. When they see the size of the group we have with us they ask if we are the ones with the settlement near here.

We admit that we are, but are curious how they know about us. The leader of the group, if there is one, tells us that they ran into three men driving an open car. The men had on military uniforms. They say they have been praying that it is true because the little ones are about done in from all the walking. One of the girls in the group says they walked from a place called Tennessee. At least that's what the signs said. They were living in a town over there and were just about out of food and darn near froze to death this past winter. There are ten people in the group, three of those are adults, four are teens, and the other three look to be between six and eight. We tell them they are welcome to join us if they don't mind working and contributing. They say they are more than willing, in fact they volunteer to help with the project we are on today.

The teens stay and help, as does the one man with the group, the two women and the little children we take back to the farm to rest and get something to eat. We bring sandwiches back for the young people who are working today. Even with as large of a work party as we have we only get about ten percent of the houses checked and emptied of all food and supplies that we can use like jars, lids, rings, pressure cookers, and things like that. Those ten percent filled four large trucks as full as we could get them. We did not take time to check them to make sure all the food is good yet. We will do that as we put it away and distribute it to the groups. I find out when I get home what a bad judge of age I am. Two of the little children in the new group are four and the other is five. One of the women, Shirley, and the man whose name is Mike have one four year old and one five year old, both girls. The other woman, Kim, is the mother of the four year old boy. The teen's parents passed away so they have been living with the others.

We continue with the process of emptying the houses for the next two weeks. There is now enough food supplies to last our whole group at least a full year even if we don't get the crops that we have planted and are planning to get into the ground yet. We have continued to look for people who may need the safety of living in a group like ours. There is no shortage of places to look and we have been finding a few every trip. The new farm that was established when we brought the group back from Rochester is catching up with the others quickly. That is as far as getting the buildings painted and yards cleaned up from the deep grass and weeds that have a tendency to overtake any patch of ground that is left unattended for even a short time.

James and Jenna are still amazed at the lack of deterioration on most of the houses, especially anything made of metal. They say the same thing that Tim and I surmised when we first came here. It appears that the radiation from the neutron blasts permeated the surface of the metal and even the wood changing the molecular structure and making it stronger or at least better able to withstand rust and rotting. We have tested the areas we go with a Geiger counter and have found no levels of radiation that would be harmful to us. James says that is consistent with the neutron technology that he studied back where we came from. The radiation from those blasts are extremely powerful and will kill anyone within a fairly large radius depending on the size of the bomb, but unlike the atomic or nuclear radiation it dissipated much quicker, leaving the area habitable much sooner.

That was the whole idea behind that technology, wipe out your enemy, but leave the cities and the usable items virtually undamaged. That way the victor could move in without having to rebuild everything as they did in the wars up to this point. Unfortunately, or maybe fortunately, everyone had the same idea at the same time. I know Ma and Gunny used to talk about how the Bible says that the world would be cleansed by fire when Jesus comes back for the second time. They as well as many other people I know felt that it might be talking about nuclear war, where all the countries on earth with that technology use them at the same time. All that we have read about that type of war would leave the world uninhabitable for thousands of years. At least for the type of organisms we know, like human beings and the animals that now inhabit the earth. It doesn't change our lives in any way, but it is nice to try to understand what brought this world to the state that it is now in.

Our families are growing, not only in size, but in self sufficiency. We are very fortunate that everyone who has joined our groups wants very much to learn everything they can. Thanks to the efforts of Frank, Eric, and Tom, we now have at least a dozen men and young men who can plow the fields, and are good enough with the equipment to cultivate the crops while they are growing. Teddy loves to drive the big plows, and according to Frank, is one of the best even though he is still young. He still hunts with the others when we need meat. We have started canning a lot of the meat when we have excess. That is not often with the size groups that we now have. The topic of being able to replace some of the things we count on is discussed often, with no real solutions. One of the biggest items is the lids we use on every jar of food that we can.

We have been able to find thousands of the lids, rings, and jars, but we know eventually we will run out. It may not be for several years, or even in some of our lifetimes, but we are thinking about what will happen as our civilization grows. In many ways we are like the pioneers that started this country. But what scares those of us that have seen the technology that the world had, is how we will ever get back to even the level of the 1960's, much less the level we knew back in our world. I guess we will just have to have faith that people will rise to the occasion and actually make the world better than it was. Perhaps all the new technology made people lazy, and caused them to forget what is important in life, each other. I'll get off my soap box for now, it's just that I can't help but wonder sometimes.

We are continuing to build homes and to setup the prefab homes. Now that I have been declared fit to work again by Doc Betty, I am spending my days either working at the mill cutting lumber, or helping build or setup homes at the different groups. Apparently, while I was injured and unable to travel the others found several locations where the prefabricated homes were being stored. We have a crew of about 30 men and women who are getting very efficient at putting these in place and getting everything hooked up.

There is an abundance of building materials in pretty much every town or city we have ever gone to.

Between Ken, Gary, Sara, James, and Jenna, they have taught our team how to do the electrical and plumbing hookups required to get the homes functional. When we first started putting the homes in place, it took us close to a month to get it ready to be lived in. Now they can get one of the homes ready to be lived in, in just about a week. We run all of our electrical wires underground, so that we are less vulnerable to attack. We have continued to put the system of tunnels between the homes as well. I had a dream the other night that we were attacked, and the only thing that saved us, was being able to get behind our attackers by having a tunnel that ran out into the woods. We all feel that the perfect place to have a tunnel come out in the woods is into a shed we built out there by the orchards, to keep the tools we use out there.

The biggest advantage to being as large a group as we are is that we can have several projects going at once. As soon as we mention the tunnel project out to that shed, we have more than enough volunteers to do the project. Billy's wife Ramona can run a backhoe as well as anyone I ever saw, and so do several of the other women in our group. Many of the teenagers in the family enjoy driving the trucks, and are more than willing to do whatever they are asked to do. In this case, we will need to get quite a bit more of the conduit and the connecting joints. We figure it will take just about a mile, plus a couple hundred yards. Fortunately we know of several places we can get what we need.

We hold a meeting to decide where the tunnel should originate, and everyone says that they feel it should come out of three of the homes in our group, and have them join into the one main tunnel running into the woods. The crews begin working on the basement walls to connect to the tunnel in our house, Tim and Charity's house, and Ken and Carries house. The other houses all connect to ours, so everyone at least in our group should have access to the new tunnel, if it is required. I think I told you that we have started putting weapons and caches of ammunition and food supplies in the tunnels. The point came up that what if someone else accidentally finds the tunnels, and uses our own weapons against us?

We decided that is a distinct possibility, so we have been getting the locking type of gun cabinets or gun safes, some of them are called, and have been locking the guns and ammunition in them, in the tunnels. I know what you are thinking. Now we have to memorize a dozen different combinations. Not really, we have the combinations hidden in the room with the safe. It is scratched into the bottom of the battery powered lantern we keep in the room with the other items in there. This particular project is going to take us most of the summer. Once the ground is dug up, and the tunnel set in place, we will have to be very careful to cover the ground over, so there is no trace of what lies beneath it.

We are also putting in vents because of the length, and we will hide them in bushes, so that they are not readily visible to someone in the vicinity. Luckily for us there is a trail just about wide enough through the woods for us to build the tunnel without having to remove more than a couple of trees in the path. Ken, who was in the Army Corps of engineers in the other world, is intrigued with this project. He says even they never did anything like this, at least while he was with them. He is our project leader, and has spent many long hours drawing up the plans, and calculating just what we will need to accomplish it. As with the other tunnels, we will be running electricity and lights the entire length of this one. We will keep battery powered lanterns at intervals, and even oil and propane lamps along the way as well.

Some of the people on this project suggested that we start at both ends and meet in the middle. We feel that is an excellent suggestion, and perhaps if we had more experience with projects like this, we would feel more comfortable doing that. Unfortunately we are afraid we may have to wind up moving the shed in the woods as it is, mainly due to some large trees along the route we have to follow. Plus, we have no idea what we will encounter, when we start getting farther out from the houses. Even digging between the houses we have found some extremely large rocks that took us a couple of days to be able to move.

All three houses are now fitted with an entrance to the tunnel, and those are now connected to what is going to be the main shaft. If anyone is watching us they will know exactly what we are doing. It is impossible to hide the kind of activity that is going on with a project of this magnitude. We have volunteers from all the groups to get this done, and it is going to take all of them. We are working on a section approximately a hundred yards long at a time. That way two back hoe operators can be digging at either end, and working toward each other. While they are digging the trench, others are going to the places where we get the conduit, and are putting it and the connecting joints along the path we will be going. That takes more heavy equipment operators to get them off the trucks and place them in the proper orientation to be put into the completed trench.

While this is being done, others are bringing large dump trucks full of gravel, to be dumped into the trench, to level the tunnel and to keep water from gathering around the bottom. The first couple of days it seems like not much gets accomplished, because the backhoes have to get the trench dug before much else besides preparation can be done, but once the first section is ready, the backhoes can move to the next section, and the others can do the work of building the tunnel. I have to admit that it sends chills down my spine to watch our extended family work together like this. For most of them, less than a year ago they were struggling to stay alive in cities, and now they are working together, building whatever we need to make our lives better and safer for all. We can all see the pride in their eyes, and in the way they carry themselves as well.

Even while we work at projects like this one, we all have guns close to hand, just in case we are attacked while we are working. I'm sure it was much like this when they built the railroads across this nation. The days go by, and the teams keep building the tunnel. Even Ken, who is pretty much a perfectionist when it comes to building, is impressed with the work that we are doing. I enjoy very much helping with this project; even if I go home every evening just about totally wore out for the first couple of weeks. Ken seems to be everywhere at once; making sure no detail gets left undone. Even as we are building this tunnel, the other teams are planting crops and cultivating them, so that we will have plenty of food for the winter. Our hunters help with the other projects until we start to run low on meat, then they go out and bring back enough to last until the next time.

We have had three small groups of between four and eight, come to our little community in the past month. They all say that they heard about us from the Colonel, who is still traveling around with his two compatriots. They tell everyone they meet about us, and how to find us. They all tell us he warned them that if they are not willing to work, then they may as well stay away. He also warns them that if they are looking for trouble they should avoid us as well, because we will give them all the trouble they could ever want. So far everyone that has come to us is pitching in wherever they are needed. We know they will need to be taught, and that is never a problem, because we all have had to learn many jobs since coming here.

We still rest on the Sabbath, no matter how much work we have to do. We also make sure we make time to have a dance, or a get together of some kind, so that we can all socialize and relax at least once a week. Our family is growing from within as well, it is now June and our family has increased in size with the birth of six beautiful baby girls, and seven handsome baby boys. The girls all teased the new moms, telling them they don't remember the winter being that cold last year. All the new people are always telling us how happy they are to have found our community to live in. We always tell them how happy we are that they found us.

Speaking of happy, yesterday which was Saturday and Ramona was working on the trench for the tunnel, and she was the farthest one out from the group. Usually, there are at least a couple of the men with the backhoe operator, but in this case they were moving large stones away from the edge of the trench, about fifty yards away. She got down to check something out, when she heard a loud grunting fairly close behind her. She turned to see a huge wild pig coming straight at her at a full run. Naturally she tried to get back up onto the backhoe, but her feet were muddy, and she kept slipping on the tracks in her haste. Just when she thought she was going to get gored by the tusks on that beast, she heard the report of a large caliber rifle fired twice, and turned to see that pig go down no more than ten feet from her.

She looked up to see Teddy walking toward her carrying his .307. He told her he was hunting about a quarter mile away, when he had this overpowering urge to come over this way. When he came out into the clearing, he saw the pig running at the backhoe, so he shot it. The first shot took the pig in the neck severing the spinal column, and the second took him in the head, killing him instantly. The shots brought all of us running with our own guns, but by that time all we could do is help load the beast into the bucket on the backhoe, and get it to the barn to be processed. Teddy just recently turned thirteen, but most of the time seems to be closer to twenty. He does have his moments when he is still a young man, and we all appreciate those moments as well as the others very much. He seems to be in the right place, at the right time for us all the time.

The summer goes on, as time has a tendency to do. The crops are growing great, and the individual gardens are growing well. This is the first time many of our family have ever had the opportunity to grow their own food, so they are as excited as they can be watching the vegetables grow. We have run into some problems running the tunnel into the woods, but we have been able to work our way through them. Many of the members of our groups have started asking why we are even bothering to put the tunnel in. They say that we have not had any trouble in almost a year now, and as strong as we are, we will be able to take care of any trouble that may come anyway.

It is easy to see why they may feel that way, but for those of us who came from the other world, or whatever it was, we have no reason to believe that we will be left alone to live our lives peacefully. It has been our experience that there are always those that think they have the right to take anything they want. Those of us with a military background agree that we will never feel totally safe from people like that. We also agree that we will do whatever it takes, to prepare our families to defend ourselves against that evil.

Our shed in the woods had to be rebuilt to accommodate having the tunnel come up inside it. We actually had to dig a basement level, and build a block and concrete room under the shed. The underground room is large enough to hold food and other supplies in case they are ever needed. We made a trip back to the outdoor store, to get as much of the supplies as we can from there. We have also made trips to military bases to get anything that we feel will be useful to us. The tunnel is complete, just about the same time that we have to start picking and canning most of the fruits in the orchards.

We thought that we had a great crop last year, but after trimming the trees last fall, the crop this year is almost double what it was then. No one is complaining though, and it is really cute to watch the children who are old enough to help pick especially the cherries and apricots. It seems like they eat almost as many as they put in the container they are carrying. It was the same way when we were picking red and black raspberries and strawberries earlier in the summer. We have so much fun, it hardly seems like work. The wheat mill is running pretty much every day, to keep flour ground for making bread, cakes, and other treats that the very creative ladies in the family experiment with. So far they have not made anything that went to waste, even if it didn't turn out to be quite as good as it looked in the cookbook.

My personal favorite is strawberries, we found a very large field of them growing wild last year, so we trimmed them out some, and this year they were fabulous. Tomatoes are another of my favorites, and it seems like the tasty dishes we make from them are fast making them a favorite for just about everyone. Dayna and Robin have learned how to make spaghetti sauce, just like Ma Horton made it. They also found recipes for making spaghetti, and many different kinds of macaroni, so spaghetti and meatballs is one of the favorite meals we can have around here. James and Jenna, who seem to know just about everything there is to know, found an area where apparently the people who lived here before we did, grew mushrooms under two of the barns.

I saw the trap door in the floor, and when I checked it out it looked like a whole mess of toadstools to me. They saw them and were as excited as the children when they were picking strawberries.

I was with them when they discovered them, so I asked them what good toadstools are. You can't eat them, they are poisonous. They told me I'm pathetic if I can't tell the difference between a mushroom and a toadstool. I informed them that I have never had trouble telling them apart before. All the mushrooms I have ever eaten have come from a can. I've never seen canned toadstools. I do have to admit that the mushrooms really add to the taste of the spaghetti sauce, and sautéed, they are great with a steak.

It is now September, the weather is still beautiful, but the nights are starting to cool off a little, which actually helps us sleep better. It's Saturday night and we had a really nice get together in the meeting hall at Ryan and Carol's group. This spring and summer they were able to add six houses to their group, and they are really proud of the success they are having with their crops this year. All the groups are, even though we consider ourselves one big family and community, there is still a feeling of ownership to our individual groups. Barbs group has grown the most in the past year. With the help of Josh, Isaac, Jake, Adam, Ben, and Hank, and some help from the other groups, they added sixteen homes to their group. They are now totally able to take care of just about any emergency that may come up.

We are just getting ready for bed when we get a call on the CB from Doc McEvoy saying that they have some strange men riding around their property on motorcycles. It is too dark to make out exactly who they are or how many there actually are. So far they are just riding around making noise and making verbal threats to the people living there. Some of the others of our group must be hearing this message, because we see lights go on in at least seven of the twelve houses we have in our area.

We hear Gary's voice come over the radio telling Doc that he and some of the other young men will be right over to see what is going on. There are similar messages from all the other groups within a few minutes. I decide to at least see what is going on, if there is no gunfire then maybe it's just a bunch of people passing by, just wanting to irritate someone. I don't really believe that, but I can always hope, can't I? Just as I get to the bottom of the stairs and start to reach for the door knob taking me outside, I hear automatic weapon fire coming from our barns. I look out the window to see the bursts of rounds being fired at our houses, and the men that are heading out to the barns, to get the motorcycles. We are walking into an ambush in our own yard, and it sounds like they may be using the weapons that we have out in the barns, just in case we need them.

The women come running downstairs to see what is going on. I have a rifle in my hands, but I don't want to use it until I can absolutely identify a target. Teddy, Jerry, and Steve have their rifles and are coming downstairs cautiously. Actually, Teddy stops at the first landing and asks me if I want him to go up into the attic to get high ground, and see if he can pick out any targets. I tell him to go ahead, but don't shoot. We don't want to draw fire at the house with the women and children still in harm's way. I am trying to see if any of our men are down out there in the yard, but the lights that are usually on, have either been turned off, or have been shot out.

We have a radio downstairs as well as the one upstairs, and we are starting to get calls from some of the men in our group telling us they are okay, but that was a close one. We are also getting calls from the other groups telling us that they ran into the same thing we did when they started to go to the Docs aid. While we are talking, trying to figure out what is happening; a voice comes over the radio that I have never heard before. He is telling us that we are surrounded, and have no recourse, but to surrender. He tells us if we do that, he will allow us to take our personal belongings and leave. That is everyone, except the women they decide to keep. The voice tells us that they intentionally fired not to hit the men the first time, but from now on they will shoot to kill, if they see anyone or if we try to resist.

Apparently they have every group covered, because we have heard from all of them, except the newest group that started the new farm, when we came back from Rochester last winter. Come to think about it, we have not heard anything from them. Tim and Charity were going over there tonight, because Ken and Carrie, along with Dan and Cassie, moved there this summer, to help them out with the electrical work that was badly needed. Don and Olivia are there as well, he has been helping them hunt, and get enough meat processed for the winter. A new voice on the radio tells us we have until daybreak to make up our minds, then they will start shooting into the windows. He says he doesn't want to do this, because then he will have to keep some of us men around, to fix the broken windows before winter. He has one nasty laugh, I have the feeling I have heard it before, but I simply can't place it right now. I know it will come to me.

The tunnel system is working great right now. Gary and Sara, as well as Billy and Ramona, come to our house to see what I think we should do. Gary says he recognizes one of the voices. It's one of the guys that got away when we stopped those guys from attacking Barbs group the day they came here. That's when we met Gary for the first time. We are trying to figure out how these guys know so much about us, when Jerry says that some of the younger men have been talking to different groups on the shortwave radio that is kept out in the barn. He says they got to bragging about everything we have done here, and when the other guys didn't believe them they told them about the guns in the barns and other things they realize now that they shouldn't have.

The first question we ask them is if they told them about the tunnels we have. He assures us they didn't. We start to formulate a plan to get the women and children to safety in the tunnels. While that is being done, I am planning to use the tunnel out to the woods, to get free and see if the new group is indeed under siege as we, are or not. Teddy calls downstairs and tells me he could take out at least two, maybe three, in the big barn. He says he has been watching all the barns from the attic by moving from window to window, and so far has counted ten men. He couldn't see all of them directly, but he saw shadows and could see some of them turn to talk to someone else. I have been on missions with trained soldiers that couldn't give me a report that detailed. I compliment him for being as observant as he is, and tell him I need him to stand guard for his mom and the others while I go after help.

We get the women and children into the tunnels, the men stay in the houses with guns, just in case anyone tries to rush them. I leave Gary and Sara along with Billy, to take care of this group, while I work my way through the tunnel to the orchard, then work my way to the new group, hoping they are not in the same mess we are. We talked about coming up through the tunnel into the barns, but decided that if anyone doing that was caught, it would alert the attackers to the tunnels. Then we would be in a world of hurt. I am saying a silent prayer just about every step of the way. The tunnel didn't seem this long the last time that I came through it just to check it out. Of course that time our lives were not in danger, and it was more for fun than an emergency.

I am carrying three weapons with me tonight. I figure any trouble I might see will be up-close so I am carrying two .45 automatics with silencers that I found at the Marine base, and my familiar 9mm Sig. I am also carrying night vision glasses, for when I get out of the tunnel. It seems like hours, but it can't be more than twenty minutes, before I get to the end of the tunnel and out of the shed. This is one of the darkest nights I can remember, it's a good thing I have the night vision glasses with me. It's also a good thing I have traveled this trail dozens of times this past summer, so I know exactly where I am going. I usually take one of the more worn paths to the other groups, but this time I am trying to go between the groups, and get to the newest group, which is a couple of miles away.

I don't dare try to call them, because they will probably intercept our conversation, and if they are not already there, may get there sooner than I can. Luckily the leaves have not started falling yet, so I can walk the path with very little noise. This fact proves to be a lifesaver at least for me, because after about fifteen minutes I hear voices coming from the area where Barbs group lives. These are definitely not any of the men from there, they are complaining about having to go to Doc McEvoys group to help out there. They don't know which group it is, but from their conversation I can figure that out. Apparently they are carrying ammunition to that group. I see them long before they see me. In fact I'm not sure they ever do see me, or the small muzzle flash from that .45. We will have to bring the backhoe out here to bury them later today.

I get to the farm without further incident, and sure enough the attackers must not know about this group, because there is no sign of any activity that is not totally normal. I know the people in these homes very well, but Ken and Tim are still very much surprised to see me show up at this hour of the morning. It only takes a few minutes to explain the situation and be on our way back with twenty good fighting men. From what I heard, Doc McEvoys place has the least attackers at it, so we decide to head there. We are all equipped with night vision glasses and just about all of us are carrying weapons with silencers, or have guns as well as a bow and arrows.

Since the attackers here are expecting their friends, when we get to the first barn, where the attackers are, Tim and I decide to go right in pretending to be the reinforcements. We are wearing hooded sweatshirts with the hoods up. There are just four men in this barn, and two of those are sleeping. The two that are awake, start to complain about us taking so long, but a six inch blade in your chest can quiet even the biggest mouth. The other two, will never wake up in this world. In the other barn, there are apparently three more men. Don puts an arrow through the chest of one of them that gets just a few feet too close to the door. Ken and Rod rush the other two taking them out without firing a shot.

We are very careful when we let the men in the houses know that they are no longer being held under siege. We now have enough men to break into groups, and go to the other groups to get them freed as well. Luckily we have the silencers, because it is not quite as easy at Barbs group. It's a good thing we get some reinforcements from Josh and his team once we finally get the attackers pinned down. We get word that the others were able to get Ryan's group freed as well. The sun is starting to come up when we start for our group, and when we are still a good half mile away from the tunnel mouth, we hear the report of a .50 talking loud and clear. We figure either they found out what we have been doing, or they have a predetermined signal to start the attack. Some of our group continues on to the tunnel, while the rest of us head for the farm planning to come up behind the barns, and hopefully catch the attackers off guard.

As we get closer, we hear sporadic gunfire, and then we hear motorcycles going in the other direction about as fast as they can go. We are hoping it's not our men running. Tim and I come up on the first barn from the rear and there is no sign of anyone in or around here. We make our way to the other barns, expecting to be shot at, but nothing happens at any of them. When we come up behind the one closest to our house, we hear people inside so we cautiously sneak in the lower door trying to see who is here. Gary sees me at the same time I do him, and it's a good thing we recognize each other, or we may shoot each other.

There is a group of our men and some women carrying guns going through the barns making sure that no one is hiding. Just as we are about to go into the house, we hear that nasty laugh and a motorcycle speeding away. Three of us fire at him, but with hand guns it would take a miracle to hit a target that far away. I decide to quit trying, when I hear the report of that .50 again and see the rider on that motorcycle fall off and roll to a dead stop. The motorcycle runs into a tree and stops much quicker than the man did. A couple of our young men have their motorcycles out now, so they go to make sure the rider is not getting up. I look up to where the shot came from and see Teddy smiling at me from the attic window. Tim pokes me in the ribs, and points to the wall of the barn.

"Your son shot that big hole in the side of the barn; you can fix it before winter gets here."

He is smiling when he says it, I think we both know what we will find when we get up to where that hole is. Everyone is coming out of the houses now. Robin comes up to me along with Melissa, Dayna, Becky, and the children all except Teddy. Teddy is walking toward us, when Karen tells me Teddy deserves a spanking for leaving the tunnel when mommy told him not to. When he gets to us he hands me my .50 and Robin smacks his butt lightly. We all agree that since the threat is over, at least for now, that maybe we should go back inside where it is at least warm, and have some breakfast.

When we are all seated around the table, Teddy tells me that Gunny and Grampa Jon came to him and told him what he had to do. They told him to get my .50 with the heat scope, find the leader in the barn, and shoot him, and anyone else he can see with that gun. They told him that the bad guys were getting ready to attack, and that some of our family would get killed unless he stopped them first. He says he was scared like he was in Rochester, but they stayed with him like they did there, and told him exactly what to do.

"When I looked through the scope, I could see a man standing in the loft of the barn, and I could tell he was the one talking on the radio, because I could see that he had the mic in his hand, talking into it. Gunny told me to take careful aim on the man's body and squeeze the trigger just like you always taught me. I did that and the man looked like he flew across the loft into a bunch of them. I aimed at the group and fired a couple more times, and the men started scattering. That's when the men came out of the tunnel in the barn, and the houses, and chased the bad guys away or killed them. When I saw you shooting at that last man on the motorcycle, I figured you didn't want him to get away, so I shot him too. I don't like shooting men Daddy. Why don't they just leave us alone? There is plenty of land for them to do what we have done here."

I tell him that's one of the biggest mysteries of life. Why some people think that they deserve everything other people work for. I'm just about the luckiest man alive to have the wonderful family that Heavenly Father has blessed me with. We are all blessed to have a man like him to call my son. We can only pray that we don't have to take any more lives in defense of our own. Gary stops in and tells me that the last guy that tried to get away was the guy he knew from when he first came to this world. That was one evil man. It's a good thing that he will not get to hurt anyone else.

Each group takes care of burying the attackers that didn't get away. It's such a shame that strong men will use their lives trying to destroy, rather than to build this world. Those who could not see any reason to build the tunnels, have all come to the council and apologized for doubting the need for it. We truly pray there will never be another need to use it for defense, but experience has shown us otherwise. At least so far we have only had to bury the attackers, and none of our own. We also pray that our lives continue in that respect as well.

14

All the crops are in for the winter, and it is a good time to work on the insides of the houses. Our wives all have long lists of things that they say they can't survive unless we do them. I remind them that they were living in a basement and moving from place to place when we met. The houses we are living in now are palatial compared to then. All that logic got me smacked, and pointed in the direction of the largest chore at the moment. None of us really mind working on the houses, actually, we are very proud of how far we have come in just a couple of years. The chore on the agenda for this week is to fix any shelves that need repair in the pantry or in the basement. Then we have a place marked off in the basement to build more shelves for storing food and other supplies.

This is not a spur of the moment project. I, actually we, have been planning it for several months now and have just been waiting for the right time. All the lumber we will need has already been cut and has been seasoning all summer. Teddy has been looking forward to this project, because we don't get to work together, anywhere near as much as we would like to. At his age he is almost always asked to work on projects with the younger people. He doesn't mind, but we do enjoy working together, and having the opportunity to talk together like men. Today he obviously wants to ask me something, and is not quite sure how to start. I am pretty sure it has something to do with Nickie, Mickie, Paige, Mandy, Collette, or Hope. That is unless there are more thirteen year old young ladies that I do not know.

When he does start talking it is a lot more advanced than I ever thought it would be.

"Dad, you know that Nickie and I like each other a lot. How old do we have to be before we can get married?"

I am not really ready for this conversation, he starts to say something else, but I interrupt to try to explain how important a decision like getting married is. Actually I have no idea what I should be telling him. Heck, I knew Dayna all of about four hours when we got married, but that was a totally different situation.

"T, getting married is a very big step in any mans or woman's life, and is not something that should be rushed into. I know that girls are so pretty and they smell so nice, but sharing your life is a huge responsibility. Before you get married you have to have a good job, and you and your wife to be have to decide if you want to rent a house or buy one."

Teddy interrupts me when I get to this point in my ramblings.

"Dad, we all have jobs that we do around the farm, and I figure when we get married we will build a house. Anyway, what I started to tell you, is that Nickie and I are thinking about getting married when we are eighteen. We asked mom if she thought that is too young, and she said I should ask you. Everyone tells us that we are too young to know whether or not we are in love, but we know we are. I know that when we are apart, we both feel like mom says she feels when you are gone for a while, like we are not a complete person without each other. Do you think eighteen is a good age?"

I tell him that I think eighteen is an excellent age. He asks if I mind if he runs to tell Nickie the good news. He doesn't have to go very far, because she is upstairs in the kitchen helping the moms make spaghetti sauce for tonight's dinner. She comes down to the basement to give me a hug. The hug she gives Teddy is so long that Robin tells them she is going to throw cold water on them if they keep it up. The project and the day fly by. Naturally our friends drop by to see how our shelves are coming, and all have suggestions on how to make them better. Teddy and I just tell them they can build their shelves the way they want to, and we will build ours. Tim tells Teddy that he used to be a nice guy until he started hanging around with me. He says that he is just too much like me now. Nickie lives with Tim and Charity, so Tim has to harass Ted about her as well.

"Sure just about the time that Nickie gets to be a really good cook she will marry T here and probably move in with you so you can get even fatter eating all the good food the ladies in this house cook all the time."

Charity hears him talking, and yells into the basement that if he doesn't like her cooking, then he can take over that little chore any time. He sure does backpedal fast. He tells her that he is just thinking about her.

"If Nickie becomes as good a cook as you, or even close, because you do everything so perfectly, then you can rest and not have to cook so many meals."

Charity yells down that we must be drowning down here because it's getting pretty deep up there. Nickie comes downstairs laughing and tells Teddy that she can't wait until they can get married. Until then she says she will learn all she can from all the great examples she has to learn from. That gets a lot of comments from the husbands downstairs and the wives upstairs. The wives finally call her upstairs and set her straight about who should be in charge, when they get married. Hunger finally drives us married men back upstairs, where we get harassed unmercifully, but it's worth it. The girls have fixed a dinner fit for a king.

We rest on Sunday, and then finish the shelves on Monday, with only a few major modifications that Dayna, Robin, Melissa, and Becky decided were necessary. They really aren't that bad, and I can see the benefit to making the changes they requested. We want some hams for Thanksgiving, which is still a few weeks away, but we figure now is as good a time as any to increase our stores of pork. We have started smoking a lot more of the meat. Our families have learned that they love smoked pork chops, plus we have some great recipes for smoked sausages that we make out of pork and beef.

Teddy and I enjoy hunting together as well. He is really very good at it for being so young. I mentioned that to Robin, Dayna, Melissa, and Becky after the young people went to bed, and as usual they set me straight. They reminded me that in the books we read about the old west, many young men and women were making their own way in the world because their parents died or simply disappeared. Even in our families we have teens that were living on their own for months or even years before we met them. They also tell me that he is so much like his dad, what else would I expect. I'm just proud that he thinks of me as his father, and hope that I can continue to be a reasonably good example to him.

We have been hunting farther from home to allow the game fairly close to stay here, so that if we ever have to we can stay close to home for supplies. We found a truck in the building materials place that has a hoist on it and a large flatbed. When we go hunting for beef or for pork we take that truck so that we can load the large animals on it after we field dress it. It works great for getting the meat onto and off of the truck. Plus it makes it much easier to deliver it to one of the other groups, if they are in need of meat. Each group has their own smoke house to smoke small quantities of meats, but we found with the large number of people combined in all the groups, we needed a much larger smoke house to accommodate all the meat we smoke.

We have become very efficient at curing our meat that way, and have done some experimenting with different woods to give us different flavors. One of the most successful experiments, at least to me is the one where we injected maple flavor into the bacon and the breakfast sausage. Melissa, Becky, Ramona, George, and Kyle kind of supervise the smoke house. We found several books on smoking and curing meats, so they have plenty of new things to try and so far I can't think of any that I consider failures. They found a book on different sausages, most of the time the entire area around our houses reminds those of us from the other world of some of the great delicatessens we used to go to. We even found a recipe for making hot dogs, but we don't make them exactly like the recipe. We use the good cuts of meat, but there are always lots of good small pieces of meat left when we butcher an animal, and we don't want to waste anything that is good.

The hot dogs were a huge surprise to Dr. McEvoy. When he was a boy his family used to cook out in the backyard a lot and hot dogs were always his favorite. When we invited him and his group over for a cookout he got pretty emotional. He thanks us every time he eats a hot dog now, which is pretty often. One of the people we brought back from Rochester has a book with lots of recipes for different sauces to eat on hot dogs and hamburgers. They made a small batch to see if we would even like it and everyone wished they had made a much larger batch. They have since then and we always have some around for the burgers, hot dogs, and the sausages we like to eat.

Getting back to Teddy and me hunting and working on projects together, it took us two days to get meat enough in for all the groups that had room for fresh meat. The girls are excited because they have some new recipes they want to try. Teddy and I both agree that we will be more than willing to be the quality control specialists on this job. There is never any shortage of people to try new foods. The teens and those just younger than them are always hungry and willing to risk their stomachs in the interest of the family. Teddy and I are just putting the truck up after delivering the last of the meat to Ryan and Carol's group. They wanted venison so we got four nice bucks. We kept two and gave them two, that's all the room they have in their freezers. We park the truck and are walking up to the house when we see a jeep pulling onto the road to our farm from the main road.

Teddy and I both have our rifles in our hands from hunting. I don't say a word, but I notice that he shifts his to bear on the jeep coming toward us. It is not in a threatening manner, but is ready just in case it is necessary. In this case it isn't, we recognize the colonel and his two assistants in the jeep. They pull up a safe distance from us and ask permission to get out of the jeep. The colonel is smiling and saying that he is happy to see that some things never change. At first I think he is talking about Teddy and me carrying our rifles, but he points behind us and we turn to see at least ten men and women with guns watching every move they make. I wave and tell everybody that there is no need for concern. I add "at least not yet" and the three men in the jeep laugh.

This time we actually introduce ourselves and invite them to dinner. The colonel, whose name is Bob, compliments us on the amount of progress we have made fixing up the farm. While we are waiting for dinner, he and his assistants, Trevor and Blake, ask if we would mind showing them around the place. We take them to the largest barn we have because we can see almost a mile in all directions. Naturally we have to move from loft to loft, but the view is pretty spectacular. We explain that when the crops are growing it is much nicer. As we take a tour of the farm, everyone wants to show them the area that they are personally responsible for. Jessica, Jenny, Samantha, and several other young ladies, show them the chicken coops, which now hold several hundred chickens. We use the eggs and have fresh chicken fairly regularly.

On their tour Bob and the guys get to meet several of the people he sent to join us. They all tell them that moving here is the best thing they have ever done. Here they feel like part of something, before they were never sure if they would wake up when they went to sleep. We finally get back to the house and the girls really put on a feast tonight. It is nothing fancy, but it is all foods that none of our groups ever tried before moving here. Bob, Trevor, and Blake are definitely impressed with their cooking. That is if quantity consumed is any indicator. They are also impressed with the sweet cider we have to go with the meal. We made a couple hundred gallons this year, and there is not much left. After dinner while we are eating a bowl of ice cream, the inevitable question comes up.

"Jon, you can't be over thirty. How is it that you have been able to turn this run down old farm into the thriving operation that we see here today? The first time we came through here it was impressive to say the least, but now it looks like there was never a war. We took the time to drive around a little before coming here and as near as we can count there are at least four other farms doing equally well. We take it they are part of the family as you all call yourselves? We have been all over this country and have not seen anything like this. We did meet some folks doing well in Texas, but they told us they had no idea about using windmills to generate power, until your group explained how to do it. They are very grateful for that information, and for all the other survival information your family has provided. How do you explain having all this knowledge that no one else I have talked to has?"

Just about the time he gets through talking, the rest of the group that has come to this world the way Tim and I did comes in. James and Jenna tell me that if I expect them to come over the least I could do is invite them to dinner. Sara and Gary say the same thing. Dayna laughs and tells them there are some leftovers in the fridge.

Tim, Ken, and Doc Betty come in with their husbands or wives whichever the case may be. I start the conversation and ask Bob if he will believe that we were all Boy Scouts, and learned all of this earning merit badges. He says he might, but he was a Boy Scout before the war and never got to go camping with anyone as attractive as Jenna, Sara, and Betty, not to mention the other wives.

The girls all like that answer, but since Tim and I were the first ones to come to this world that we know of, we tell them how we got here. The others relate their stories and we all tell them what we have brought to this world that has helped us all live better lives. They all give Tim and me credit for getting the first group out of the city and starting the settlement that we all enjoy. We don't feel that we have done any more than any of the others. In fact if it wasn't for all of them we would be better off than in the city, but nowhere near as advanced as we are. Bob and his team are not as surprised as we thought they would be. That in itself is confusing to us, he explains.

"If you had told us what you just did a month ago, we would have had a pretty tough time accepting it. As it is we ran into another group of people, not as efficient as you are, but doing much better than the average groups of people we meet. This group of about sixty is being led by a young couple who claim to have come from another world, or dimension just like all of you. They are living in a city called Minneapolis, actually just outside the city. They do not have the knowledge of growing crops and storing food that you have, but they are living off the food in the stores and the homes in the area. I told them about your group here, and I probably put my big foot in my mouth when I told them that I believed that you probably came from the same place they did."

We assure him it is not a problem, but what does the group in Minneapolis have to do with us. As soon as the question is asked, I know exactly what it has to do with us. Dayna and Robin who are sitting on either side of me with the children on our laps, both elbow me in the ribs and tell me I am not going to get those people. They are whispering in my ear, but they are heard by just about everyone in the room. Bob says funny they should mention that. The people in that group are hoping we may be able to help them get down here, and maybe help them get established like we did.

"Jon, everyone, they really hate to ask for so much, but they do not have the expertise that you had getting cars and trucks going, so they have no way to get to a warmer climate unless they walk. They have thought about that, but they have many babies and children in their group, and they are afraid they will not be able to take the trip. As you know in the colder climates the food does not last as long, and they only have enough food to last a few more months. We will be more than happy to accompany you on this mission. Will it be okay if we sleep in one of your barns for a couple days? Please think about it, and discuss it among yourselves. I know I have no business asking so much of you. But those people will probably not survive the winter where they are."

We assure them that they are more than welcome to stay in the barracks that the young men built in the large barn. There are still several young men, who sleep there, but there is plenty of room, and it is very comfortable. When they leave, we all agree that we will not leave those people to die up north, when we have so much here. The biggest question is who is going to go. We will need several vehicles just to get them back, and at least one for supplies for the trip. Luckily it is still early enough in the winter that we shouldn't run into much snow. Robin and Dayna both still say they don't care who is going, but that I am not. They say that they came too close to losing me last time, and are not taking any more chances. The point is brought up that with me on a mission like this one they have a better chance of success. I can't see how, but then Tim points out that I am not only the family's best tactician when it comes to fighting, but that I am trained in medicine, and the family cannot afford to send Doc McEvoy or Doc Betty along.

We set the team to go on this mission of mercy, Bob's words not mine. Dayna and Robin are not real happy because I will be going. I promise not to do anything dumb this time, although I can't think of anything I would have done different last time. I start to ask T if he will stay home with the women and he tells me not to even think about it. He says he is going to make sure I come back. We talk with Bob, Trevor, and Blake in the morning and lay out our plans for them to see what they think. What we have decided to do is kind of risky, but will save us several hundred gallons of gasoline. Bob says that like in every city they have ever been to, there are plenty of cars, vans, trucks, and buses just sitting there. Actually they have been traveling around for years siphoning gas out of cars along the way they are going.

We are going to take just one vehicle up carrying the supplies we feel we will need and those of us who are going. When we get there we will find the vehicles we need to get everyone back, and get them ready for the trip. Naturally doing it this way, we will need Ken, Sara, Gary, Marty, Chip, and of course Jenna and James. No matter how much I argue, Robin has decided to go on this trip. She says she has to make sure her two men come home in one piece and with no serious wounds this time. We decide to leave tomorrow, so we spend the day getting ready for the trip. We decide not to take more than a couple five gallon cans of gas for the large van we are taking. It is more like a small bus and is actually quite comfortable and holds quite a bit of supplies. Bob and his companions are a great help, because they know what we can expect to find along the way as far as food and other things we will need.

One of the first things we do is call the groups together and discuss where the new people can live. Barbs group has been working very hard putting up the pre-manufactured homes and have even started bringing in some homes from trailer parks in the area. Barb says that her group can easily take in twenty or twenty five, and should be able to get a couple more trailers in before we get back. Ryan and Carols group has been busy adding on as well, and say they can take any that are left. Ray and Carol's group say that if we wind up getting more people than expected, they can absorb them. For the first time since coming here, we have a small group that says that we should let any others fend for themselves. We don't have time to address this new attitude right now, but when we get back, we will definitely have a talk with those that feel that way.

15

We take off first thing in the morning, knowing that we will be gone at least a week and a half, and possibly as long as two weeks. The first part of the trip goes very well, and we make great time because the roads are not in too bad of shape, and there are only a few areas where the road is blocked by vehicles in the road. We have fitted all of our vehicles with armor plate to protect the radiators, so we can just push any vehicles out of the way as we go. Usually someone has to jump out and steer the vehicle to a place that is off the road, or at least out of the way. By early afternoon we need gas. I'm not sure if I mentioned it or not, but between Ken, Sara, James, and Jenna they have come up with a small generator that we can use when we go to gas stations, so that we don't have to try to get the generator in the station running, if they even have one.

We do have to rewire the tanks, but for that bunch of thieves it only takes a couple of minutes. We are always teasing Jenna about all the ways she comes up with to bypass systems, and doing things that may be considered somewhat shady. One example of that is when we found a vehicle in one of the cities that she and James really liked. It's a great looking full size pickup that for its day was state of the art. We couldn't find the keys, but Jenna just jumped in and hotwired it in less time than it takes to tell you about it. Naturally we had to fix the tires and push it to get it started, but we will never let her forget that incident. Bob, Trevor, and Blake are really impressed with our ingenuity. As I said before, they have always just siphoned gas from vehicles along the road, which is also a great idea, but you can wind up with a mouthful of gas real quick that way.

We were discussing that point just this morning, so coincidentally when we get to the station we decide to get gas from, Jenna finds a small hand pump on the wall of the station that is used just for that purpose. She hands it to Bob and tells him to think of her every time he doesn't have to gargle with gasoline. Ken and Sara demonstrate their generator to the guys, and tell them that if they would like them to, they can fix them up with a generator very similar, and show them how to jump the wires to make the pumps work. The way they say they would like that tells me that they may have something else in mind. I have a pretty good idea, but I don't want to say anything right now. I'll let you know if I'm right when the time comes.

The first day goes by without incident. We actually make better time than we thought we would, and are farther along than we even dared hope for. Day two goes much the same, until we stop for gas. We pull into a station on the outskirts of a fairly large city. I think the sign we passed said that this is Missouri, but I'm not totally sure. That's irrelevant anyway, but what greets us isn't. As soon as I get out of the vehicle I feel like something is wrong. Ken and Gary stop no more than a step or two from the van, then turn back and get their guns. Apparently they feel it as well. Ken asks Sara if she can hook up the generator herself, because we feel the men need to stand guard.

Trevor says he will help Sara so that we can be ready in case something happens. He no sooner gets the words out, when we hear women screaming. The sound is coming from about two blocks away so Ken, Chip, and I tell the others to hold our position, while we check out what is going on. There is still a lot of noise coming from that direction as we head that way. Teddy wants to come, but I tell him I need him to watch after his mom. He understands that, when last I saw him he had his .307 ready for whatever comes. We get to the area where the ruckus is coming from and we see what looks like a band of men dragging women toward some motorcycles that are parked a short distance away. Actually there are four men dragging women, while five or six more are shooting at some people who are throwing stones at the men dragging the women away.

The women are fighting for all they're worth, and are definitely not going to be taken easily. In fact with us here, they are not going to be taken at all. Reflex takes over and I head straight for the attacker closest to me. When I get to him and the young lady fighting with him, I jump and kick him from the side knocking him down and freeing the young lady. She isn't waiting around for introductions. She takes off back toward her group of family or friends, whichever applies. The guy I kicked gets up and takes a swing at me. It's a good thing these guys never really learned to fight. I block his punch and with a couple well placed kicks, he is back on the ground scrambling to get back to his friends.

The others are doing pretty much what I just did and it appears that the attackers will leave without anyone getting killed. A couple of the attackers start shooting at us, but Ken has an AK47 automatic weapon and fires a few short bursts at the ground in front of them, sending them scrambling to their bikes, to get the heck out of here. We turn to look for the people that were being attacked and they are nowhere to be seen. We spend a few minutes trying to find them with no success, so we decide to head back to the gas station. As we are walking away, I speak as loud as I can, telling the people that if they would like some help, please come to the gas station a couple blocks over. We walk about four steps when a voice comes back asking what is a gas station.

We have to laugh at that, I tell them that they can follow us from cover, and if they feel threatened when we get to where we are going, they can simply disappear, or they can come down and talk to us. We promise we will not hurt them, or make them do anything they don't want to. It only takes a few minutes to get back to our group. The men are standing guard while the women stay inside the garage. The van is already filled with gas and we can leave as soon as we are ready to. We are telling the others what happened when a man in his early twenties, and a woman that appears to be in her late teens, come out from behind the building across the street. When they see we have women with us, the rest of the group, which totals twenty-four comes out and joins us.

This changes the complexion of this trip somewhat. Sara and Jenna say that they remember seeing a small bus that looked to be almost new. They both laugh and say it's probably no more than thirty years old. We find the bus they are talking about, and they are right, it is in excellent condition. At least on the outside, it takes a couple hours to round up tires and to get the bus started. It runs as good as it looks, after it has a chance to work the bugs out. The women have been getting to know the new people, and have been telling them about where we come from. At first they didn't believe them, but when they saw how we got the bus running and the tires changed, they are starting to believe. We agree that Marty and Chip will take the new group back to the farm. By the time they get them there, we should be in Minneapolis and be able to call them on the short wave radio.

Our new friends tell us about a couple of smaller groups they have seen in the city so we decide to go looking for them. We actually find three smaller groups that are more than happy to get out of the city and go to somewhere that it is relatively safe. By the time the bus pulls out it is just about full to capacity with new people to join our family. The rest of us continue on and even with the big interruption, we still get to Minneapolis on Friday about midday. Bob, Trevor, and Blake know exactly where to find our new friends. Even they are surprised because the group has grown from sixty to eighty-five. They are correct in their estimation that this group wouldn't make it all the way to our farms walking. Of the eighty-five, at least fifty are children and babies.

We get to meet the leaders of the group who are the ones that told Bob they came from another world. We get the short story for now, knowing that we will have plenty of time on the trip back and when we do get home, to find out all about each other. Actually, they are a lot like James and Jenna. Their names are Morgan and Mike. They are so much like Jenna and James that at first I tell them we will take everyone, but them. Naturally I am only kidding, well kinda. Apparently Mike was a contractor for the Air Force, he and Morgan went on vacation, they both have their pilots license and went fishing up to the Upper Peninsula in Michigan. When they came back to the base here in Minnesota, there was no one at the base and everything was old and broken down. They went looking for any sign of life, and when they went back their plane was no longer there. They met a small group of people and it continued to grow much like when Tim and I were in the city.

Ken sets up the radio as soon as he finds a building with an antenna. Some of us go with a couple of the group members to gather food and other supplies we will need, while some of us go looking for vehicles enough to get us all home. We are able to find two large vans that will hold approximately thirty of the people, and get them running before we have to quit because of darkness. It sure is cold here at night, even with Robin and Teddy snuggled up close I am freezing most of the night. We decide we do not have enough drivers to use vans to get everyone back, so we go looking for a decent bus or two. While we are looking for a bus, we find a group of five walking into the city looking for food and shelter. It is a mom, a dad, her younger sister, and their two children. When we explain what we are doing, they ask if they can come along. They can't see how they have anything to lose.

We find the bus we are looking for, but it takes a little longer than we thought it would to get running, so we are now a little behind schedule. I mention this to Robin when we are getting ready to go to sleep, and she laughs at me. She tells me I am the only one in the entire family who is so hung up on time. I guess it is just a carryover from my past life. As a Navy SEAL time and schedules were very important. If you miss the extraction team, for whatever reason, it meant that you now have to find your own way back. In this case it is different though, because one day or the next doesn't mean that much.

Actually in this case it does, because we get over a foot of snow overnight and now the bus is having trouble holding the road. The vans are not much better. We are about to quit for the day when we find a pickup truck with a plow on the front. It takes a couple of hours to get it in shape to run and we take off south again. Somehow or other we are going back on a different road than we came up on and nothing looks familiar. We have maps to help us find our way back so we are not worried. The plow moves enough snow going first to allow the vans and buses to get through with minimal trouble. When we finally stop for the night, we have ninety scared new family members. We find a motel for the night, so we can at least take hot showers and order room service. Yeah right, we do stay at a motel, but it has been abandoned since the war.

It is out of the cold though and there are plenty of rooms for everyone. When we get out to the vehicles in the morning, we have ten new friends sleeping in the bus. It's a good thing we have the pickup, because we have just enough room for everyone to sit with two people in the cab of the pickup with the driver. At least today we drive out of the snow, so we can make better time. When we finish for the day, we figure we will get home probably early afternoon, the day after tomorrow. The day goes by quite boringly, when around mid afternoon we get about twenty motorcycles driving all around us, cutting in and out of the paths of the vehicles. They are shooting guns, but up into the air, so no one is getting hurt. The bikes are gone as quickly as they came upon us. It's a good thing, because although all the men are driving at this time, the women can shoot every bit as good as we can. We really don't want to kill anyone who doesn't mean us any harm.

We don't see the riders again today, but we post guards to make sure we don't wake up to any major surprises. We have been discussing how we are going to find housing for all of the people we are bringing back. We were expecting sixty, and between the first bus and this group we have more than twice that number. Before we get home, I can't remember what day this is, we are telling everyone about the farms we live on. When we get home there are several people from each group here to greet the newcomers. The new people are all in awe of what we have here. Everyone gets fed a good meal before we determine where everyone will live, at least for the time being. Everyone has been busy getting housing ready since we have been gone. They have brought ten trailer homes back to the groups and have them at least in place, even if they do not all have electricity to them yet. It looks like we will have to put up a few more windmills to take care of the increased demand. We have had to do that already, so it is not like we don't know what to do.

Barb takes us aside and tells us we have a major problem on our hands with the group that didn't want to allow any more people to join us. They have been openly hostile and rude to the new people that came back just before we got back. Apparently the leader of the group told Barb that if she didn't like it, then she and the rest of the people that think like her can pack up and leave. We have too many people to find places to live at the moment for us to address this problem, but we will be speaking with those people first thing tomorrow.

When we finally get everyone settled in, and have dinner, it is after nine at night. We can finally relax a little and discuss the trip. Bob, Trevor, and Blake come to the door asking if they can speak with us for a minute. Naturally we tell them they are more than welcome anytime. Bob is doing the talking and isn't quite sure how to ask what they want to know. I think I know what they want, so I tell them they are more than welcome to stay with us, as long as they are willing to do their share of the work. They are very relieved to say the least. They tell us they are just tired of running around the country all the time looking for something that we have, a home. By the time they go back to the barracks in the barn, which is full to capacity now by the way, we have decided that they will stay here with us, but will travel around looking for people to join our settlement.

16

In the morning we no sooner finish breakfast, when we get a call on the radio from Barb. She says we need to come to her group as soon as possible, because there is definitely going to be trouble between some of the new people, and some of the not so new people. The ones who have been causing the trouble have not been here a full year yet. They are some of the group that came down when we went to Rochester last winter. Apparently it is only a handful of men and women, but it is the first trouble like this that we have had. On the way over to Barbs, we are discussing the issues and so far we have come up with throwing them out, trying to talk some sense into them, and exterminating them. Of course we will try talking some sense into them before we do either of the other options.

When we get to the farm there is definitely tension that is about to erupt into violence. Several men are carrying weapons and are threatening some of the new people, as well as established members of this group. We brought the members of the council that live in our group and the other members of the council from the other groups arrive only a few minutes after us. The first thing we do is ask the men with the guns to put them up where they belong and we will discuss their concerns as civilized people. We have never subscribed to the principle that the strongest are right and everyone has to do what they say. At first they are reluctant to put the guns down, but with the presence of all of us, they agree to talk. We are under no delusions, the only reason they laid down their weapons is because they are outnumbered. I don't know how the others feel about these discussions, but I do not hold much hope for keeping our family intact.

It bothers me that we will most likely be losing some of our friends today, but in my opinion it is inevitable. History has shown that most people simply cannot live the way we do. The Bible refers to it as the natural man. I interpret it as the ego and the greed of most people. I have been hoping that perhaps the way our people had to live before coming here, would be incentive enough to make living the way we do inviting enough to stick with it. Unfortunately as Ma Horton would say:

"No matter how fresh the fruit is when you pick it, eventually you will find a rotten apple in the basket and that one bad apple can ruin several before you find it."

Well it looks like we have found some rotten apples, now what we have to figure out is how many they are taking with them. Tim and I are no longer part of the council, but when we held the elections about two months ago it was decided, almost unanimously, that we should be included in all decisions, because just about everyone feels that we were responsible for us settling here. We are going to meet in the large meeting house that this group has. We have the entire council which is made up of representatives from each group. Seeing who the trouble makers are, I remember that these same guys complained at the council nominations that none of them were picked. It was explained to them at the time, that the nominations are made by the members of each family. If they were not nominated at this time, it is quite possible that their family members don't know them well enough.

That time I was in the mood to be diplomatic, this time I'm not. Several members of the group that is causing trouble are still carrying guns when they start to file into the meeting house. The council came in first to hear what has been going on and to bring everyone up to speed on why we are here. I tell the first one through the door that he and anyone else packing a gun, will have to leave it outside. On second thought we tell them to leave the guns on the table at the back of the room. At first they say they are not carrying guns, but when I tell them the meeting is over they have ten minutes to pack and leave, they agree to leave their guns in the back. I whisper to Tim and to Gary, who is one of the new members of the committee, that we better be ready for an attack. The attitude of these guys tells me that they have something planned, and probably have some accomplices. They are just too sure of themselves and are way too cocky.

The meeting comes to order and the leader stands and tells us they are tired of taking orders and they feel that they should be able to form their own group, where they can do whatever they want to. Marcy, who is from Ryan and Carol's group, asks them if they don't work who is going to grow the food and keep the buildings in good shape. One of the others of their group says they will buy food from us, and maybe even pay us to keep their buildings in shape. The smirk on his face makes me believe that these guys actually think they can overpower us and take over. These guys are either total idiots, or they have a lot of friends coming to help them. Just as I am thinking this I recall the motorcycle guys that harassed us the other day. There were a bunch of them, there were about twenty that we could see, but there is no way to know how many were hiding or were elsewhere at the time.

I no sooner get this thought when we hear the dinner bell sounding and gunfire. It's not dinnertime, so someone is sounding it to let everyone know that there is an emergency. The gunfire tells me that we under attack, plus the guys we are meeting with are trying desperately to get to their guns at the back of the room, but Billy, Ken, Chip, Rod, and Marty just stepped into the room and picked up the guns back there. Tim and I draw our 9mm's and duck out the back door. I know what you're thinking, we made them leave their guns in the back, but we had ours all the time. We're the good guys. We are not planning to make any trouble, well except for the bad guys. We get outside just in time to see several motorcycles speeding away up the road, and several lying on their sides, with what appear to be the riders lying on the ground near them.

Billy and the others are prodding the guys from the meeting out into the street. They are surprised to say the least. They also no longer appear to be so cocky and self assured. Coming across the yard are Teddy, Jerry, and Steve with their rifles trained on the backs of several more of the guys who came from Rochester last year. We meet in about the center of the yard. The leader of the rebels, I guess we can call them, asks if we are going to kill them. I tell them of course we are and I get smacked by Dayna and Robin for saying it. We have discussed what we should do if a situation like this ever comes up. We all hoped it never would, but knowing human nature we were pretty sure it would eventually. I tell them that we tried to listen to their complaints, but they obviously had much more devious intentions than we first thought. Therefore we are left with no alternative than to ask them to leave our settlement. They can take anything that they brought with them, except guns or ammunition. We tell them they can use the motorcycles of the men who were killed in the failed attack.

None of them even go to their homes to retrieve personal belongings. They just grab a motorcycle and take off heading south. We bury the dead, and go on with what we need to do for the rest of the day. Bob, Trevor, and Blake come up to Tim and me after everything has settled down and tell us that we haven't seen the last of those fifteen that left. We assure them that we are well aware of that, and will probably wind up killing them, or they will kill one of us before all is said and done. Hopefully they will learn their lesson and leave us alone.

At dinner I finally get to find out how Teddy, Jerry, and Steve managed to capture the guys that they did. Teddy says they just got lucky, but Jerry and Steve are more than willing to talk about it. They say that when we went into the meeting, Teddy told them to go to the other two barns and hide in the loft with their guns and wait to see if anybody shows up with guns, or if it looks like anyone is going to hurt the others. They both say they did as they were instructed. Teddy is the same age as they are, but they look up to him, and will always do as he asks. They waited for what seemed like a long time, when finally two of the men from Rochester came up into the lofts with guns. They overheard them talking about shooting anyone who puts up a fight, when the guys on motorcycles get here.

They both say they were scared, and were not quite sure what to do, when they heard the motorcycles coming and the men in the loft started to raise their guns, like they were getting ready to shoot. At that moment, they stepped out from behind the hay bales, where they were hiding, and told the men to drop the guns or they would shoot them. Apparently the men believed them, because they dropped their guns, and when the shooting was over they brought the men down to the street, where they met us. We are all impressed with the initiative of our young men. If there had been six more guns firing from the barn lofts, we definitely would have lost some people today. I look over at Teddy and he smiles and tells me he learned from the best. Bob says that Teddy is right about that, he tells him his dad is the best he has ever seen. Teddy smiles, and says he was referring to Gunny and Grampa Jon. I tell him that's more like it; we can all laugh about it. Bob, Trevor, and Blake just look confused which makes us laugh even more.

In the morning we all get to meet Morgan and Mike. They get to compare notes with all of us from the other world. They are very much impressed with the progress we have made here. Mike and Morgan are manufacturing specialists. They were on contract with the Air Force, working with companies that manufacture things that the military uses. Since we don't manufacture anything, we can't see how they are going to be very helpful to the group, but they are welcome anyway. We have found that it is not always obvious what our family members can bring to the group as far as skills. So far everyone that is staying here is more than willing to do their fair share of the work, and often contribute in many ways that may not be seen by most.

The women are always helping each other, and if someone is not feeling well, there are always others to help her with her housework and children, or to do her job if she has one on the farm. The main interest right now is to make sure everyone has adequate housing for the winter. Bob, Trevor, and Blake are proving to be a huge help in this area. None of them have ever done this kind of work before, but they have traveled all around the area, and seem to have a photographic memory of where the trailer parks are, and even where there are large numbers of pre-fabricated homes. Our other option is to refurbish another farm, or even groups of farms, for the new people. Actually, several of the people who have been here from the beginning, like the idea of establishing another farm, as long as it is not too far away.

We have been searching the area for a couple likely spots and we are really excited about the farms we found today. They are only about two miles away, but they are set back off the main roads where we have never seen them before. They are kind of southwest of us, and would only be a little over a mile from Ryan and Carol's group. We found them totally by accident, when our hunters were out in that area looking for game; they came upon the farm from the woods. There are five large homes, and four large barns, right at the farm site and we found three more homes about a quarter mile away that are obviously part of this group. All we have time to do today is check them out quickly, because it gets dark fairly early this time of year. We are going back tomorrow morning first thing with Sara, Gary, Ken, Jenna, and James, heck too many of us are going over to tell you all the names. Let's just say if we decide to fix these homes up, we will have a good enough crew to get a good start on it.

In the morning we pile into one of the vans, and two pickups full of supplies, so that we can tell if it will be worth doing. The supplies we have are enough parts to rebuild a windmill or two, and a couple of pumps to make sure that these places have good water. We also have a portable generator to check out the electricity in the homes. Bob and his team have already asked if we decide to settle this farm, if they can be part of the group coming over. I noticed that when they asked there were six people asking, not just three. It seems that the trip back from Minneapolis was very romantic for some of those who went. It only takes a couple of hours to determine that we are going to enlarge the groups to include this farm. Once the decision is made, a few of us decide to check out the roads we are on to see if there are any other possible farms.

The roads we are on are all just barely big enough to be called roads. We will have to cut some of the woods out that have all but overgrown the roads. A little over a mile to the south we find three more homes and a large barn. The road runs past here, but turns west at the end of the third house. The names on the mailboxes show that the same family lived in these homes when they were alive. The road goes in a square that is approximately a mile wide, and just about two miles long. We had to cut away some brush to be able to get through, but when we tell everyone about what we saw, they all want to go back with us and see it too. There are a total of sixteen homes on this farm, with plenty of woods for firewood and game. Just like the farms we have already settled, each home had a large garden behind it, and there is plenty of farmland that can be cleared and planted in the spring.

Many of the people, who came today, are those who were with us when we found our farm. They are just as excited today as they were then, only this time they know we can make this run down farm a home just like ours. The evening is spent outlining the plan to fix these homes up to be lived in. We want to open up this project to those who really want to do it. We feel that it will take a mixture of people who have gone through the experience of starting a group, and new people, so they can learn what is needed. The biggest problem with becoming as large as our group is now; we can no longer meet in any one building on any farm. That is why the council is going from group to group this evening, explaining what we want to do and see if anyone is particularly interested.

We already have some great leadership in the group that will be settling these farms. Billy and Ramona, along with Frank and his wife, and Tom, Dayna's dad, with Roberta, who is Billy's mom, all want to be part of this project. One of the houses has very high ceilings, and like eight foot doorways, so it will be perfect for Billy, who is over seven feet tall. There are three other couples in our group that really want to be part of this project. They are newer young people, who have gotten married since joining us a little over a year ago. Jessica and Jenny, along with Samantha, want to go along so that they can help them get started in the chicken business. Rachel and her sisters have agreed to continue taking care of our chicken coops.

The other groups are as excited as we thought they would be. Most of the newer people want to help, but they really have no idea what to do yet. We assure them that they will learn the same way we did, by doing. They will have a slight advantage over us, because we had to read how to do many of the things that we now know well, so we can save them a lot of time, along with trial and error, until they get it right. By the time we get back to the house tonight we have enough people to fill the first eight houses, that's the five right at the farm, and the three that are approximately a quarter mile away. Isaac, Jake, Adam, Ben, and Hank, along with their wives asked if they could take the three houses that set apart from the others. They feel that they may be better able to take care of themselves if attacked before everything is in place.

The plan is for them to move in as soon as the houses are cleaned and the electricity is hooked up. There are still plenty of new furniture and appliances in town. We are going to hit the new farm in groups tomorrow to take care of everything we can, in as little time as we can. Frank and his team of field hands, who are our experts in plowing, planting, and taking care of the crops that we count on so heavily, are already checking out the fields. They are in just as rough shape as ours were when we came here, but with a little hard work, we can make them usable again. The first order of business is to get the remains of the families, who lived here out of the houses and barns where they fell, and bury them appropriately. All the homes on this farm are large two story homes with large attics. They all seem snug enough to make excellent living space. The young people in our groups agree with that assessment. They are always looking for places where they can live together, young women, with young women and young men, with young men.

I am not going to tell you that everyone in our community is totally righteous, but we discourage the young people from living together, until they can get married. The weather this time of year can be very unpredictable, but we have a great day to start this very important project. All the houses get cleaned out completely, and all but two have new furniture and appliances in them. The other two will be completed tomorrow. As with our houses, the people who lived here used windmills for electricity, and did an excellent job building them and controlling the number of homes using the same power supply. Mike and Morgan know quite a bit about windmills, so they are more than content to work with Sara, Gary, Ken, and Ryan getting the windmills set up and working properly.

James and Jenna are still overwhelmed by the shape of the buildings after such an extended period with no one taking care of them. They are keeping notes in case they ever get back, or if they ever meet someone that comes over as we did. They have a theory that the vegetation even stopped growing for a period of time, otherwise they say we could expect all these fields to be overrun by the woods. There is some of that, but nowhere near as much as even we expected. Today they found a very large above ground tank that they surmise was used for catching rain water, and was used to water the backyard gardens during the summer months. The way it is situated, with the proper piping, it could have caught the runoff from at least two of the houses and possibly three.

We also found an above ground gasoline tank that they obviously used to fill up their farm vehicles, of which there is a great assortment that made Frank, Eric, and Tom act like kids at Christmas in all the barns. Those of us with mechanical experience are being pulled several directions at once. It makes us feel good, because just about all of our newer people want to learn all they can. We have found at least one reason why Morgan and Mike are here. What those two don't know about windmills and electricity is not worth knowing. The windmills we find here were built in the late 1960's. Since then there has been a tremendous amount of research into the shape of the vanes and other things that I am not sure what they said, but Sara, Gary, Ryan, and Ken are excited about it, so I guess it was right on.

Teddy, Tim, and I are busy getting the farm machinery going, so that Frank, Eric, and Tom will get off our backs. Since we are taking so long, they decide to go and borrow a thrasher from Ryan and Carol's group to cut the tall grass in the fields. We may as well bail it for bedding, plus in a pinch it will do for food for the dairy cows we keep. They will be doing the same thing here, if the ladies that are planning to live here have their say. The young men are clearing paths through the brush and woods to get to the fields, which seem to run the extent of the area in between the road that runs around it. They no sooner get the road cut through the brush, when Frank and Tom get back and drive right thru it. The amount of game they kick up is astounding. Wild turkeys, pheasants, and all manner of game birds fly up in front of and around the thrashers. Frank and Tom are careful to watch so that they don't run any animals down.

We all take a few minutes from our tasks to watch the cutting of the tall grass. Trevor sees a large buck standing not fifty yards from us, watching the thrashers go across the field. He starts to go to the truck to get a rifle, but Teddy asks him if he would hold off shooting the game this close to the house. It may or may not scare the game, but if they feel comfortable this close to the buildings, they will stay around and we never know when we may need a supply of meat close by. Teddy, Andrew, Dan, and Don volunteer to take Bob, Trevor, and Blake deer hunting the first chance they get. They tell them that they always use a bow and arrows for hunting, unless it is a large steer or one of the huge hogs that roam these woods. Those three have tasted the pork, but have never seen one of the hogs that we get it from, so they think the boys are teasing them about the hogs being huge.

We all return to work, but as luck would have it, we are surprised to hear several of the young ladies in the group screaming and yelling, as they run into the barn we are working in. In this case it is my daughters Kathy, Karen, Lisa, and Christy. They were helping Jessica, Jenny, and Samantha round up chickens for the coops in the barns. Apparently, a particularly large hog, decided he doesn't want the young ladies in what he considers his woods. Tim, Teddy, and I grab our rifles and go out the back door of the barn, where the girls just came in. Bob, Trevor, and Blake, along with many of the others, heard the girls screaming and came running to find out what the problem is. They see us looking toward the woods and turn that way just as the biggest hog we have ever seen comes walking toward us from about fifty yards away. Blake mumbles that it looks as big as their jeep. Tim tells Blake if he would like to ride it, we will help him put a saddle on it.

The hog has not stopped coming toward us, but he is walking slowly. There is no fear in this animal at all. He has survived in these woods for several years, and that's not an easy thing to do. Bob asks me how we usually kill something that big. My answer, "as quickly as possible", doesn't make him feel any better. Tim tells Trevor to run across the field, and draw the hog that way, so we can get a side shot at him. The hog is only about thirty yards away now. Teddy has been walking to the right, as we have been talking. I am doing the same, to the left. We both raise our .307 rifles at the same time and take aim. The angle we have is not enough for a side shot, but at least we are not shooting straight head on. Tim fires at the head just above the eyes, and the bullet hits the very thick skull bone and glances off cutting a furrow in the thick skin, but not even slowing him down.

He is mad now, and is speeding up coming directly at us as Teddy and I both fire, hitting him just in front of the ear trying to hit his brain and stop him cold. It has always worked in the past and does this time. Just about everyone has backed up to the barn, but the huge animal drops about twenty feet short of the closest person. Blake and Trevor start to go toward him, when we tell them to hold back for a few minutes. Just as we say it, the huge legs kick out in the animal's death throes. A kick from one of those could break any bone in our bodies. Dan, Don, and Andrew ask Bob, Trevor, and Blake if they feel up to field dressing that tank. They are willing; they agree to at least help. Dan and Don go back to our farm to get the flatbed truck with the hoist. By the time they get back Andrew, Teddy, and their three students have the beast field dressed, and just about ready to be loaded.

Normally the young men would just take the pig home, quarter it, and put the meat in the freezer in the big barn to butcher later. Since Bob, Trevor, and Blake are so curious, Dan and Don take them with them to take care of that little task. This incident reminds us of another very important project. Tim and Rod go looking for which barn has the butchering, and the big freezer. It is in the back of the second barn in the group. Just like at our farm, the ground falls away behind the barn, so the room used for butchering is actually below ground level at the front of the barn. It is much like ours in that you can drive a backhoe or even back a wagon into the room through a very solid double door. The tables in the butchering section are very large stainless steel tables, and the room is well stocked for its intended use. Tim and Rod are able to check the freezer, because the electricity is already on to the first two houses and barns.

The day flies by, but we have completed a tremendous amount of work. Everyone is pleased with all that has been accomplished today. Billy and Ramona are planning to spend the night in their new home, as well as those who will be living with them. The evening is finished off with a triple wedding with Bob,

Trevor, and Blake marrying the young ladies that I told you about earlier. The first two houses each have five or six bedrooms, depending on how they wish to use one of the rooms. The guys and their wives are only going to stay in the second house until one of the three houses down the road is ready. The way things are going, we figure by the end of the week. In the morning we start all over again, only this time we have slightly different jobs. All five houses in this group have been cleaned, and according to our electrical staff, will have power by lunch time.

They are setting up the windmills as they are, but Mike has promised that as soon as we can show him to a couple of manufacturing facilities where he can find the sheet metal and the equipment that he needs, he and Morgan will show us how to improve the efficiency of all our windmills. This morning we move to the group of three houses, and do the same thing we did with the other five. We thought we were being very efficient when we first came here, and cleaned up our homes and made them livable again. With the crews we have now, we can get a house livable in less than a day. Of course they are going to need some minor work on the outside, and definitely painting of the inside and outside, but they are livable and can be done as we go along, just like we did. Some of the rooms are already getting painted as we go, especially the first house in this group. This is the one that Bob and the others are going to share. Their new wives noticed that we have lots of paint left over, and asked if they can use some to paint the rooms, before they move in. It's a good thing it is too cold to paint the outsides, or I know what I would be doing.

By the end of day two, all five houses have power, and all three in the second group are ready to be moved into. There is no shortage of people to move into them, and it is reassuring to see that there are no arguments about who will get which house. The committee is ready to help settle all disputes, but there simply are none. With the new groups, we do not need so many of the pre-fabricated homes, at least not yet anyway. When Bob and the guys decided to settle down and get married, we thought that they had changed their minds about continuing to look for people to join our community. On the contrary, their new wives are excited about the prospects of traveling, to find those who may wish to join us. The house they moved into is quite large, and has six bedrooms, so they are sharing it with more of the people who came here from the Minneapolis trip.

17

    We found that from the corner that group of homes is on, is less than a mile from Ryan and Carols group, but we have to cut a road through the woods to connect the roads. The road we cut is not a direct route, but we try to take the path that will allow us to leave many of the very large beautiful hardwood trees that abound in this area. We only cut it wide enough to accommodate one large vehicle at a time, but we put some places where we can pull to the side, if two vehicles happen to pass on the road. We paved the road with gravel from the piles we found at the public works buildings in town. We are building this, as the rest of the houses in the group are being made ready for habitation. Isaac, Jake, Adam, Ben, and Hank, along with their wives, are waiting for the last group of homes to be ready. That group will be the farthest away, and the guys all feel that it could need a strong group living there. None of us can see any flaws in their logic.

    We are getting on close to Thanksgiving, and we all wish that we could find or build a group meeting house that is large enough to hold everybody. We did okay until the last few groups, now we have more than four hundred people in our community. Since these great farms were sitting here hidden from sight for the past two years, we have decided to check out the surrounding area, to see if we are missing any more great places to settle. Our hunters are more than happy to check out every dirt road and path in the area. On the Friday before Thanksgiving, Dayna, Melissa, Robin, and Becky are saying what a shame it is that we can't all celebrate the holiday together. They are even more disappointed that we will not be able to celebrate Christmas all together. Everyone seems to feel the same way, because I have heard the same concerns in all the groups. We are trying to figure a way to at least get everyone together for a prayer, when Teddy, Jerry, and Steve come home from a day of hunting and exploring the area.

    They are all smiling and talking, until they get into the kitchen where we are all sitting, then they get very quiet. I am relatively new at parenting, but even I know when to start worrying, and when teenage boys are being quiet, there is definitely something to worry about. They all head to the refrigerator first thing, so that part is normal. Teddy takes out the milk and pours a big glass for him and the other two. Something's wrong, the boys usually get their own, and leave the milk for the others to get theirs. Kathy and Lisa come in from the living room, where they were reading, and ask their brother if he will pour them a glass of milk as well. He agrees and even smiles, when he tells them it will be his pleasure. When Jerry and Steve offer theirs to their sisters, this is more than the women can take. They ask the boys what they have been up to this afternoon. Robin tells them if she finds out they were in the barracks with their girlfriends this afternoon, they will be grounded for a month.

    Teddy smiles and pats his mom on the head, she hates it when he does that, and smacks his behind with the towel she is drying her hands on. He apologizes, and then asks us if we would like to see our new meeting house. That surprises all of us, as you can imagine. Teddy, Steve, and Jerry all start explaining about the meeting house at once and nothing makes sense, so I tell them we can only handle one conversation at a time. They tell us to grab our coats and they will show us, after all one picture is worth a thousand words. We call the other leaders on the radio and tell them what the boys just told us. They are excited to say the least, and by the time we start for where the boys want to take us, we have about fifty people going. We had to find out which direction we are going, because Billy and many of the people in that group, and Ryan and Carol along with many from their family are interested too.

    It is a brisk fall afternoon, and we still have about an hour and a half until the sun goes down, so we decide to walk to where the boys are taking us. We only go about three quarters of a mile toward the new group, when the boys turn into what looks like a game trail in the woods, on the side of the road. We go back into the woods about a hundred feet, where there is a large clearing, and what was once a very nice brick church building. There is no cross on the building, but it even says it is a church in the name written on the outside. We are communicating by radio with the others, and within a few minutes they join us. The doors to the church are closed, but not locked, for which we are grateful. We find out why when we go into what is obviously the chapel area. The pews are about half full of what was probably the congregation. It looks like they were having some sort of service when the bombs hit.

It is difficult to see the families that perished here, and not think how we would feel if that had been us. We leave the chapel behind, and explore the rest of the building. This is one of the most unique churches any of us have ever seen. Most of us, who are familiar with churches, are used to the large cathedral type. This is more what I would describe as a meeting house. It is very practical, and seems to be set up for use, more than just to worship on Sundays. There are many smaller rooms that look like classrooms, and behind the chapel, separated by large folding doors, is a larger section that looks like a gym. There are even basketball hoops and nets at each end of the room. There is even a stage at the end of this large room with storage compartments under it. Upon further investigation, we find that the compartments are full of stacked chairs and folding tables.

Even though everyone is very excited, no one is speaking above a whisper. It is starting to get dark out, so we decide that we will come over again in the morning, to start the process of cleaning the building. Later we are discussing the building, and whether or not it is right to use it for a meeting house. Gary and Sara are visiting with us this evening. Sara says that the building was a Mormon church before the war. She recognized the name, The Church of Jesus Christ of Latter-day Saints, on the outside of the building, and picked up a copy of a book called the Book of Mormon while we were inside the building. I have known a couple of Mormons in the other world, but never really learned much about their beliefs. The one belief they had early in the history of their church is the practice of plural marriage. The only reason I remember that one is we found something about it in a history book, and we practice the same belief. Anyway, one of the guys in the unit Tim and I were in was a Mormon. He was always telling me I should join his church. Then they could call me Gorman the Mormon corpsman. We would all get a good laugh about it.

To get back to Sara, she says that she had several good friends who belonged to that church, and they always told her that they built their meeting houses with the intention of being used seven days a week. They believed that your religion isn't somewhere you go on Sunday or Saturday, it's the way you live your life. She says she thinks that if the people who attended that building could talk, they would tell us to use the building, but don't abuse it. Knowing the people of that faith that I did, I tend to agree with her. In the morning, we ask some of the others who came from the other world, and they all agree. We start this project as all the others. The first order of business is to bury the remains of the people in the building. We mark the graves the best we can from identification in wallets or handbags, and try our best to keep families together.

This part of the project takes longer than usual, because there were a large number of people here. The inside of the building will require very little work compared to the houses we have found. There is some mold and mildew on some of the interior walls, but some bleach and a good coat of paint takes care of that. The churches front yard apparently went all the way to the road. It looks like they probably had a row of pine trees across the front, and over the years they just kept growing and multiplying, until they covered the entire front of the building. We consider leaving the woods as a kind of cover, but decide that the cover could work against us, if someone decided to attack us while we are inside. The young men are clearing the woods in front, and are putting gravel down on the road leading in wherever it is needed.

When all the bodies are buried properly, the women go to work cleaning the inside of the chapel, and all the rooms in the building. We found the parking lot in the back of the building, with all the cars still parked there. We also found a kitchen in the building, which makes all the women in the family happy. This way when we have an activity here, we can bring the food already cooked, and warm it up when we need it. This building must not have been powered by a windmill, but it does have a propane generator that we are able to get running, so we have power. Even resting on the Sabbath, we have the building ready for our Thanksgiving dinner. We find enough tables and chairs under the stage that we only have to bring a pickup truck load from the farm. The women have been cooking for two days, to make this meal the occasion that they want it to be.

The young men brought home six very nice wild turkeys, and the hams from that huge hog are smoked to perfection. We have white potatoes and sweet potatoes from our fields along with corn and green beans. The ladies fixed several dozen pies and cobblers for dessert, and everyone eats until they have to stop, or their stomach will burst. At least I do, and the others are eating just as much as I am. It's a good thing we started early, because after the meal, everyone who wants to say what they are thankful for gets the chance. We even have a microphone so everyone can be heard. That may not have been a good idea, because everyone in the building is crying by the time we are done. We are looking forward to celebrating many more great occasions in this building. There is still a lot of work to be done, including changing the electrical over to windmill, but it will definitely be a labor of love.

Now that we have room for more friends to join us Bob, Trevor, and Blake are getting itchy to go look for some. When they announced they were anxious to get started again, we had to tease them and ask them how their wives were going to fit in that little jeep they have. After our wives smack us, we ask them which vehicle they would like to take on the trip. They really like one of the small buses we found up in Minneapolis, so we help them load enough supplies for about a week, and they take off. We went over the map with them of where we have been, but we all know that most of the people left are nomadic, so just because no one was there when we went through, doesn't mean they will not be there now. Those guys and their wives have become pretty good mechanics, and are carrying a portable generator to use when they need gas. Bob even made sure to show Jenna that he is taking along the hand pump she gave him, in case they need to siphon gas from other vehicles.

While they are gone, we are using this time to plow the fields at the new location, and we are continuing to work on the church building and the grounds. Mike finally got to go into the city, where he found what he was looking for. He was able to find what used to be a manufacturing facility, with sheet metal forming and cutting equipment. They also found many different sizes and sheet metal of different materials, as well as hundreds, if not thousands, of feet of bar stock. Before they brought what they wanted home, they cleaned up enough space in one of the barns to build a small metal working shop. Luckily we setup windmills to cover the barns separately from the houses, because when Mike is using certain power equipment the lights in the other barns dim a little. Many of us have been taking turns helping him and James manufacture new vanes for our windmills.

We were even lucky enough to find some epoxy resin paint, to cover and protect the vanes from the elements. Jenna and James say that they don't think the vanes need it, because of the way the molecular structure in the material has changed. Mike and Morgan who have worked extensively with different metals agree that this material is much different than what they are used to. I don't mean to start any trouble when I suggest that we can't really be sure about what caused the difference in the strength of the metals, because this is a different world, even though it is very similar that could be one of the major differences. All four of them look at me like I just grew a second head or something. James finally says he thought about that when they first came to this world, but dismissed it. They are now walking past me like I am not even here, headed for the door. Now they are going back to the manufacturing facility where they got the material, to see if they can find any certs for the material we have. Don't ask me what they are talking about. I'm just repeating what they said.

Dayna is coming toward the barn to see when I will be home for dinner. She gets here just in time to pass the four of them getting into a car, and heading for town. She knows me pretty good, because she asks me what I said to get them all wound up like that. They walked past her like she wasn't there as well. I explain what I said, and she says no wonder they are upset, they're nuts. We laugh and head for home, where it is warm and I have little Timmy waiting for our nightly wrestling match. He is almost two now and lets me know when he doesn't think he is getting enough attention. Tammy and Tina, the twins, are almost seven but they still like to roughhouse with Timmy and me. We almost always have a houseful of children and their parents, I never know exactly who is going to be there, but I always know we are going to have a good time.

I lose the wrestling match by the way. Robin was the referee tonight, and she always cheats for the children. My shoulder was a good half inch off the carpet, when she slapped her hand down saying that Timmy pinned me. Besides Tina was helping him and Tammy, and he didn't even tag her hand. After the treat that they earned by beating me, the children all head off to bed. Dayna wonders out loud whether or not the others found what they were looking for. As if on cue they all walk through the door and join us in the living room. Jenna continues on to the kitchen to see what we may have to eat in the refrigerator. Morgan who had sat next to Mike on the couch gets up and joins her. They find some left over roast pork, so they cut it up and make some sandwiches for all of them. Mike takes a bite of his sandwich and asks if we have any barbeque sauce. We have recipes for ketchup, mayonnaise, and even mustard, but we don't have one for barbeque sauce.

Mike and Morgan vow to make several gallons of barbeque sauce tomorrow. They remember why they stopped by, and tell me that my hypothesis was not correct. Mike and James take turns explaining that the material certs, the chemical composition of the metal, are pretty much the same as they were in the other world. Both Mike and James worked extensively with metals and had to specify the chemical composition of the material. They say however that they did find a device to test the hardness of the metal and compared the hardness of the metal against what the specifications call for. This tells them that the fallout from the neutron bombs definitely reacted with the metal, and probably all the building materials within a certain radius of the explosion. They talk some more, but most of what they are saying is beyond me. They get up and excuse themselves, thanking me for questioning what they were accepting as fact. They say they will see me bright and early so we can finish those vanes for the windmills. The girls remind Mike and Morgan that they are going to make barbeque sauce tomorrow as well. They even volunteer to let them use our kitchen.

We do not complete the vane project today, but the barbeque sauce project is a complete success. Something tells me that by this time next week, we will have at least a half dozen different recipes of barbeque sauce in the groups. For example we all agreed that the sauce is good, but we also want to try the same recipe with more honey to sweeten it. The days are flying by heading toward Christmas. We are all busy working on projects and as we get close to completing one project, we find two more that we have to do. With five days to go until Christmas we have cleared as much of the woods out from the front of the church as we want to, and have completed the gravel road around the new settlement. All the houses are fixed up to where they are livable, and have happy occupants living in them. We are continuing to search for more places to settle, within a reasonably close proximity of the others.

The young people have been busy cutting firewood for the new settlement, and have a very nice supply ready for winter. Luckily it has held off so far, but we are hoping for a white Christmas. Our hunters have been bringing in plenty of meat for the holidays, and just in case we get some inclement weather. The women and some of us men have put several dozen quart jars of beef, pork and venison up so far this winter. With four days left until Christmas, we are all wondering what kind of luck Bob and the others are having finding people to join our settlement. Today after helping set the windmill in place, and helping run the wiring to the church, I get home about an hour before suppertime. I no sooner get my coat off, and start getting comfortable when Teddy, Jerry, and Steve, along with Nickie, Mickie, Paige, Hope, and Mandy come in and tell us we have to come and see what they found. Actually the girls are the ones who shout it out, the boys were going to drag it out for a while.

Since it is getting close to dark we decide to drive, if the young people didn't say this is important, it could have waited until tomorrow. We go about a half mile past the church, when the young people tell us to stop right here. There is nothing, but woods, we can't even see a game trail into the woods anywhere near here. The girls jump out of the truck followed closely by the boys and show us a very dim trail that leads into the woods. Once through the overgrowth we can see that there was once a small road leading back deeper into the woods. We go barely a hundred feet when we see what used to be a very neat small farm. The road doesn't go any farther than the two houses that are sitting there, with a single good sized barn about fifty feet beyond the second house. We take a few minutes to check out the houses and the barn and they all look just about like the ones we live in. The houses both seem to have five bedrooms and are well built. There do not appear to be any bodies in the house.

We find a mailbox that has fallen down outside, and Dayna seems to remember the name as one of those we found in the church. It is almost dark, so we head for home to tell the good news to the others. In the morning we meet at the new farm, and discuss the best way to use this new property. We decide the first order of business, is to get the road in cleared enough to at least drive in, and then see what we should do from there. Today is Saturday so we do all we can, which is just about what we wanted to accomplish, figuring that we will come back on the day before Christmas and start cleaning the houses, so someone can use them.

On Sunday we hold our church service in the new church building. Many of the young people have been asking if they can come over here to play basketball or volleyball sometimes. We can see no problems with that, as long as there is some adult supervision. Robin is always telling Teddy and Nickie that they can do anything they want to, as long as they have adult supervision. They always turn red, which makes Robin and the other moms extremely happy. We know we should not be working on the Sabbath, but we also know we may not get a better time to set up the tables and chairs for our Christmas celebration. We are planning to have a group meal on Christmas Eve, and leave Christmas day for the families to be together and to visit. Knowing us we will wind up back here on Christmas to visit with everyone anyway, but so far that's the plan.

We are really starting to worry about our friends who are out looking for others. We have even considered sending out a search party for them, but we have no idea where they may be. We discussed a rough area where they were going to look, but as we all know when you are looking for others; you never know where you will wind up. We all remember them in our prayers when we turn in on Sunday night hoping that they will make it home in time for our Christmas Eve celebration. During the night I have some disturbing dreams in which our friends have come under attack and can't get back to us. In the last dream I had, I could see that they were holed up in a building, in the city that is about seventy miles to the southwest of here. There were several armed men keeping them from being able to leave.

When I finally wake up, I can remember all the dreams I had, as clear as if I was actually living them. I am telling Dayna and Robin about the dreams when Teddy knocks at the door asking if he can talk to us. He comes into the room and recounts a dream he had that matches the one I just had exactly. We have to hurry downstairs to answer the door before Sara and Gary kick it down. Tim is right on their heels with Charity and the baby. Sara tells me we have to go kick some butt, because our people are being attacked. Tim agrees with her, and Ken and Dan along with Carrie and Cassie make it unanimous a few minutes later. The fact that we all saw the same things in our dreams is a pretty convincing argument, but all we have to go on is the dream. We decide that the worst that could happen is we drive to that city and find nothing. In which case my wives inform me they have a list of items I can probably find there for Christmas presents. If it is true, our friends will definitely need our help.

It only takes us a few minutes to get everything ready for the trip. There is no shortage of volunteers when the others find out where we are going and for what purpose. Robin doesn't want Teddy to go, but he tells us he will simply wait until we leave, then he will follow on a motorcycle, so we may as well let him go. That young man is getting to be too much like me. Robin, Dayna, Melissa, and Becky tell me they will all kick my butt if anything happens to Teddy. In the van that we are using to get there, I tell Teddy what a pain in the neck he is sometimes. He just smiles and tells me that Gramma Horton is always telling him how much like me he is. He says that Grampa Gunny always says the same thing, except he doesn't say pain in the neck. He refers to another part of the anatomy. All of my good friends tell him that Gunny is absolutely right.

The trip to the city seems to take forever. We all saw the same buildings in our dreams, and we know exactly where they are. We drive to a place a couple of blocks from there, and decide to go in on foot. On the way here, we discussed the best way to handle this situation. The women at home all asked us to at least try to handle the situation without killing anyone. They reminded us that after all even the attackers are Gods children, even if they don't realize what they are doing is wrong. I am going to try to establish high ground, big surprise there, and the others are going to work their way into position to come up behind the attackers. That is if there are any attackers, so far all we have to go on is our dream.

Teddy is going with me. There is an old church with a tall steeple, less than a block from where we think our friends are. We get to the church, and work our way up to the highest point we can get to and still have a view of what we need to see. On the way up we hear gunfire so we are pretty sure of what we are going to find. The scene is exactly like we saw it in our dreams. This is hard to believe, we can see the buses parked outside the building where we saw our friends pinned down, and we can see the attackers working their way around the buildings across the street from there. I am telling the others what we are seeing. They are working their way around to get behind the attackers. It doesn't look like it is going to be too difficult to end this fight.

I get a very big surprise when I hear a familiar voice come back over the radio, telling me I am underestimating them. I can see the man talking into the radio in the building, so I take aim at him with my .50 caliber rifle. Before I pull the trigger I remember what the girls asked for, and I tell the man that I can kill him and all five of the people with him, before he can set the radio down. I ask them to please surrender and they can walk away from here. He laughs and says he doesn't believe me. They are in a very secure position. The man is sitting on a chair with the front legs tipped up. I tell Teddy to shoot one of the legs out from under the chair, just to show them that we can do what we say we can. Teddy takes aim and we see the man fall to the floor as quickly as we hear the report of the gun.

He is surprised to say the least, so are his friends, but they all say they quit. They really didn't mean any harm to our friends they just didn't want them getting back to the settlement. Our friends have surrounded them by this time, so they come out of the building we can see, plus the one next door to it. We are more than a little surprised to walk up and see the same people that left our settlement only a few months ago. Bob and his group come out, along with thirty-seven new members for our family. We tell Karl and his group that they are free to go. They hesitate then ask if there is any way they can return to the group. They say they realize how foolish they have been, and hope that we will give them one more chance. We have to have a meeting and we even call back to the settlement to see how the others feel about it.

We wind up taking them back with some pretty strict stipulations. When that is all settled, I can look for the stores that I can find the long list of items that I was asked to get. Everyone gets into the spirit and we spend at least a good hour combing the stores in the city for treasures. We can finally get underway back home. We get home just in time to get ready for our Christmas Eve celebration. Karl and his group say they will probably not be welcome after all they have done, but we insist that they have done nothing any dumber than most of us. Only two out of the thirty-seven remember what Christmas is and they had forgotten about it, but that doesn't stop them from enjoying the friendship and the great food. We even have a Christmas movie to show after we all eat.

Everyone thanks Teddy and the others for finding this great church building. When we get home he tells us that he can't take credit for finding the building. He says he found that the same way we found out our friends were in trouble, only that time his grandparents came to him in a dream and showed him where to look. He says it was funny, because he was walking down that road with all the grandparents and when they showed him the trail back to the church, Grammas Anne and Diane told our grampa's that if they went inside the church, it would probably fall down. I can remember

Ma Horton telling Gunny that all the time. It looks like they are taking care of me and my family even after they are gone.

We can finally go to bed and get at least a little sleep before Christmas morning gets here. It's funny how quickly the children have become accustomed to getting presents, but they also enjoy hearing the true story of Christmas. I have a great dream where I am talking to Ma and Gunny, as well as my real parents. They all tell me how proud they are of the way I handled that situation yesterday and for giving those people a second chance. To be honest I wasn't sure how Gunny would react to that. He seems to know what I am thinking, because he tells me that he has a different perspective on life, now that he is where he is. He even says he wishes he had been a little more forgiving when he had the chance. The dream seems to go all night and I am really enjoying talking to everybody when I feel my eyelids being pulled open, and I am looking into Timmy's eyes as he tells mommy that daddy is awake now. He tells her that he didn't even poke me in the eye this time.

It's great sitting here watching and listening to the children open their presents. I wouldn't change this moment for anything in this, or even the world I left behind. I am always telling our family that as far as I am concerned, my life didn't begin until that day Tim and I found our way into this world. We had a discussion last evening, and decided that the new farm we found may be a good place for our prodigals to settle. Of course we will help them every way we can, and they are as much a part of our family as anyone, but they may enjoy being off by themselves, at least a little. My children drew me some really beautiful pictures for Christmas that will definitely have a place of honor in our home. I think I will start breakfast and give the girls a break this morning. I found out last evening that by next year at this time our family will be at least two members larger. Dayna and Robin are both expecting, naturally I had to hear from Sara about having too much time on my hands, if I can accomplish that.

We have some really great breakfast sausage that we put maple flavoring in. I think I will fix some of that and some pancakes to go with it. We had a great maple syrup crop this year. Well I should have known that if I start cooking something that smells this good, all of my freeloader family will come over looking for breakfast. Maybe if I lock the door before they get here I can keep them out. Too late, Dayna let her sisters in with those bum husbands of theirs, so I guess I will see you later.

PART III

1

The New Year has begun, and with it many new challenges for our little community. Karl's group is now settled on the small farm, and seems to be very happy about it. A couple more of the people from Rochester wanted to join them, which is fine with all of us. So far they have worked very hard to make their farm to be as nice as all the others. Of course they get all the help they need from the rest of us. They worked well with us before their rebellion, so they all have the skills it takes to run a farm. So far they kind of keep to themselves when we have a multi group function like the party we had on New Year's Eve, but we feel that may be at least in part due to embarrassment for leaving the way they did.

We have had a couple of council and group planning meetings since last we visited. With the new people we have, especially Mike and Morgan, there are some very interesting suggestions for things we could do to perhaps make our lives a little better. Apparently Morgan was raised in a home where her mother loved to make quilts, knitted, and crocheted all the time. Her parents passed away when she was sixteen, but she still remembers how much she enjoyed working with those skills. All the beautiful quilts and handmade blankets and other items we have found in the homes we have settled in, have reminded her of those memories. In the attics of all the homes we found the frames that the people who lived here before, used for making quilts, along with dozens of magazines and books showing different patterns and styles of beautiful quilts.

We had a quick course on quilting materials, so now we are all experts on what we need to look for, so that our wives and the other women in the families can make quilts. There is quite a bit of supplies in the attics of the homes we live in, but there are also fabric stores in town that are full of all kinds of great material and the other necessities for making quilts and other great things. We have also been instructed to bring back all the yarn and materials for crocheting and for doing needle point. Needless to say the women and young girls are going to have plenty to keep them busy during the winter months. I know the girls in our family are always saying that they wished they had something other than reading to do in the evenings, now they do.

Jenna remembered everything her mother taught her, and even Sara remembers what she was taught, although she enjoyed working with her father more. Some of the women that grew up in this world even remember how to knit, and the skills are coming back to them as they get more experience. The women in our family are making a quilt out of pieces cut from the clothing they were all wearing when we came to the farm. I thought they had burned those clothes, but Dayna, Melissa, and Robin have kept all the clothes that we and the children wore, as a reminder of how they lived before. Becky still has the clothing that she and her children wore as well, so they are all making quilts to remember the bad times, as they refer to the time before we came here. I remember Ma Horton working on quilts when I was younger. She loved to get together with some of the other women on base and make quilts for the women having babies.

If making the ladies happy is the main purpose for doing this project then this is one of the most successful things we have done since coming here. All the girls talk about how much fun they are having all the time. They have even tried to teach me and the other men how to knit. I think that's a lost cause, but the younger men like Teddy, Steve, and Jerry are actually taking to knitting quite well. I think that's because Nickie, and the other young ladies their age, told them they thought that it is quite masculine for a man to know how to knit and sew. I really tried, but my hands are just not made for those needles. It did bring a lot of laughter and good natured kidding in our home for the week I tried it.

Frank, Tom, Eric, and some of the other men who are in charge of our crops, asked if we could find some different kinds of seeds to plant this year. I think Morgan and Mike are behind at least one crop they want to try. Morgan loves the jams and jellies we make, but she is always saying how much better it would be if we had some peanut butter to go on the bread with it. We have found some peanut butter in cans that has been okay to eat, but there is not very much of it and we could use a lot more. The guys came to us asking if we could look for some peanut seeds, so we could grow them and make our own peanut butter. We promised to look next time we go to any stores that might have carried those before. We would all love to be able to make our own peanut butter.

It is getting toward the end of January and the weather has been considerably colder this year than the last two winters. One evening Tim and Charity are talking to some friends on the short wave, when a group that they have never spoken to comes on. They say they are in southern Georgia, one of their group can read. They also say that they are running out of food, and are hoping someone might be able to help them. According to them, there are twenty-six people in their group now. They have heard us and other groups talking on the radio about how we banded together for safety, so they did that as well. Their group is mostly women and children as well; they have many small children and are afraid to try to walk any great distances.

This sounds like it is right up Bob, Trevor, and Blake's alley. After what happened last time they went out, we decided to send a couple of better trained fighting men with them next time. Mike, Teddy, and I decide we will go with them this time. Naturally Gary and Sara, along with Jenna and James, want to go to see how that part of the world fared the war. It only takes us a day to get ready then we head for the location where they said they are. We figure since we are going through peanut country, we should look to see if we can find some seed. See we have more than one agenda for coming down here. Naturally the people are more important than the peanuts, but there is no reason why we can't accomplish both. We stop at a couple of farm stores on the way down and find that there is plenty of seed to be found, so we plan to pick it up on the way back, along with some other items we would really like to have.

We stop at an outdoor sports store to grab a bunch of cold weather clothes for the people we are picking up. One of the things they mentioned is that they have been unable to find enough warm clothes this winter. Apparently it is colder than usual down here as well. We all know it feels it to us; the thermometer has not risen above the freezing mark since New Year's Day. Usually we get a couple days in the forties and maybe even the low fifties, but not this month. We have to move several cars out of the way on the roads down, so the trip takes a little longer than we were hoping for. We get there on the morning of the third day out. The people are very happy to see us, and they are in exactly the condition they described. We did not bring a bus with us to save gas, so we have to find one and get it running.

Gary and Sara, along with James and Jenna, take care of that small detail, and we are ready to head back home the next morning. We radio home the night before we leave and find out they have received a call from a group about a day's drive farther south in Florida. We send Bob, Trevor, and Blake along with their wives, back with the new group and the rest of us head for Florida. The roads down here are much worse than we have seen anywhere, except right along the coast of the Carolinas. That's probably because of the hurricanes and tropical storms that hit this area regularly. For the first time since we have been traveling around, we have to find our way around the route we have laid out, because a bridge that crosses a river has fallen down. We have to backtrack several miles, but we do find a bridge that we can cross on that is still solid.

James and Jenna and Morgan and Mike are fascinated by what we are finding. Personally I would rather be home with my family, but we do not want to leave anyone out here alone, if we can do anything about it. We get to the city where the people said they are staying, and we can't find them. It is kind of late and is just about dark so we decide to find a place to spend the night. We have done a considerable amount of traveling since coming south and have never really had anyone try to steal our vehicles until tonight. We never sleep without posting a guard to make sure our vehicles are here in the morning. Tonight James and Jenna are taking their two hour slot when they come over and tell me that they hear someone or something around the truck and small bus we are driving. I am up instantly heading for the door to check out the situation. Teddy is right beside me before I go five steps, so I ask him to cover me from the door while I check it out.

I slip out a side door and start toward the vehicles, which are parked in front. I am wearing night vision glasses that we found at one of the bases we have visited, so I have a pretty good view of the surrounding area. When I get near the bus I can hear voices talking low. It's obvious from the conversation that they are not sure what they are supposed to do to steal the bus. The voices are whispering, but I can still tell they are female. I work my way up beside the door that one of them is standing at, the other one is in the cab of the truck. I take off my night vision glasses then reach up and tap the person on my side of the truck. I am not at all ready for what happens next.

The young lady that I tap jumps out of the truck onto me and starts punching, kicking, biting, scratching, and if I had enough hair, I'm sure she would be pulling that as well. Now I know what Gunny meant when he said someone fought like a bag full of bobcats. It's definitely a woman or at least a well developed young lady. It's all I can do to finally get a hold of her hands and keep her from punching me anymore. She is still kicking and trying to bite my hands, when Sara and the others come out to see what is going on. The other young lady is climbing out the other door, but Jenna talks to her and she at least doesn't attack anybody. Sara and Morgan are talking to the armload of dynamite that I am trying to hold, and she finally settles down enough for me to feel safe letting her arms go.

Both of us are pretty much winded. Sara tells me she is going to tell Dayna, Robin, Melissa, and Becky that I am trying to assault young girls. When I can finally say something, I tell her it was the other way around. We invite the two young ladies into the building we are staying in to get out of the cold, while we sort out what kind of mess we have here. They are both wearing one of the coats that we brought down with us from the outdoor store up in Georgia. Apparently they had more time in the truck and bus than we thought. Inside we can turn on a lantern and see that our desperate criminals are a pair of young ladies around sixteen or seventeen, I would guess. They are definitely more afraid of us than we are of them. The one that I was trying to talk to asks us what we are going to do to them. Sara answers that we are not planning to do anything to them.

"We came down here because we received a message that a group of people needed some help. We have a settlement up in Virginia and we are always looking for anyone that would like to join us. We live on farms and are pretty much self-sufficient; we grow our own food and make most of what we need to survive. Our homes have electric lights and heat so we can stay warm in the winter. We have cows to give us milk, chickens for eggs and food and we even have some horses that our young people, like both of you, like to ride."

The same young lady who has done all the talking so far, tells us that she doesn't believe it.

"Nobody does anything for anyone unless they are looking for something in return. I bet if we go with you we will be used for sex then thrown away when you are tired of us."

Jenna tells them that she doesn't blame them for feeling like that. We have met some people who would do exactly like she says. All we can do is assure them that we are not that way. Teddy tells them that we would never treat anyone like that. He explains that he is my son and how that all came to be. It looks like they are starting to at least believe what we are telling them. I apologize for scaring her so badly, and ask them if they are part of the group that contacted our group. The young lady, who hasn't spoken yet, says that they are. They are not sure whether or not to believe us, because the people they talked to on the radio sounded different than we do. I tell them that's because we were already in Georgia when they called, but we know who they talked to, and if they would like we can radio them back, and they can find out that we are who we say we are.

Sara, Jenna, and Morgan agree to go with them while they contact Tim and the others back home. They are only gone a little over fifteen minutes, when they come back with the rest of their group. There are ten people, all women and children, in this group. The leader is not much older than the two young ladies we already met. Her name is Kayla. The two girls we met are Lindsay and Hope. They say that they always have to run to get away from men who would capture them and take them away. They tell us that they lost four women just yesterday, to some men who come from the east. Lindsay, the young lady that I was wrestling with, says they took her once, but she was able to escape before they could do anything to her. We ask if she remembers where the men live, so that we can go after the others.

She leads us to a small town about ten miles away. We can see smoke rising from a building near the center of town. I take my rifle and look for high ground near where we see the smoke. What I don't know is, as soon as I leave, the women tell the others that the men have never shown them any guns. Armed with this information, Gary, James, Mike, and Teddy decide to see exactly what we are up against, which violates every rule we have ever discussed. Anyway they sneak up on the people in the building, and look into the windows on either side. They can see the four women, but they don't look like they are in any danger. They are tied to some chairs, but they are fully dressed, and even have blankets wrapped around their shoulders, to help keep them warm. There are four men in the room that appear to be cooking something over a grill that is just outside the back door. The guys decide to go in and see if they can take them without bloodshed.

During this time, I have been working my way through a run-down three story building across the street, making my way through piles of debris to get to the third floor. I am talking to myself, telling me, that in no uncertain terms this is the last time I go looking for people to join our group. It's too darn cold, and I am getting too darn old to be climbing around like this. I no sooner get into place, when I get a call on my radio asking me if I am in place yet. I am still a little upset, so I tell them that yes I am in place, and as soon as I can catch my breath I will give them a report. This is what puts the frosting on the cake. I start to look through the scope of my rifle, when I hear Sara's voice telling me to look to the right side of the building across the street. Now what the heck is she up to?

I look through the scope, and there are all my friends, and the people we found along with the four women and what appear to be the four men who kidnapped them. Sara is smiling, and asks me what I am doing way over there, when they are all way over here. I am sorely tempted, but I don't shoot her, at least not yet. I work my way back down those same stairs that I worked so hard getting up, just a few minutes ago, and walk across the street to see what is going on. I may shoot someone just for the fun of it. Teddy meets me halfway and tells me he is sorry that I went to all that trouble for nothing, but that the truth is really funny. I tell him that I will be the judge of that, and right at this moment I can't think of anything that will make me laugh.

I meet everyone at the door to the building, and I think they can tell I'm in no mood for humor right now. I ask the men what ever happened to doing things the way we planned. At first they tell me to lighten up, but then say they are sorry, and fortunately there was never any danger. We will discuss this later, now I want to know what the heck is going on. Gary and Sara come over and start to explain what happened.

"Jon, when we looked in, we noticed that the women did not look like they were being treated badly, and the men didn't appear to have any firearms, so we decided to see what exactly is going on. We walked in with our guns raised ready to fire if need be, but the women told us to stop, and the men threw their arms up so fast they dropped the big forks they were cooking with. It only took a couple of minutes to find out what has been happening. Did you ever see a movie about seven brothers who kidnap seven women?"

I inform Sara that I don't see seven brothers standing here, so what has that got to do with this situation.

"In this case there are only four brothers, but the story line is the same. They have been trying to find wives, but whenever they went near any women, they would run because they were afraid that they wanted to sexually assault them. They kidnapped these four young ladies, and have been trying to show them that their intentions are honorable. They are only looking for wives."

Actually, looking at these guys, it's easy to see that it would be difficult for them to capture anyone that could fight like that young lady earlier. These guys look about as tough as the three that Dayna called her brothers, when we first came here. You would

173

never know that those three are some of our best fighting men and hunters now. I ask them what we are going to do about this new development. They say that they were waiting to ask me what we should do. I ask the guys and the women, if they think they can live in the same community together, knowing that the men are not going to assault them. They say they are sure they can, Lindsay says she will kick anybody's butt that tries to assault her. I have no doubts about that. We have just about enough room for everyone to fit into our bus, so we decide to take everybody back. We find another woman and her two children on the way back, but we can squeeze them in.

We go back a different way than we came down, and we find some very interesting buildings, and other items on the way back. There is room for our new people to move into the farm where Billy and Ramona live. The young men we brought back are staying in the dormitory for now. Now that the women know they are not predators, they seem much more interested in getting to know them. When we finally get everyone settled and taken care of, Teddy and I get to go home and relax. Naturally Sara is just leaving when we get there, she smiles and tells me she thinks I could take Lindsay, if we went more than three rounds. Then she pats me on my behind as I walk past her. I know exactly what is coming, Teddy does as well. He is already smiling when Dayna, Robin, Melissa, and Becky ask how my trip went, then start laughing. I forgot to mention that my eye is almost swollen shut from where Lindsay caught me with her elbow, when she jumped at me. The kisses that I get from my young ladies and not so young ladies make it just about worth the whole trip.

2

The days go by, and the new people thank us every time they see us for coming to bring them back here with us. Bob and his group stopped on the way back to get a couple very large bags of the seeds to grow peanuts. Frank, Tom, and Eric are reading everything they can to learn how to grow some different crops. The young lady Lindsay, and her sister Hope, brought back something that I didn't even notice at the time, but it has sure caused a stir in our community. They brought back, what I consider a very nice, acoustic guitar. I know that's not exactly an item that should cause much discussion, but you have to remember that just about all of our family has known nothing more than to survive, until recently. Lindsay and Hope can strum the strings a little, but don't know how to play very well. Actually just being able to strum the strings gives them an edge over my musical talent.

Fortunately, many of our family members that came from the other world have much more talent musically than I do. Morgan and Jenna seem to be the most talented people in the family, followed closely by James, Mike, Ken, Sara, Gary, and even Tim, have played a musical instrument when he was young. Doc Betty plays piano and says that she has really missed being able to relax by playing sometimes. I asked her why she hasn't played the ones that we found in the church. She says she has not seen any there, but should have guessed there should be at least one, if not more. We remembered that every time we have used the chapel portion of the building she has been busy watching someone sick or injured, or delivering a baby. We went over to the church for our music experts to see the pianos, and they all fell in love with them at first sight.

There is a large piano in the chapel, and two upright pianos, in different rooms in the building that look like they were used for meetings as well. They need tuned; at least they all say they do. To my untrained ear they sound pretty good, and our family members can play them as well. All this talk about musical instruments prompts a visit to the city, to see if we can find enough instruments to satisfy everyone who wants to learn to play one. There is actually a store in the city that sold musical instruments, along with instruction books and sheet music. Our musical experts come along, and direct us unmusical types, to load every instrument in the store into the truck, and bring it back to the farm. I can recognize trumpets, clarinets, flutes, French horns, violins, guitars, banjos, mandolins, a trombone, and several types of drums. It takes two trips to get all of the instruments, and the books and music. We even found two upright pianos that went to Doc Betty's house, and Mike and Morgan's house. We are continuing to look for pianos and other instruments, because it seems like everyone wants to learn to play something.

    It seems as fast as we can bring the instruments to the group that someone asks if they can learn how to play them. One of the most popular instruments is one called a recorder. It's kind of like a flute, but instead of blowing in the side you blow into the end. Many of the children love these, because they can learn to play simple songs fairly quickly. The young men all seem to want guitars or drums. They can make a lot of noise, but so far it doesn't sound too much like music. Those that know how to play these instruments are going to start having classes to teach those who wish to learn. To find more instruments, the young people go from house to house in the city looking for them. It's surprising how many people have guitars, pianos, and other musical instruments. We manage to find enough to give one to every member of our community that wants one, and have some extras, in case others join our group or someone decides to change instruments.

    Most of the women want to learn to play the piano, as well as other instruments. Luckily we found enough of them to put one in every home that wants one. It was really funny, because some of our people found out they already have pianos in their homes, and had no idea what it was. Once people started learning what musical instruments look like, they are finding all kinds of them in the homes we live in. In most cases they were put up in the attic because they had no idea what they were. I have to admit that our once peaceful evenings in the winter, are now filled with the sounds of almost music, coming from every house in all the groups. The young people all seem to want to get good enough to play some of the songs we listen to on the records we have found. Our teachers are being very supportive, they tell them that the people on those records started exactly the way that they are.

Some of our people are learning very fast, Dayna, Robin, Melissa, and Becky are all doing very well learning to play the piano. They take turns watching the children and practicing every day. The other families are doing much the same, the children practice every day, and are more than willing to show we parents what they are learning. The young adults practice in the barns. There are several groups of them learning different instruments, so they seem to band together to help each other every evening when chores are done. Our talented people are so excited about teaching they can hardly stand it. Especially Mike and Morgan, they have felt like they don't contribute as much as some of us do. We all tell them that they contribute all the time, in many ways that perhaps aren't as obvious as some of the others. They are very good teachers, at least in my opinion, and have much more patience than I would have teaching.

The winter is slipping past before we know it. We have all been very busy with chores, and learning to play the instruments that most of our people want to. Our teachers formed two bands to highlight their talents, and have performed a couple of concerts for all of us the past month. They are very good. They do some songs from those we have records of, and some from the world we came from. The audience always enjoys the concerts very much, and just about everyone who is learning to play something, wants to be able to put on a concert someday as well. With the progress that just about everyone is making, none of us have any doubts that they will be able to entertain us all. As you can see, when we have a project that everyone is interested in, we become almost obsessed with it. Luckily for us most of our projects are much simpler than the musical one, but we give it our best whatever we are doing.

A couple of months ago, James mentioned that the pork we eat tastes stronger than the pork he was used to, in the other world. He thinks this is because the pigs we kill have been running wild their entire lives. Personally I like the pork we get, I have not had any that I didn't enjoy eating, but I admit I am no expert when it comes to meats or vegetables. Most of the last six years before coming here I ate chow hall food, which most people will tell you is not that tasty. I liked it, so maybe that tells us something about my taste buds. James suggested that we could try to capture some young pigs, and raise them here on the farm, to a good size to butcher, and then we can compare the meat. The ones raised on the farm would be fed left over vegetables and grains.

As luck would have it, our hunters spotted some pigs, that although not real small, weighed somewhere around fifty pounds. It was not easy, but we were able to capture six of the beasts, and put them in a pen that we reinforced, because Frank told us when he was a boy his family raised pigs, and they almost always got out of their pen. Admittedly these are not your average barnyard pig. These animals have run wild since they were born, and they really don't seem to enjoy being in the pen, nor do they like people coming into the pen with them. In fact my daughters, Kathy and Lisa, who are both twelve now, fell in love with the cute little pigs when we first brought them home. Yesterday, when they came in from feeding the pigs, they asked me if they could shoot them when the time comes.

Every time they even start to go into the pen, those cute little pigs attack them trying to gore them with their tusks, which we cut off shortly after bringing them home, bite them, or simply run into them knocking them down whenever they can. Our pigs are getting very close to the size that James says they should be butchered in order to get the best meat to fat ratio in the meat. Everyone that lives within fifty yards of that pen can't wait until it is time to butcher those pigs. The smell is terrible, even if the meat tastes a lot better, I still prefer to let the pigs run wild and hunt them when we want pork.

The big day comes for us to butcher at least one of the pigs, and see if there really is any difference in the taste of the meat. We are doing this very scientifically, Don brought in a very large hog that he shot about five miles away from the house, and it was butchered yesterday. There are some very nice hams and other cuts that are getting ready to go into the smokehouse as soon as the meat from the farm pig is ready. Since Andrew actually has a scar on his leg, where he got gored by one of the pigs when it was small, we are letting him have the honors. I know that sounds cruel, but we raised the pigs for meat, and you have to kill them to eat them. That's a fact of life on the farm. An animal is either here to work, as a pet or for food. Pigs are not much good as work animals, and they are not very good pets either, so that leaves eating.

We decide to just use one of the pigs for our experiment. We reason that the meat should be consistent across all the pigs, since they were all captured at about the same age, and fed the same food for most of their lives. The first thing we all notice is that the farm raised pig has much more fat than the wild pigs we butcher. The hams and all the other cuts are much smaller than the others, but James assures us the taste of the meat will be much better. He doesn't sound quite as sure as he was when this experiment started. The cuts that go in the smokehouse are all put in there, and the rest of the meat is left to season or age properly before we cook it. The big day arrives, and Jenna says she will cook a large roast from each of the animals, and a panel of taste testers will make the final determination. We will do the same thing with the bacon and the hams to be fair, and cover at least most of the types of meat.

This little experiment has attracted quite a bit of interest, because just about everyone in all the groups likes pork, they are curious to see if it can be even better than what we have been eating. We have a panel of judges, which I refrained from, since I really like the wild pork. Jenna fixes a shoulder roast from each animal, but when it is cut in the kitchen, it is put on identical plates that are marked on the bottom, where no one but her and those helping with the food knows which meat is which. I am really impressed with how thorough everyone is being with this, what I consider kind of a silly experiment. I do cheat and taste the meat in the kitchen, and to be honest I can't tell any difference in the taste of the meat. The farm raised meat has more fat, but taste wise I could eat either and be happy.

Our taste testers are taking this job seriously. They taste the meat from first one plate then the other. It takes all of about fifteen minutes for the judges to agree that they can't tell the difference in the meat. Even James agrees with the findings, we suggest that perhaps he and Jenna might want to try seasoning the meat different, if he really doesn't like the taste. He says he likes the pork fine, he just thought that if we controlled the pig's diet, the meat would be better. We all agree it was worth the effort to at least see if it made a difference, and we also all agree that if we were to really domesticate some pigs that the meat may be better. But since none of us care that much, and we really don't need the added work involved with farm raising the pork, we are going to let the remaining pigs loose, and wait until they get as big as a small car to butcher them. The pigs waste no time leaving when the gate is opened. Their tusks are already growing back, so they should be okay in the woods until they fill out. We tear the pen down, and use a backhoe to move the stinky dirt to the area we keep our compost for the gardens. We want to make sure no one gets the idea of keeping pigs around this farm again.

3

I mentioned that we were going to try our hand at growing peanuts this year. Frank, Tom, and Eric have been obsessed with this crop since it was first mentioned. They went a step further and decided to try planting some pinto beans this year as well. After researching both crops they found they are actually very similar. We traveled to Georgia again to get as much information as we can, and to get as much seed as we can. We felt a little foolish when we were in town with some of the wives, and they found several large bags of Virginia peanut seeds right here. We decided to plant a couple of acres of peanuts and beans on each farm to see if the soil is any better for these crops on any particular farm. So far they, along with everything else we planted, are doing quite well. Some of our winter wheat is not doing as well as it did last year. Frank says he thinks we got too much rain early this year, and some of the seeds couldn't grow because of it.

We know we cannot expect to get great crops every year, that's why we plant almost double what we think we will need, so that even if we have a mediocre season, we will still be able to get by. Plus when we do have an excess we preserve it to be used when needed. I love spring time because everything seems to come alive after the long cold winter. Putting in the crops keeps most of us pretty busy, either actually plowing and planting or keeping the equipment running. Once it is in the ground, it has to be cultivated and taken care of, but we are not quite as busy as with the planting. This year we found two projects to keep us busy after the crops are all in, at least for now. We stagger some of the planting to keep everything from being ripe at the same time.

The children have some books that show children playing on swing sets and using slides and other wonderful toys in the yard to amuse them. Our children asked me why they don't have those same kinds of toys in our yard. I really didn't have a good answer, other than I have never really thought about it. Since that's not an acceptable answer, we went looking for swing sets, and all the other great things children love to play on. We find exactly what we are looking for in one of the small public parks in town. Between there and the schools in town, we find enough heavy duty swing sets and slides for each group to have some. We even find some monkey bars, and other things for them to climb on and around.

When James and Jenna heard what we are doing, they drew up the plans for some really great areas that the children can climb on and in, like a clubhouse that we can build with wood. Each group has a team of people that are setting these areas up for the children. I don't know who is more excited, the adults setting them up or the children. We are building platforms that they can climb up to, rope bridges and monkey bars connecting two or more of the platforms and little clubhouses. Even the not so young children, say they would love something like this to use to get in shape. Teddy is voted to be their spokesman, when he comes to me to ask if it would be possible to build an obstacle course, like Uncle Tim told them about. I am very diplomatic; I tell him I'm sure Uncle Tim can build them a beautiful obstacle course.

Actually I have missed running the obstacle courses we used to do regularly in our training. Between all of us with military experience, we come up with what we feel will be a very challenging course, but that will be a lot of fun as well. As soon as we finish with the playgrounds, we will start on the obstacle course. You would think we have enough to do, but with so many willing workers just about every project is fun. The playgrounds take a little longer than we anticipated, because the mothers want swings and teeter totters big enough for them to use, while they watch the children. We are now into April, and both Robin and Dayna are getting quite large in their pregnancies. According to Doctor Betty they are due about a week apart, around the middle of May. Little Timmy is two now, and is getting to be quite a handful. He is taking after his sisters Tammy and Tina, the twins; in fact he may actually be as much of a handful as the both of them were.

He thinks he is invincible when he is playing outside with his sisters and cousin, Jon, who is about a month younger. It's a good thing that Zeus and Missy, our dogs are as diligent as they are, because those two will try to go wherever they see somebody they know. We fenced in the playground in all the groups, to make sure the little ones can't go very far. I for one never realized how difficult it can be to watch little ones, like our sons, until I was watching them outside one day. Unless I was right beside them when they decided to take off and go somewhere, I had all I could do to catch them quickly. Between the fence, the dogs and us parents and older brothers and sisters, at least we can keep them in the playground. We have some small objects to keep them busy, and some sand boxes for them to play in. This parenting stuff isn't as easy as I thought it was.

We can finally start the obstacle courses, and the older young people are very happy to help. As I said, those of us with military backgrounds have designed what we feel are some real challenges yet fun for anyone doing the course. We decided to use the natural lay of the land in the woods between the groups in our area, and to build a second course in the woods near the church. Both woods are different in the way we set them up. The woods near our group do not have much water in them, but we are able to put a couple of rope bridges across the stream, and a place where you have to jump out and catch a rope, to swing over the stream. It's not as easy as it sounds, because the bank on the opposite side is steep, and you have to be careful not to come up short or you will fall back into the water.

We tried to make the obstacles tricky, but not necessarily difficult. We built a wall that you have to get over. There is a series of logs that you have to run the length of. There is about thirty feet of logs that are about two feet off the ground, if they get slippery from someone falling off the rope bridge, they can be a challenge. I think the most challenging obstacle, is the one where we have logs high and low in two layers starting at just above ground level, and going up to a height just about six feet up. You have to go over one log and under the next weaving through the entire obstacle that way. If you fall you have to go back and start that obstacle over. I think the young people like the climbing towers the best. We have at least two on each course that you have to climb up one side then go down the other side, using a rope to get down. At the end of the course there is another swing across a small ravine, when they get over that, there is a rope climb of twenty feet. At the top we put a bell, so that if you can make it to the top, you get to ring the bell telling everyone you made it.

The young people helped build every obstacle on both courses, and had excellent suggestions on how to make it better, and even more challenging. Many of the young people keep track of their times and are constantly trying to better them. The young men are not the only ones who enjoy the obstacles, just about all of the young ladies fifteen and up enjoy running them as well. We have decided to build another obstacle course, for the younger people who are not quite up to the more challenging courses yet. They are helping us design and build it as well. Please don't tell the young men about this, but when we, meaning those of us with military experience, ran the course for the first time, we didn't do as well as some of the young men did. Teddy, Don, Dan, Chip, and Marty all beat our times by a minute or more. Some of the other young men like Josh, Isaac, Jake, Adam, Ben, and Hank beat their times convincingly.

At least we can laugh about it, the worst part is that Jenna, Morgan, and Sara beat our times as well. Melissa and Becky finished just a little slower than we did. Now Dayna and Robin can't wait to have the babies to see if they can beat my time. We think this is a good thing, because it shows us how much we need to stay in shape, even if we are very busy making a living. We have a pretty well equipped gym or workout room, set up in the barn where the dormitory is, so we have been using that since our rude awakening. We have also started running in the evenings at least three or four days a week. We always have plenty of company when we run. It looks more like a parade than a bunch of old guys trying to get back into shape.

The weeks go by so fast when we are as busy as we are. I don't think any of us have ever worked any harder than we are now, but we all enjoy what we are doing so much, it doesn't seem like work. Dayna has another baby boy. He comes into the world complaining about pretty much everything in general. We name him Thomas, after Dayna's father, he weighs in at a solid eight pounds, twelve ounces and is twenty-two inches long. Not to be outdone, Robin has a boy that is no less loud in voicing his opinion, and weighs almost a full pound more than Little Tom. We seem to be on the Grampa kick, because Robin asks me if I mind naming him after her father, whose name was Allen. Our daughters were all hoping for a little sister, but since the last eight babies born in the community have been girls we really need some of the opposite sex, just to survive.

    Mike and Morgan are causing trouble again. Not really, but they did come home today with a suggestion that was more in the form of a request. It seems they were out checking the countryside for farms that we may be able to use, when they came across an old golf course. Naturally it is totally overgrown, but they think that with a little, actually a lot of work, it could be playable. I have never played golf, so to me it would not be worth spending the effort to get the course playable again. I much prefer to sit on the couch with my two new little men, and relax after working in the fields all day. That is if I could get them away from the girls, who never seem to get tired of taking care of their little brothers.

    Naturally Jenna and James want to go and see what will be required, and now it seems like everyone, but me, thinks it would be a great idea. They all say we don't have enough ways to relax, and golf would be a very good way to. The course in question is closer to Doc McEvoys group, and since he played golf before the war, he is interested now. First thing in the morning we take a walk over to see the golf course. It is not as big as some courses, but looks like it is definitely salvageable. It will probably never be as nice as it was before the war, but we could definitely make it playable. We find a large building that appears to have all the equipment they used to mow the grass on the course, and pretty much everything we will need to get the course back in playing shape. When the children hear about the golf course, they ask if they can play golf. Of course they have no idea how to play it, but they are excited to try anything that looks like fun.

    The women didn't want the others to know that they have no idea what golf is, so they wait until we get home to ask me. I am explaining it to them when Teddy and Kathy come into the kitchen where we are sitting, and show them some books they have that show people golfing. They are still pictures, so I explain that you hit a small ball with a club designed to hit the ball a certain distance. The younger children hear the word ball, and come running into the kitchen to show us a couple of golf balls they found today at the course. They are excited that they have the right kind of balls to play golf. Dayna still looks confused, so I ask her if anything is troubling her. She asks me if there is such a thing as miniature golf. I tell her that there definitely is, I have even played miniature golf. I ask her where she heard of that.

    She says that there is a place in town that has a big sign that says "Miniature Golf". I don't recall ever seeing that sign, but I have no doubts that it is there. I explain the difference between regular golf and miniature golf, and everyone at least in our family, agrees that it would be fun to try it. We decide that we will check it out in the morning. We get up and do our chores as usual then I tell Tim, Ken, and Gary what we have planned. Tim says that Charity, who had another baby boy a week after Dayna did, heck I never even noticed that she was pregnant, remembers seeing the same sign Dayna did. They named the baby after Tim's dad, his name is Kevin. To get back to the conversation with Tim, I tell him that I am concerned because I am always hearing about things and places in town that I have never even noticed. As a SEAL, we depended on powers of observation, and our memories to keep us alive. I am afraid that I am beginning to get careless, and not observing as I should be.

    Tim tells me that I'm absolutely right, I'm getting careless, and I am not noticing everything that I should. I was hoping for a little less blunt answer, but if you can't take criticism don't ask for it. I start to tell him that I will be more careful when he, Ken, and Gary start laughing. Tim slaps me on the back and tells me he is only kidding. They all tell me that the miniature golf course is on the edge of town, in an area that we have only been to once, when we first came to this area. Our wives know about it because they were driving when the youth were emptying the homes in that area of food and canning supplies. When we went through we were looking for guns and food, not entertainment.

When he mentions that, I do seem to recall seeing something like that, and thinking that sometime down the road it might be fun to play that game again. I mention that and they all laugh and tell me that I'm pathetic.

"You can't even admit that you are getting senile Zeus. You may not be much older than we are, but all that sex takes a toll. When we came here just a couple years ago you didn't have any children. Now you have how many, ten or is that twelve? You better slow down Jon boy; we need a healthy Zeus to keep the bad guys away."

Dayna is coming toward us and hears what Tim is saying. She smacks Tim and tells him and Ken that if they keep it up, she is going to tell her sisters that they are trying to ruin her sex life. Charity and Carrie are walking toward us and tell her she doesn't have to tell them, they heard every word, and they better not hear it again, or they will not have to worry about aging prematurely. Ken and Tim act properly chastised, and we can all laugh about it. I know I say it a lot, but it really is great to have good friends and family to joke around with. Dayna asks me if I am ready to take her and the children into town to see the miniature golf place. Charity, Cassie, and Carrie all want to go along, and if they are going, so are their husbands. Hope and Lindsay have become our best babysitters, as well as very helpful working around the farm. Dayna already asked them if they would watch the babies while we go into town, so Charity, Cassie, and Carrie leave the children under five with them at our house.

When we get to town, Teddy and Nickie know exactly where the miniature golf course is. They explain that they saw it when they were cleaning out houses, and although they had no idea how to play it, they thought it would be a great place to go for a date, under other circumstances. The course is in pretty good shape, considering how long it has gone without maintenance. All the supplies you need to play are right here, so we pass out putters and balls to everyone, and show them how the game is played. The boards where the ball rolls are raised up in places, so the ball doesn't roll like it would if it was smooth, but everyone thinks it's great anyway. We men let the wives and children continue playing, while we discuss the best way to go about this. We all agree that this would definitely give the young people, and those of us who are not so young, a way to relax and enjoy ourselves.

Since the course is not in bad shape, we decide that we will try to move the entire course to the farm and set it up there. We are discussing where we can put it, when Dayna and Charity come over and tell us they think it will go perfectly between two of our barns, in an area that is only used for walking anyway. Plus those barns are only used for equipment and not for animals. We know exactly where they are talking about, and agree that this should fit into that spot nicely. It is difficult to pull the young people away before they finish their game, but we really have to get back and outline this project to the committee, then get started moving everything. The young people and the wives say that we can start right now by taking all the balls and putters, along with the boxes of scorecards home with us.

The children can't wait until we can get the course set up. Some of the adults feel the same way about the full size course as well. When we present the idea to the committee, the vote is unanimous to proceed. There was one suggestion that we put the course more centrally located for all the groups, but we all agreed that it should be in a group since the children will be playing. We don't want them wandering perhaps into the woods, or trying to find other groups. We will probably wind up with more than one course eventually so that each group can perhaps share with one or two others. The transfer of the course from its current location to the farm goes much smoother, and with a lot less problems than I would have guessed.

Each hole is put together in sections, so all we have to do is separate the sections and load them on the flatbed. Some of the wood frames crack, and a few even break, while loading or unloading, but we have plenty of good lumber to repair anything that needs it, and all the help we could want. We even find some carpet or floor covering that matches the covering that is supposed to be grass. We bring several rolls of that back with us on one of the trips as well. It takes us two weeks to get the entire course moved and set up ready to use. Of course we have had a group repairing and making each hole usable, as we bring them over, so every day the young people get to play the holes that are ready. This has been one of the most popular projects that we have ever done.

We have had help from the other groups, who also enjoy coming over and playing on the course as well. Even though there is almost always a line waiting to play, there have been no arguments so far. Now that this course is complete, except for some minor things, we want to change; the other groups are looking for courses that can be set up in their areas. We will be happy to help them, some of us men and women have expressed an interest to design and build some holes that are more challenging than the course we have. We feel that it can only help the children if they have to figure multiple angles, to get the ball close to the hole while playing. Most of the current holes require one or possibly two bank shots to get the ball into the hole.

When we mentioned making bank shots it reminded some of us that we used to enjoy playing pool. I know it appears that we are only thinking about entertainment, instead of our safety and our survival. Actually, that's all we have thought about for the past couple of years, and now that the threat of invasion is at least much lower than it used to be, and our crops are growing, we feel that some entertainment is not a bad thing. Plus the miniature golf and other things we are thinking about doing, gives us something to do as families, and keeps the young people occupied in a good way. Our young people do have bicycles, and the younger ones have all kinds of toys, but the miniature golf is something we can do as a family.

When Bob, Trevor, and Blake return with their wives from searching for other people to join our community, they have ten new people, who are more than happy to be out of the cities. When they see the miniature golf course they just laugh, and say that they enjoy going away and coming back, because they are never quite sure what they will find when they return. They, along with the new people, get to try their hand at the game. I have to warn them not to bet against any of our young people, male or female, because they will more than likely lose. Many of us parents have already learned the hard way.

The summer is slipping past and we are still as busy as ever, but we always find time to rest on the Sabbath, and to spend time with our families. Bob and his team are out looking for others again. They always manage to find at least a couple of people that are more than willing to join our family. They have been gone as long as a month, at least once this year, although the average time they are away is about two weeks. We did find some pool tables in town as well as in the city that is in the opposite direction. Since we use the church for meeting in when we have a large group, we put three pool tables in our meeting house, and we still have room for our entire group to fit in comfortably. There are also several homes in all the groups that have pool tables in them. I enjoy playing once in a while, but not as much as some of our younger and older people do. Frank and dad love to play pool, as much as they do playing checkers and cards. We found a small table in one of the stores we were in, and they love playing on that.

Our peanut crop is getting close to harvesting. According to the books we have read on the subject, there is a short window that the ripe peanuts must be picked. If you wait too long, they will break off the plant and stay in the ground, and if you pick them too early, they will not be ripe. We have been marking the days on the calendar to make sure we don't forget. When the time comes that they are finally ready we will make sure we have plenty of help, because the plants have to be picked by hand since we don't have a peanut harvester. The plants have to be pulled out of the ground, with the peanuts holding on to the roots. The plant is turned upside down to let the peanuts dry for a few days in the air. This last trip Bob mentions seeing a couple of things that catch our attention.

One of those is that they went past a large farm that was marked as a peanut farm. They took the time to check it out quickly, and they found several barns full of equipment that was probably used to harvest peanuts. We waste no time getting a group ready to check that out. As it turns out they do have three harvesters on this farm which looks huge. We also find very large ovens that were used to dry the peanuts after they are picked. They must have made their own peanut butter as well, because we find at least two presses in boxes that show that's what they are for, and two others that look almost just like them. We also find dozens of bags of seeds in the barns that they were probably going to plant the year the war ended almost everything. It takes a couple of trips to get everything we can use, but it is definitely worth it. We also find hundreds of cases of jars and lids that are just the right size for peanut butter, along with many more books with information in them.

Our peanut crop turns out to be a huge success, but then we have been praying that we have a good crop more than planning how to use it. Our expectations are high in how the peanut butter will taste, but we are fully aware that our soil may not be as good as it should be for this crop. Our pinto beans did much better than we thought they would. They are pretty easy to store as well. We simply put then in five gallon plastic pails with lids that we found in town, after seeing them in the basements of most of the homes here. Naturally the beans have to dry first, but after that they will last quite a while. That is if we can keep from eating them all. When they ripened we cooked a large batch, and mashed them with some cheddar cheese that we make. Everyone in all the groups loves them, so next year we are going to double the area that we plant.

Our other crops are doing quite well also. We have more tomatoes this year than we did last year, and our sweet corn is doing great. I remember when I was young, helping Ma Horton cut the corn off the cobs, and get it ready to either be frozen or canned in jars. When the corn is ripe we have large groups of people in the meeting house sitting and cutting the corn off the cobs. We have some tools that help the process, but we wind up cutting at least some off with a knife. This is the third crop that we have had, and we can all honestly say we have not heard one word of complaint from any of our family. We are still concerned about being able to replace the lids that we use for canning. The rings and jars can be used over and over again, but the lids only work once. We tried using some twice and it didn't work very well at all.

That's the other surprise Bob had for us when he came back last time. We got so busy harvesting and canning that we haven't been able to do anything about it. He told us that in their travels, they saw a factory that has the same name as the lids and jars that we use for canning. They did not go inside, but they say it is a pretty good sized factory. Mike is excited about it, he says that he may be able to bring some of the machinery back here, and we might even be able to make our own lids. That would be great, but even I know that it will take many processes to make the lids, but maybe they have a good supply of them in the factory. Bob says the factory is just about a day's drive away, so in between harvests, we plan a trip over to see what we can find. At this time of year we are busy harvesting, and preparing foods for storage, but we feel this is important enough for a few of us to check out.

The trip over is uneventful, which is what we always hope for. The factory is larger than I thought it would be, and we are definitely not disappointed. We enter the factory from the front, and go into what appears to be the offices of the people that ran the company. Sara, Morgan, and Jenna are with us as well as James, Mike, and Gary. The women all say they would love to have some of the office equipment, even if it is pretty much all antiques compared to what they are accustomed to. Mike heads into an area of the offices that is marked engineering, the rest of us head out to the production area. There are machines and equipment all over the place. We can see the lids and rings that we use for canning on punch presses where they were being punched out. They are connected to conveyors that carry them to hoppers, that I'm sure got taken away to the next step in the process when they were full.

I would have loved to see this factory when it was running. There are other machines that appear to be where the completed lids were fed into, to get the coating of rubber that seals the jars shut. Mike joins us when we are at these machines, trying to figure out how they work. Mike has some notebooks that he says are the process instructions for operating this equipment. He is excited and confident that if he had a couple of days, he could actually get this equipment running again. Around the machines we are looking at, there must be fifty or sixty thousand lids, waiting to have the rubber put on them. At the end of the process there are thousands more that have gone through the process, and are being put into the little boxes automatically. At least they were when the factory was working. There is another line where rings are coming off being boxed as well.

Looking at the number of rings and lids right here, we will have more than enough for a couple of generations. It would be great to get the machinery running again, but just seeing what we are is a huge relief. What we find when we go to the shipping area is almost mind boggling, because here we find pallet loads of boxes of the finished product. The pallets are marked with who they were going to, and how many are on that particular pallet. Just adding the quantities quickly in my head, I can see that there are over a million lids sitting here on the dock. They must be affiliated with the jar company of the same name, because there are thousands of jars in the stock room and on the shipping dock. We find that we can back our truck right up to the dock, and load the pallets onto it using one of the fork trucks sitting here.

They are electric, so we will have to recharge the batteries, and hope it holds long enough to load the truck. Gary and Sara are looking around and find a propane fork truck that we are sure we can get running. We spotted a store on the way here, so while Gary, Sara, and Ken get the fork truck running, some of us head to the store to see what we can find there. The store shows signs that people have been visiting here recently. The stock room is still full of canned goods, and there are a lot of canning supplies here as well. We decide to see what we can get on the truck from the factory, and then see if we have any room. We only take enough food for our trip then head out to see if there is anyone around.

We see a sign that says Sporting Goods, so we head that way to see what we may be able to use. They have just about everything you could want in the line of sporting goods. There is a barrel full of different putters, as well as a whole wall covered with golf clubs, balls, and clothing. We also find a very nice almost new, thirty years ago, truck with about a fifteen foot box on the back. Naturally we have to see how much work it will be to get it running. Since we are going to spend the night anyway, we figure why not and get to work on the truck. James and Jenna head back to the factory to tell the others what we are doing. They come back with the pickup with the compressor and generator on it, and we have the truck running in no time. Gary and I take it for a drive to make sure it is going to stay running.

We turn down a street a couple blocks from the store, and we see a woman and two small children running for cover in a building, a few doors down from where we are. Naturally we stop and call to the young woman, telling her that we mean them no harm. They have disappeared by the time we get to the building, so we continue on, hoping that maybe we can find them before we leave. We mention what we saw to Sara, Jenna, and Morgan when we get back and they want us to take them to where we saw them. We are on the block before where we saw them, when Sara tells me wait here for a moment. We are walking, so I just stop where I am and watch them go into the next building. They are in the building probably five minutes, when they come out with four women and seven children. We recognize the ones we saw earlier, so that is a relief. The woman says she heard us call, but she was too frightened to stop.

With the new truck, we have just about room enough for everyone to ride back to the farm. The women we found tell us that as far as they know, they are the only ones living here. In the morning while the truck is being loaded, some of our group decides to take a ride around town just to make sure we don't leave anyone behind. On the far side of town they find a family of four that are walking into town from the north. They are more than happy to join our group, and the father in the family even helps us load the truck. We are able to fill all of our vehicles at the factory, which had its own gasoline pumps right there. The weather is not bad, so rather than spend another half day getting a vehicle running, some of us volunteer to sit in the back of the pickup on the way home. When we get there everyone is excited about the quantity of lids, rings, and jars we found and they are just as excited about the golf clubs, and balls we brought back, as well as the other balls and games we found there.

As usual the new people are excited to join our community. There is plenty to do and since they are all more than willing to help, we know they will be good additions to our family. We are continuing to harvest our crops that include the fruit trees we have. At first the new people were afraid that they would get into trouble if they eat some of the fruit while it is being picked. But then the children told them that they do it all the time, especially when they are picking apricots and cherries. They all seem to like the peaches, apples, and pears just as much. The orchards seem to be doing better every year. Frank says that's because we are pruning the trees properly each fall, so that they don't have a lot of wasted branches that prevent fruit from growing. We have plenty of each crop to can some, dry some, and eat just about as much as we want fresh.

    The faces on the new people make going after them all worth it, especially the children. They have never known a time when they can have a full belly on good nutritious food, and sleep in a warm comfortable bed. We have a large number of children under ten living in all the groups. We always have to be careful in the farm yards, because there are always children riding bikes and other riding things, and just playing around the yards with the other children. The dogs and puppies keep them from wandering off, besides the moms and the teens take turns watching the little ones. If there is mischief brewing you can bet that Tammy and Tina are right in the middle of it. Fencing in the playgrounds has helped keep the little ones where they are supposed to be, plus we try to keep adding to what they have to play with to keep their interest.

    One of the things we have been doing at least this summer and fall so far, is taking bike rides as a family. We found some little stroller like carts that can be fastened on behind a bike for the younger children. Some of them even have plastic covers, to keep dust off the little ones, and to protect them better. It is not uncommon to see thirty or forty people, and bikes riding from group to group on an evening. We love to go bike riding to visit our friends in the other groups. We get to visit with our friends and get some great exercise doing it. Our hunters have started taking their bikes to ride farther from home to shoot game, to keep what we have local just in case. They always take a radio with them and call when they are ready to have whatever meat they have killed, picked up.

We have been talking about raising our beef in the pastures, instead of letting it run wild. Personally I have been studying the animals in the woods since we came here and they seem to be breeding and multiplying fine on their own. Most of the cattle we see in the woods are not even afraid of us, and on most days you can sit on the porch and see several large groups of them, along with deer grazing on the deep grass on the other side of the road. That is not counting our cows that we keep for milk and other dairy products. We usually just let them graze behind the two barns that we bring them in to milk. When we first came here, and we started having cows come into the barnyard, there were several calves along with the adult cows. We now have ninety-seven head at last count that we milk every day.

That's another improvement that James, Jenna, Morgan, and Mike have made since coming here. They know a lot about dairy farming, and have been able to get the automatic milking machines working, so the job of milking the cows is much easier than it was. Each group has their own cows, so they had to go from group to group and teach those in charge of that chore how to use them. Anyway, getting back to raising our own beef cattle, we discussed all the pros and cons and decided that we may be getting into something that will just add more work, with no real return on investment. We all agree that when the area becomes more populated with other than our groups, then we will probably need to do something, but as it is we simply don't need to do it.

This year we planted oats as one of the new crops that we wanted to try. I honestly don't know much about harvesting and preparing them, but I definitely enjoy the oatmeal and the oatmeal cookies that the ladies always seem to find time to make. We found grape arbors at the farm where Billy and Ramona moved, so this year we have grapes. We were even able to make some raisins this year, much to the delight of the children and some of us who are simply young at heart. The wives have started cutting up dried peaches, apricots, cherries, and apples and putting them in oatmeal cookies. Between that and the ice cream made with the fresh fruits, you can see why we need the exercise we get from riding our bikes.

We do eat well, but we work hard as well, so none of us seem to be getting fat, at least not yet.

I have been able to get back into good enough shape to beat the teenagers at the obstacle course. They are still very popular with the groups that can use them. The younger people got so good at running the course we did for them that they have pretty much all started using the bigger one. The wives love to race me on the course, but they always cheat so they can win. I won't tell you how they cheat, but I don't mind losing, if that helps you figure out what they might be doing. Fall comes and turns into winter before we realize it. We are getting ready for another Thanksgiving already, and our family has grown by twenty new members. They are fitting in with the groups as if they have been here from the start. We continue to have babies and our couples continue getting married. Melissa is expecting in January, the twins are about as excited as they can be. They say they know this baby will be a little sister, time will tell.

Dayna, Robin, Melissa, and Becky chastised me, because when we talk it seems like everything is going along without a hitch here in our community. Things are going very well, and all of us are doing much better than we did before we came here, but we do have our share of setbacks. For instance, this summer we had a tropical storm that made its way inland and blew down a windmill in Barbs group, and two of them in Ryan and Carol's group. We were able to get them back up and running within two days, so the impact was minimal. Everyone involved agreed that compared to what they lived with before coming here that was a minor inconvenience. Not all of our crops grow as we would like them to, but we plant almost twice what we think we will need, so we still get more than enough for our needs.

Just like in any home, water heaters go bad, pumps stop working, and have to be repaired or replaced, but we work our way through these small inconveniences, just as you have to when they happen to you. I prefer to talk about the good things that are happening, rather than dwell on the small problems. We have been very lucky, and have not been attacked in almost a year. That doesn't mean that we let our guard down, because we are still ever vigilant. We continue training the new people and giving refresher training to everyone. There has been nothing in any of our lives to make us believe that we will never be bothered again. We continue to check with other groups on the short wave radio. Tim, and many of the others, are always talking to someone, mainly in the evenings. The group in Arizona has been dropping some hints that all may not be as well as they would like. They have been growing much like we have, only not to the extent that we have.

In their conversations, Tim says it sounds like they are having trouble getting enough food, and other necessities, for the larger group that they have become. After our get together on Thanksgiving, Tim raises them again, only this time they come right out and ask if there is any way we could send them some of our people who know farming, mechanics, and electricity. When they only had thirty some people in it, they were able to sustain fairly well, but they have had twenty people join their group, and now they don't know what to do. Clark, the leader of their group, even asks us if we are being honest when we tell them we have over four-hundred people in our group.

We assure him that we have more than one group to accommodate that many people, but we do have that many, and are able to accept that many more if we can find them. He says he knows he is asking a lot, but they are afraid they will be no better off than they were living in the cities, without some help. We assure them that we will do something to help them. We give them some advice to maybe get them through until some of us can get there, but he tells us they don't have vehicles like we do, and they have no idea how to get any. We assure them we will have some help on the way shortly.

We call an emergency meeting of all the groups on Friday, after Thanksgiving. Our group has already discussed the situation, and we have some volunteers to go. Bob and Blake, along with their wives, say they will be happy to go. Trevor's wife is expecting anytime now, so they don't think it's a good idea to go. Chip and Marty, along with their wives, say they could use a vacation. Those two, along with Troy have come so far from the first day I met them. That day they were running faster than Dayna could from the predators in the city. Now they are some of our best fighting men, as well as being able to do just about every job on the farm.

Sara, Gary, James, Jenna, Mike, and Morgan all ask if they could be allowed to go, because they want to see how that area survived the war. They will definitely be missed, but we're pretty sure the other group needs them more right now. Doc McEvoy and his wife want to go along as well. They say they spent their honeymoon in Arizona, and feel like it's time for a second one. Teddy wants to go to teach them how to hunt, but we assure him that we need him here. Andrew volunteers to go for that purpose, so they have a very good group of people to show them what we know. Just after everything is settled, and it's decided that they will leave in the morning, we have a wedding that no one expected. Well, actually we have been expecting it for a while, but with Andrew leaving for an extended period of time, Lindsay told him in no uncertain terms that he is not going without her. She also told him she will not go with him unless they are married. So now they are married.

For supplies they are mainly taking only emergency rations, and twenty gallons of gas, just in case they hit a stretch where they can't find any vehicles or stations to get it from. They are taking plenty of guns and ammunition, although we are sure they will be able to find plenty on the way, and when they get there. They are taking a small bus, and a pickup equipped with a small generator and a compressor. We have also started taking along a couple of extra tires, just in case. We learned the hard way that tires don't last forever, and they can be difficult to find, when you really need one. They are also taking a short wave radio, so that they can keep in touch with us on the trip. Tim and I would like to be going on this trip, but we are needed by our families, so we will stay where we belong and leave this mission in the capable hands of our friends.

Hello everyone, Jon asked me to tell you about our trip to Arizona. I'm Doctor Donald McEvoy, please call me Don. My wife Emma and I are excited to be accompanying this wonderful group of talented young people to Arizona, to help some dear friends of ours there. We are starting out on Saturday morning, and are not exactly sure how long it will take to get there. We are not even sure how long it will take to teach them how to be as self sufficient as we are. When we heard of the group started by Jon and Tim, we couldn't believe that anyone could be living as they claimed to be. When we found them, we were astonished at the progress they had made, and just how self sufficient they were. Since then we are continuously astounded by the things that our friends and families are able to accomplish.

Getting back to our adventure, most of our party has been on at least one trip except Emma and me, so this is rather exciting to us. Bob, who is the unofficial leader of this trip, is a very interesting man. He used to be called the Colonel, and very much looks the part, but after meeting Jon he dropped the title Colonel, and is now known simply as Bob. Jon is a most remarkable man, if you ask him he hasn't done anything except help out a little in our community.

However, if you speak with those who were the original group settling in Virginia, they will tell you he is the only reason they are still alive, and is the driving force behind our success. I have spoken in depth with Tim as well, and even he says that Jon is the one that made everything happen. Tim says he would like to be able to say he helped some, but it was Jon's idea to join forces in the city, and to find a place where they could live without counting on others. Just like when they were in the world they came from, he was content to follow Jon and do whatever he could to help.

We are able to make better time than any of us anticipated, mainly because Bob knows the roads and is able to navigate us past the worst places, with little or no delays. So far we are able to find gas stations when we need them, and have even found food close to the stations. The first time we stopped for gas, we found a young couple with one child living in the city we stopped at. We drew them a small map how to get to the community, and they assured us they were heading there as soon as possible. We stop for the night at a motel that used to be part of a large chain. James and Jenna tell the rest of us that they have stayed here before, and room service is terrible. Those two are always joking around, but when there's work to be done, you would have to look very hard to find someone working harder than they are.

Day two of our trip is uneventful, but interesting. We simply drive all day, except when we stop for gas, and to spend the night. It's Sunday, so we spend part of the day reading the scriptures out loud, so our drivers can partake of the word as well. On day three we find another couple with a small child. We are too far from home to send them there, so we take them along with us. On day four we find five more people, and now our vehicles are becoming full, but none of us can just leave them to fend for themselves with winter coming on. I know you are thinking that they have survived this long without us they should be able to last another winter. Being a doctor, I have seen people healthy one day, and pass away the next. I for one will never turn anyone away that needs my help. We pull into the farm, of the group we are here to help, just before dark, on the fifth day. We were not sure what we would find, so we stopped at a store in one of the big cities on the way, and was able to get enough food for a few days anyway.

Clark, the leader of the group, is happy to see us, but is not quite so happy to see the people we picked up along the way. We assure him that we will take them with us when we leave, and will be responsible for their food and safety while we are here. We can see a huge difference in this group and ours. For one thing, they are settled in the lower mountains here in Arizona, and there is very little around it in the form of cities. The original founders of this group lived in a fairly large town, but all the food has been gone from there for quite a while. The farm they are living on does not have room for more than the thirty people who settled here. They do not have electricity, and most of the people are sleeping in the one barn on the property. We decide to sleep in our truck and bus tonight, and discuss possibilities in the morning.

In the bus we have a pretty lengthy meeting, discussing how best to help these people. One suggestion is to find a couple more vehicles, and bring them back with us. That would obviously be the quickest and easiest fix, but would not help any other people who may be living alone in this part of the country. By the time we get to talk to Clark and his wife Susan, we have a plan to propose to them. We get to tour the place in the daylight, and it doesn't look much better than it did in the failing light last evening. Bob has been to this group and tried to prepare us for what we would find, but I don't think any of us quite believed it. After breakfast and a tour, we decide to be totally blunt with them. We recommend that they move from this location to one a little closer to the desert, where there are still four seasons, but that are not as severe as in the mountains or on the desert.

Some of the group is afraid to make a change, so we tell them we will take their leaders, and go looking for somewhere that will give them room to live, and even to expand as they want to. We tell them if we don't find a place, we will help them fix this place up, and help them get some vehicles so that they are more mobile. On the way here we passed some likely places that our people are going to take them to first. It's a good thing I came along, because they have several people that need medical attention. This is where we meet the young man who came here from the same world Jon and the others came from. We use the short wave radio which is a hand crank type and call our group back in Virginia. After making sure we are all right, and letting us know the people we sent to them arrived with a couple more people, they ask us what we think of our mission.

Sara outlines the situation very accurately. Tim and Jon tell us that if we think it would be best, to go ahead and bring them all back with us. We tell them that we fear if we do, that there will be nowhere for the others that may be in the area to go to, and they may perish. Jon tells us we should do exactly what we are doing, and find somewhere worth fixing up. He tells us what to look for and when he is done talking Sara tells him, "Yes daddy Zeus." Even Jon laughs and says he gets carried away sometimes. Sara laughs and tells him if he wants to get carried away out here with us, he is more than welcome. We have all expressed that we would feel safer if Jon was here with us. When he is around we all feel that everything is under control. We have to end our discussion and see what we can do in the interim.

We ask if there are any cities or towns where we might be able to get some food and other supplies. Brian, the young man who came from the other world, says they have walked to all the towns within a day's walking, and they are all just about empty of food. He also tells us he was a registered nurse in the other world, but he has nothing to work with here. Luckily I brought some medical supplies and herbs that I know help heal common ailments. Chip and Marty, along with James and Jenna, decide to go looking for a small city that is supposed to be about twenty-five miles away, at least according to our map. Some of the newer people say that there is a city over that way, so our guys figure they may as well go over to see what they can find.

The groups get back to the farm at just about the same time. The ones who went to look at another location seem to be somewhat uncertain about what to do. Our men and women, who went to the city nearby, had very good luck in finding food supplies, as well as winter clothing and other essentials. We have a meeting to discuss the proposed move with the group, and it really doesn't look like they want to move. Clark keeps saying that they should be able to make it work where they are, and we are simply pointing out the weaknesses of their position. Still no closer to a solution, we decide to call the group back in Virginia to see what advice Jon and our council might have. As soon as Jon gets on the line, he tells us that if it was up to him, he would help the group improve their living conditions, and if the new people who have come to the group would like, we can help them start their own group somewhere else.

The new people all say they will be very happy to go to another location, where they can be self sufficient, because living here is not really any better than living in the towns. We were not planning to start two communities, but it looks like that is what we need to do. Chip and Marty say that there are plenty of good vehicles in the city they went to, as well as a farm store where they can get pretty much everything they need. When our team starts something, they are pretty much unstoppable until the project is done. Sara, Gary, and James start looking to see how this farm was powered before the war. Bob, Jenna, Mike, Morgan, and my wife and I go with the new people, to show them the farms we passed on the way here. All of the others get to work helping them find equipment in the barns, and checking out the area for the best fields to plant crops.

The new group is very much impressed with the farms we show them. The best one we saw on the way up has four houses and three barns on it. They are very similar to the group we settled back in Virginia. We spend a little more time exploring the area, and find a larger place just a couple miles away. The people wanting to move in say they can be happy in either location, so we recommend that they settle the largest group first, knowing that they can expand to the other location when they get big enough. The bigger location has six houses and four barns, along with several miles of farmland in three directions. There is game grazing in the fields of tall grass, and the woods are just about as close as they are to the original group in Virginia.

As in Virginia there are mountains in the distance, but right here it is quite nice. The temperature seems to be at least ten degrees warmer than it was up at the other place. Since they are at a higher altitude, it will probably be colder up there most of the time. While the people, who will be staying, get to work cleaning the houses, our team gets to work figuring out how to get electricity to the homes. Mike comments that he has never seen such wide spread use of windmills as a source of power. This world must have been ahead of our world in that technology, but since our world suppresses so much technology, that would cost the big companies money, it is hard to tell. Either way they find three windmills, two of which are still standing, but the vanes need repair to get them to turn properly.

Our group anticipated this, and brought enough supplies to totally rebuild all three, but they only need repaired to be functional. By nightfall, two of the houses are cleaned well enough for everyone to stay in them, and there is even electricity to those two homes. They found several hundred jars of canned vegetables and fruits in each house, just as we did, so they are already in pretty good shape. We found a map in one of the homes, that shows there is a city only about fifteen miles west of us. Jenna comments that although this state is similar to the one in the world they knew, the cities are not in the same locations here. That's probably a good thing, because it will be much more convenient this way. A trip into the city shows that there are people living there, but the stores still have a large quantity of food in them. We see smoke coming from a couple of blocks over. When we investigate, we find a man with two women and four children, standing around a fire in a large drum.

We explain what we are doing and they decide to give it a try. They have nothing to lose. At a car dealership on the edge of the city, we find some excellent vans and trucks. It never ceases to amaze me how quickly our people can get a vehicle running, and get the tires changed. I get the honor of teaching Brad, who is the oldest member of the group, how to drive. He learns quickly and is beaming over his new found abilities. By the end of day two, our new group has four houses cleaned, and with electricity. They have a new van, and enough food to last at least a couple of months. They are also seven members stronger than they were yesterday. We made one discovery that is a big plus. These homes all use the electric baseboard heaters, so we don't have to try to find any and hook them up.

While we were in town yesterday we found some guns, as well as bows and arrows, for hunting. Andrew and Chip came down early this morning to see how we are doing. Apparently the group up north is not doing quite as well as we are. They must get much worse weather up there, because the windmill on that property is totally busted, so they will have to build a new one, and the wiring in the house is pretty bad as well. Chip says that they believe that the place up there was not a self sufficient farm like the ones we live on, and this one. We found a short wave set in the barn, so we call up to see if anyone hears us. Apparently there is no one listening, so Bob volunteers to take Jenna back up to speak with the others, and so that she can see James.

Our group is proceeding to make this a home. By the end of the day, all six houses have electricity, and two of the barns. We were able to recharge the coolant system on a very large freezer in the largest barn. Just like back home it appears that these people butchered their own meat and prepared it here. Andrew and Chip promised the people here that they will teach them how to hunt, and take care of the meat tomorrow. It is so gratifying to see the faces of the people whose lives are changing so drastically. It reminds Emma and me of when we first joined the groups in Virginia. You can see the pride of accomplishment in all their faces, instead of the desperation that was there. The fear and distrust of each other seems to be leaving as well. Working together toward a common goal can do that for you.

In the morning, we are getting ready to work on cleaning the barns. Chip took a look around yesterday and is excited about the farm equipment they have here. He and Andrew are taking Brad and Todd, who is the man we met in town, hunting this morning. The freezer seems to be working fine, so they figure now is as good a time to fill it as any. Brad and Todd ask why they don't just shoot the cattle or deer that are in the field's right near the houses. They explain that if they hunt those animals first, then they will have to go out farther all the time. If they go away from the farm first, the game will stay close, in case they ever need it. We have our walkie-talkies and within an hour we get a call to come and pick up a large steer, and a good sized deer. The men spend just about the rest of the day butchering the meat, and getting it hung in the freezer.

Towards the end of the day, we are surprised to see our people, accompanied by those from up north, pull into the driveway. We can tell by the looks on their faces that they are surprised to see the progress that has been made here. I would not blame the people here if they told the others they are not welcome, because that's what they did to them. However I am pleased to see them welcome the other group and they are all excited to show them everything they have accomplished. We have a meeting of all of us from back home, where we find out that the group up north finally realized that where they were, is not adequate for what they want to accomplish. They are going to settle in the first location we found when we came down here. For tonight though they get their first taste of sleeping in a warm house, with electric lights. If there were any doubters among them, they have all been converted.

6

In the morning, the group from the north head to the farm they will be moving into. We start the process of cleaning, and getting everything setup just like before. Now that they know what it can be like, they are working as hard as they can to make it happen. We get all of our supplies from the city. We have also found ten more people to join the groups in that city. I feel like a complete waste when it comes to farming and building. Everyone tells me that I am a doctor, so I am not expected to be able to plow fields or build houses. I can paint, so I at least feel like I am doing something constructive in the homes of our new friends.

The days turn into weeks, and our new friends are fast becoming self sufficient. Clark's group has grown to forty people, and Brad's group now has fifty-two people in it. They are looking for areas to expand because it seems that every week we get people coming, asking to live here. The area here is very similar to where we live, at least in the way the farms are set up. We have found two more farms that will be perfect for when the groups want to, or need to expand. The people here have learned very quickly, we show them once and they can usually accomplish most any task with minimal help the first time, and can manage on the second or third with no help.

The weeks turn into months, and before we know it we are getting ready to plant crops. This is always an exciting time of year for me. I always love to watch the plants grow, and produce vegetables and fruits that are so delicious. The groups have really come together here. There are now three groups, totaling one hundred and ten people. I have had the privilege of delivering five babies since coming here, and Brian has assisted on all of them, so he can take over when I leave. He grew up on a farm, so he is invaluable to these people. All three groups now have dairy cows, chickens, and are able to hunt and process their own meat. We found a wheat mill and brought it back here. We hooked it up just like back home, using a river that flows near here for power.

We had to teach them how to grind and use wheat by using some that we found in sealed buckets, and hundreds of plastic bags, much like we found when we first started out. We planted winter wheat, and it is starting to come up beautifully. Chip and Marty have trained our new friends how to fight, and they have needed it on a couple of occasions. On one occasion a group of men rode in on motorcycles, and told the people to leave. They did not see the men working in the barns and the fields, but the men saw them ride up. A couple of the men started after some of the women, and found out that these people are not to be taken lightly. Clark asked them to leave politely, but when they went for their guns, they were just a bit slow. They are all buried near the woods.

To see the farms they look very similar to ours. They have found gasoline trucks on the highway and in the cities, and brought them home. They have done the same for propane trucks, and now have a pretty good supply of both. The crops are in and so are the individual gardens. While we have been here we have been in contact with our groups back home as well as other groups around the country. We have been in contact with a group up in Utah that seems to be doing at least as well as we are. We have also talked with groups in California, Washington and Oregon that seem to be doing exactly what we are doing. We have had small groups ask if they can join one of the established groups, and they have always been invited to join the closest group. During the winter we made a trip to northern Arizona to find a group of twenty that was in pretty desperate straits. They have been a very welcome addition to these groups.

The people that we found on the way here have become a part of this family. Actually, when you live and work as closely as we have to, it is hard not to become part of the family. Spring turns into summer, and we are harvesting the winter wheat we planted. Everyone is working hard to get the wheat harvested and bagged, to be used for flour when it is needed. The fields are again planted with crops that can be used to feed the groups for the winter. During the summer some of our people have been asked to go over to California, to visit with our friends there and see if we can make any suggestions, or learn anything from them. They have a very nice community going, that seems to be growing much like ours, and the one in Arizona.

Sara and Gary are able to teach them some things about cars and trucks that help them quite a bit. Mike and Morgan help them with their windmills to get more out of them. The best thing about going over there is that we are able to bring some oranges back with us. We were feeling guilty until we radioed home and found out that Trevor and Ryan went down to Florida looking for a small group that asked to join ours, and found oranges growing wild. They tried them, then picked as many as they could, and brought them back as a treat for the family. Everyone says they miss us as much as we miss them. Our technical people are on the radio at least once a week talking to other groups, and giving them advice. Some of them obviously have people from the other world helping them, because they understand everything they are told.

Summer is almost over and we have started harvesting the crops. We have been stocking up on canning supplies, whenever we go where we can find them. We have found enough to last this group a couple of generations. We did the same thing our groups did back home, going from house to house in the cities, gathering food and other useful items. We brought our calendar along to share, if they even care about the days. We found another Mormon church near the community that they now use like we do. There are actually some people of that faith in this group, as well as the one over in California. Emma and I have had some very nice conversations with them. We have been reading their Book of Mormon, and so far have found it fascinating.

We have never really believed in a God, or a divine head of the universe. After seeing and living through the almost total annihilation of the world's population, it was difficult to think that any God would allow that to happen to his people. After meeting Jon and the others that have come to our world from another world, to help us get our civilization back, Emma and I have started rethinking our beliefs. We have always believed that the way we live in our community is the right way to live, but until we joined these fine people we spent our lives running and in fear of our fellow man. For us it is simple, either live your life working and helping others, or find somewhere else to live. That doesn't mean if you are ill, or if you are pregnant and can't work, you will be thrown out. Quite the opposite, if one of us is unable to do their chores due to illness or other good reasons, the others are more than happy to pick up your share of the load.

The crops are now mostly harvested, and the people here are doing very well. They have learned pretty much everything we can teach them, the rest they will have to count on trial and error, or read about it in the books they have gotten. Reading and writing are also skills that we passed along to these fine people. They are now capable of everything that we have done and are continuing to do. Lindsay has been worth her weight in gold to these people. She showed them how to get chickens to come to the coops, and has also shown them how to milk their cows, make butter, and other dairy products. The groups now also have the electric milking machines to make their job easier. Finally the day comes when we are saying goodbye and heading for home. We talked to Jon and the group back in Virginia and they are excited that we can now come back knowing that these fine people will be able to take care of themselves.

It is a tearful farewell as we are getting ready to pull out of the farm yard. We have made some very good friends here that we hope to see again in the future. When we came here there were fifty-six people, and today as we leave there are one-hundred-fifteen people living in three groups. Each group has the room to almost double in size, plus they have been working on other farms in the vicinity, getting them ready, because people will come if they know they will be safe. Last evening while we were talking on the radio, we found a group that started up recently in Missouri. They heard our conversation with our people back home, and asked if we would mind stopping on our way back, just to give them some advice and maybe a little help. It takes us two days to get to the new group, we also found ten people on our journey that are more than happy to come with us.

When we pull into the farm in Missouri we are surprised to say the least. This farm is almost identical to Ryan and Carol's group back home. There is no one around, which is also surprising, because this time of day and year this should be a very busy place. We ask the ladies to stay by the vehicles while we check it out, but you know Sara and the others. We have to run to keep up with them heading for the first house in the group. We get about three steps from the porch when someone opens the door and steps out onto the porch. We stop short from surprise, because the first one through the door is Rod from back home, and following him are Ray and his wife Carol, and George, Kyle, and Thomas, along with their wives. We all hug and exchange pleasantries, and then I ask the dumbest question imaginable. I ask them what they are doing here. Even Emma rolls her eyes at that one, and she's used to my inability to grasp the obvious.

They came here on a mission just like the one we have been on in Arizona. While we are talking, Don and Olivia come driving into the yard with a huge steer in the bucket of a backhoe. They stop long enough to give us all a hug and say hello, then Don is back driving the backhoe, apparently to the barn to butcher the steer. The occupants of this fine farm come out to meet us rather shyly. We tell them they have no reason to be shy, we are all one big family, whether we live in Virginia, Arizona or Missouri. They get over their shyness quickly, and are very happy and proud to show us around their farm. This group has four houses and two large barns much like Ryan and Carol's group back home, at least when they first moved in. They tell us there are two other groups that are actually part of this group, just like all of our groups are like one. Naturally we all want to see the other groups, and now Don can join us, because he turned the steer over to the group members that handle that chore.

The other two groups are as impressive as the first one we saw. Actually they are both larger than the first one, and are in just as good condition. We can tell that these people have done a tremendous amount of work. We talk for over an hour about the projects they have completed and some of the projects they are planning. The question comes up as to whether or not they have ever been attacked yet. Rod tells us that they have successfully fought off several attacks, and have had to rescue some of their people from those who meant them harm. He says in fact when we pulled into the yard today, there were at least ten guns on us until they knew for certain who it was. In one way that makes me feel very relieved, but it also makes chills run down my spine, knowing that I was in the cross hairs of someone's high powered rifle.

They have a special meal planned for us, made from the crops that they harvested this year. After dinner we are treated to some of the best ice cream we have ever tasted. This is when we hear the whole story behind these people, and our friends being here. It seems that the leaders of this group, or as they prefer, the people who helped get this community started, met Bob, Trevor, and Blake about a year and a half ago. That's when they were looking for others, and they offered Trent and his group a ride back, but they said they would walk. Well, they were walking toward Virginia when they met David and Kimberly, a young man and a young woman who seemed to be completely lost. They told them this fantastic story about being in the military in another world, and coming to this world after being caught in a terrible storm in the gulf of Mexico. They claimed that they had chartered a boat to scatter the ashes of his foster parents, who had died in a terrible car accident, a few days before that.

While they were on the water, a storm came up and tossed the boat every which way, they were sure they would be joining his parents at any time. Finally the storm quit, but then the worst fog they have ever seen settled around them, and they had no idea where they were or where they were headed. They fell asleep, and when they woke up the boat had drifted into a dock and the fog had lifted, at least enough to see a couple hundred yards. They went looking to see where they were and found no sign of life, although there were cars parked on the roads everywhere, some with skeletons in them. They went back to where the boat was, and it was no longer there. In fact where the boat was, there was now a large boat that was sunk, and almost totally rotten and covered with seaweed and barnacles.

They didn't waste any time trying to figure out what was going on. They found a nice pickup truck that they could change the tires on, and get it running, and headed north to see if the whole country was like this. They met Trent and the group of people with them on the highway walking east. They decided to join the group and see what there was to see. They got enough vehicles running to carry everyone and continued their journey. They drove for about a half a day when they were surrounded by some nasty looking characters on motorcycles, so they got off the main road looking for a place to hold the bad guys off. They came to the first farm we were at today, and used one of the barns to fight from, and were successful in chasing them away. Trent had told them what we had done in Virginia, so when they saw the potential where they were, they decided to try what we had done. As they said, if they fail, they can always see if we will let them join us.

As it turns out David is very good with mechanical things whether it be a car, truck, tractor, or anything else that runs on gasoline or diesel fuel. Kimberly was an electrical engineer in the Air Force, and worked as an electrician since she was ten. Her dad was an electrician and worked on just about any kind of circuit you can name. Her mom passed away when she was ten, so her dad took her to work with him and taught her the trade. Her dad passed away when she was eighteen, so she joined the Air Force to get an education, and because she had no family or even any good friends where she lived. That's where she met David, and they fell in love the first time they met. David's parents passed away when he was ten, so he went to live in a foster home. He was treated very well, and learned about mechanics from his foster father, who had a garage where he fixed cars and pretty much anything with an engine.

He was very sad when his foster parents died, but now neither of them have any ties in the world they came from. Both of them say they have been happier since coming to this world, than they have ever been. I tell you their story so that you can understand how they have been able to be so successful here. They elaborate on how they started pretty much the same way our groups did when they first came to the farms. They were able to get the electricity hooked up and to find a couple of small cities nearby, where they found food as well as people to join their community, but they didn't know anymore about farming than our groups did when they first started. That didn't stop them any more than it stopped Jon and the others. They plowed a couple of fields and planted some seeds they found here on the farm.

They were talking to Tim and Frank one night in late spring, and mentioned that they could use some help with planting and raising crops, if they have any advice that may be useful. Two days later the group of our people that we see, pulled into the farm yard to help them get started. They taught them how to figure how many acres are needed to produce enough food to feed however many people, they have showed them the value of having smaller individual gardens to grow smaller amounts of the foods you eat a lot of. In our gardens back in Virginia we always grew some different varieties of tomatoes, cucumbers, lettuce, different kinds of squash, and things like that. They are doing the same thing here. Since our people have come over they have had two older men and their families join, much like Frank and Connie back home. They were farmers before the war and have missed being able to raise their own fruits and vegetables. They didn't have a spectacular crop, but by planting much more than they needed, they have been able to harvest more than enough so far to feed them all winter and beyond.

They know they have some very large challenges in front of them, but like us they are excited about the possibilities. While we are talking, a small group of six comes walking into the yard. We can see they are embarrassed to ask if this is the place that takes in people who are willing to work for a living. Trent and his wife Patricia run to meet them and welcome them warmly. They make sure they get a good meal and that the children are cared for before they come back to the porch. They continue expounding on the plans they have and the things they want to accomplish for another good half hour. When they have completed their dissertation, I ask the second dumb question of the day. Again this one is even dumb for me, which Emma will be happy to tell you is difficult to do.

I ask them what exactly they need our help to accomplish. Trent, Patricia, David, and Kimberly look totally confused. Rod who is always the diplomat, tells me that maybe we should see if we can raise Tim or Jon on the radio, so he can explain why we are here. I think I have figured it out by the time we manage to get them on the phone. Tim is the one who answers, but he says he just sent Teddy and his shadow to go and get Jon. At first we are not sure what he means then Sara says that Teddy and Nickie must still be seeing each other. Tim tells us that's an understatement, but yes that's what he means. Jon takes over the mike and we can hear Teddy tell Tim he will show him about his shadow. Jon starts laughing and we can hear Teddy and his Uncle Tim wrestling around in the background. Jon who is still laughing, tells Teddy to take it easy on Tim, he tells him Tim is too old to be wrestling anyone stronger than Kevin, who is Tim's son who is just about a year and half old now.

Jon tells us this better be important enough to take him away from reading stories to his favorite young ladies and young men. I tell him I'm afraid that I am the reason he got called away this evening. I apologize and tell him we would like to know what he would like us to help these fine people with. I start to tell him that they are doing a fabulous job, when I hear him laughing at the other end. Now, I am getting just a bit perturbed about his attitude. Just when I am about to give him a piece of my mind, he stops laughing and tells me he is sorry.

"Doc, I owe you an apology. The only reason we wanted you to stop there is so you can see what they have done, and to drive home with the rest of our group. Unless there has been a change in plans, they are planning to leave there tomorrow morning, to come home. Colonel Bob, see what you started by traveling around? You have no idea how much good you and your team have done for people."

Bob is turning red, he doesn't like the spotlight. He tells Jon that he knows he was never really a Colonel. He starts to elaborate when Jon interrupts him and tells him he will always be the Colonel to us. I tell everyone that they must be saints to be able to put up with me sometimes. I can never quite see the obvious, and I am always asking foolish questions. Sara, Jenna, and Morgan all give me a hug and tell me that's part of my charm, and they hope I never change. Jon is always telling me how much he enjoys being part of this family that can kid and joke around with each other. I know exactly what he means, Emma and I have never been as happy as we have been since joining these wonderful people. Jon tells us unless there is a change in plans, they will be expecting us on Friday. He says they have saved all of our chores since we left for us to do when we get back. Gary tells Jon in that case, he will be staying right here. Sara tells Gary that there is no way he is staying here, because she is going to kick his butt on the golf course, even if they haven't played for a year. Gary laughs and says he guesses he will see Jon on Friday after all.

When the call is completed David and Kimberly ask Sara what she was talking about when she said golf course. We explain all about the golf course we have, and the miniature golf and other games we like to play with the children. Rod says he forgot to tell us about the bowling lanes they set up at the farm after we went to Arizona. We also tell them all about the obstacle courses we built for exercise and for fun. They are writing all this down while we are talking. Trent and Patricia say that they may be calling in the spring to get some advice about getting some of those forms of entertainment for this group. We tell them we will be happy to come back and help them in any way we can. We are all hoping for a long happy relationship with these groups. To all of us they are part of our family even if they are a distance away.

In the morning it is difficult to leave, even though we have only known each other for a short time. We are only on the road for about an hour, when we see a group of twenty walking down the road. When they see our vehicles they try to hide on the side of the road, but we assure them that we mean them no harm. They say they overheard a conversation on the radio about a settlement near here. We have a bus large enough to hold them all, so while the rest of us wait here, Rod and Marla take them back to join our friends.

The trip from there on is uneventful, which is something we all appreciate. The others are bringing us up to speed on what has been going on in the groups. We could probably make it in one day, but it would be very late when we get there, so we decide to stop for the night. It gives us a chance to fill all the vehicles from a station next to the building where we are spending the night. I am so excited to be going home that I have trouble falling asleep, and when I do it seems that I am awake just about every hour. In the morning we get an early start, so that we can be there before noon. Until we went away, Emma and I never realized how much we would miss our home and our family. When we pull into the driveway, my mind races back to that day four years ago when our little group from Erie, Pennsylvania, pulled into this very same driveway and prayed that these kind people would somehow let us stay.

Emma must be thinking the same thing I am, because the tears are flowing down her cheeks as freely as they are mine. She pats my hand and tells me we are home at last. That's exactly what she said that day when Jon and the rest of our new family showed us the farm they had already started cleaning up. They said that they just knew that Heavenly Father was going to send them some very nice new friends to move in, and love it as much as they do. Just about everyone in the vehicle we are riding in have tears in their eyes as well, when we see the reception that is waiting for us. Jon and his family are waiting next to the area where we park the cars. We never drive them into the yard, unless we are unloading something very heavy. That looks like Teddy standing next to him, but that can't be. That young man is at least two inches taller than Jon. The twins look like young ladies instead of little girls, and Kathy, Karen, Lisa, and Christy are all teenagers now.

It seems like we have been gone much longer than a year in some ways, and in other ways it seems like we never left. I am getting so emotional from all the hugs and our family telling us how great it is to have us back that I will let Jon visit with you again. I have enjoyed getting to know all of you. I hope you haven't been too bored listening to the ramblings of an old country doctor. I'm sure we will meet again. Emma and I are looking forward to it. Goodbye for now.

7

Hello everyone, I'm back. Doctor Don and the rest of our wandering family members are home, so the women are cooking up a huge barbeque for later. We have a couple hundred pounds of ribs, as well as other kinds of meat, like hot dogs, and hamburgers. That's the first thing Doc asked for is a hotdog. The first thing some of the others said is that now they have other games and sports to kick my butt at. Three guesses who said that and I'm betting you don't need more than one. You're right, Sara, Jenna, Morgan, and Lindsay. I asked their husbands how much red meat they have been eating lately, because it seems like they are even more aggressive and competitive than they were when they left. When they first got home they came up and hugged me, telling me how much they missed me, then all four of them punched me in the chest, and told me I better be ready to run the obstacle course against them on Monday.

Naturally Dayna, Robin, Melissa, and Becky have to laugh and encourage them. I have been working out a lot lately, along with our normal chores which never seem to be completed. We had an excellent crop this year, so we have been blessed with the privilege of canning, freezing, and drying, more than any other year since we have lived here. We also have many willing hands to help with the harvest, so it's really not bad at all. I should bring you up to date on what has been happening around here for the past year. Melissa did not disappoint the twins. She delivered a beautiful baby girl, making all the women in the family happy. We named her Julie after Melissa's mother. Her personality seems to match some of the other ladies of this family, whom I shall refrain from naming, at least if you take into account the amount of complaining she does. She is almost nine months old and yells at me every time I don't pick her up the minute I walk into the house.

Between Timmy, Tommy, Kevin, and Julie, I am kept busy playing with children pretty much all evening, every evening. Luckily the other children are getting old enough to help me play with the babies, or there would be a lot more complaining than there is. Becky is expecting anytime now, she says she is sure the baby is a girl, because when she had Jerry she had heartburn constantly, and with this baby she has not had heartburn. I got yelled at and smacked, when I asked her if that could be because she is eating better now, than with the first three pregnancies. Lisa and Christy are on my side, they tell their mom that Jerry still gives them heartburn all the time, and they are not even pregnant. Kathy and Karen tell them that is a byproduct of having a brother. They say Teddy gives them heartburn too. Can't you feel the love our girls have for their older brothers?

Getting back to what has been happening for the past year beyond our little family. After we set up the miniature golf course, we did the same for the other groups, only we changed the shape of the holes on each course, so that when you played on the course at Ryan and Carol's group, it was totally different than our course and different than any of the other groups as well. We did make some of the holes like par threes, not because of the distance, but because of the compound turns that we built into some of the holes. Some of the holes are even a challenge to get the ball in the hole in three strokes. Frank, Dad, and some of the other older men in the group found some wooden balls in one of the barns, and decided that they are for a game called Bocce, which they all remembered enjoying when they were young playing it with their families. Naturally when we find something new the children all have to look it up in the books we have, and found out that the game can be played in an open yard or in a boxed in area similar to a horseshoe pit.

We already have horseshoe pits at each group that everyone big enough to toss a horseshoe far enough enjoys playing. Why not build some Bocce pits to play the game in. Most of the younger children just play in the yard. It's the older children, like Frank and Dad that play it in the boxed in area. So far none of the young children argue about the game, but Dayna, Roberta, and Connie have had to tell Frank and Dad that if they can't play nice together, they will have to quit playing. Anyway the Bocce reminded some of the older people, as well as Tim and I that we used to go bowling, the older people when they were younger, Tim and I before we came to this world. Naturally there were a couple of bowling centers in town, so we investigated how difficult it would be to move some lanes to each group, so that we can all go bowling again.

The first item on the agenda was to get a building to put the lanes in, so we had to decide how many lanes we wanted in each group. The lanes in the bowling centers in town were pretty good sized, with one of them having thirty-six lanes, and the other having sixty-four lanes. We decided to put ten lanes in each group, but since our group has more people than the other groups, we wound up with fourteen. We poured the concrete slab that the building and the lanes will sit on then built a building to house the lanes. We decided to use some of the prefab homes, with some modifications of course, to make them long enough to house the lanes, and the equipment for setting the pins. The lanes were not too difficult to move and we have not been able to make the automatic setters work properly yet, but we all enjoy bowling together. We take turns setting the pins for each other, and usually bowl as families. With as many lanes as we have, several families can bowl at a time. We are hoping now that Mike and James are back, they will know how to make the pin setters work the way they should.

Other than that things have been pretty boring. We did have to drill a well in Karl's group, because they have been expanding, and they wanted to put some houses where none were before and they needed water. A challenge like that excited everyone, so as usual we had plenty of help. Frank remembered helping his dad and uncles drill for water on their farm once, so we have an expert. What more do we need? I was not sure how we would go about finding where to drill the well. We found the rig for drilling in town, at of all places a company that had a sign saying, Wells Drilled and Repaired. In the office they had pictures of a guy using what Frank called a divining rod, to find where they should drill the well. For the life of me I couldn't figure out how a forked stick could find water sixty or seventy feet below ground level, but if Frank says it works. Who am I to doubt it?

We went over to where they wanted to build the houses, and Frank made a big show of walking around with the divining rod, until it miraculously pointed straight down at the ground. He had been walking with it parallel to the ground up to that point. We set up the drilling rig that is mounted on the back of a one ton truck, along with all the pipe and drills we should ever need, and started drilling into the ground in that spot. It's a good thing Ken knows about this stuff from when he was in the Army Corps of Engineers, because even Frank was lost once we started drilling. It took us a day and a half to drill the well, and another half day to run the pipe down the hole and hook up a pump. Oh yeah, Frank was right on, we found water first try. Of course when I found out that there was a geological map of the entire area showing the underground water patterns, I have to admit I am questioning Frank's ability to use a divining rod.

According to the map it would have been difficult to drill anywhere on that property and not hit water. We were able to move three of the prefab homes into that location, which opened that area up for more people. Karl's group loves that small section and has been no trouble at all. In fact they helped tremendously the only time we were attacked in the last year. I'm not even sure we can call it being attacked, because there was not even a single shot fired. Ryan and Carol's group had some men on motorcycles causing trouble one evening. They called us because they were not sure if they should shoot or not, since the men bothering them didn't appear to be armed. We were on our way over when some of the men from Karl's group came up behind the men on motorcycles with guns drawn, and convinced them that they really didn't want any trouble. The men rode away, but returned the next day and asked if they could possibly join our community. Karl's group took them in to watch them, which wasn't really necessary, because they have turned out to be some of the hardest workers we have and with our groups that's saying something.

Monday morning comes around and I have to race against Sara, Jenna, Morgan, and Lindsay on the obstacle course. I have my strategy all thought out, where I can lose this race a little at a time and not make it look too obvious. Just about everyone in our group and several from the other groups show up to watch the race. Naturally I have to joke around, so I ask everyone if they don't have work to do somewhere else. The race goes pretty much like I thought it would. I don't have to work too hard to lose against these girls, they are plenty fast enough. When the race is over, my daughter in law, they're not married yet, but we are sure they will be, comes up and tells me a full minute off my average time. Sara and the others come over and tell us and everyone in general that they knew I would not win, so that they could feel like they kicked my butt. Then they get all mushy on me and say that I have been putting others ahead of myself ever since they met me.

Sara says she wants a hug so I start to give her a hug, and the little brat grabs me around the neck causing me to be off balance, and she along with the others drag and push me into the stream that runs through the obstacle course. That's more like it, now I know for sure my little sisters are home. We spend the rest of the day harvesting, and preparing crops for food storage. The days and weeks seem to fly by when we are harvesting, canning, preserving, and drying foods for future use. We were talking the other day about how much work it can be getting all this work done. Cassie who is Dayna's youngest sister, and has been with us since the very beginning, says that to her no matter how hard we work here, it is still ten times easier than when they lived in the city. All the others that were working together that day agreed whole heartedly, and I had to agree as well.

Our group isn't getting as many new people as we were last year at this time. There are groups like ours springing up in many different states, and as far as we can tell from listening to the radio and talking with them, they are all doing well. We still get requests from other groups for some of our people to come over and perhaps help them, but usually it only takes a few weeks or maybe a month at the most. Sometimes we can explain what we did or do well enough over the radio, for them to get the job done themselves. We were on our way back from a trip to the factory where they used to make lids, with another full truck, when we heard on the CB that there is another settlement near there. We took a detour to stop and meet them. They have a very nice group that has been living there for about six months now. Many of the people met trying to find our settlement and decided to try it on their own.

They have two young men with the skills it takes to make something like that work, and they are close enough that we can go over periodically if they do find out they can use some help. We left them enough rings and jars to last at least fifty years, to go along with the stores of them that they have already accumulated. Mike still wants to see if he can get the equipment running, and we will probably have time during the winter. We all agree that we probably will not need them, but when we checked the facility closer, we found several hundred thousand lids that have already been plated and all they need is to have the rubber applied to them to be usable. Mike and James are sure they can get the machines to do that running, so why not let them. We have found some great jars that have a glass lid that is fastened to the jar with wire. The glass lid presses down onto a rubber gasket and has a clasp to seal the jar and its contents. We have several thousand of these jars, but could not find the rubber gaskets until we found that manufacturing facility.

We not only found the gaskets but we found the machine, the rolls of rubber, and the process to make them. We will be going back in a couple of weeks to spend a few days and see whether or not Mike, James, and the rest of us can get those antique machines running. We are making some strides toward getting the people in this world closer to where they were when man decided to destroy each other. At least it looks like the worst ones killed each other off, and left those that may have a chance to make this world the place that Heavenly Father wanted it to be in the first place. Only time will tell, and I'm sure that will not be answered in my lifetime, but it feels great to be the small part that we have been privileged to play so far. We still have some apples to be made into apple sauce, and we always like to dry a bunch to eat as snacks, instead of cakes and ice cream all the time.

Becky brought the female baby population in our home to a tie. She gave birth to twin daughters and both lovely ladies and their mommy are doing fine. Sometimes I think that they are competing with Julie to see who can complain the loudest and longest, but they don't have to complain long before one of their big sisters, or many moms pick them up and fuss over them. Of course their daddy can't let them think that he doesn't love them just as much, so I pick them up every chance I get. Nickie makes such a fuss over her new little sisters all the time, and is always telling Teddy she can't wait until they can have some of their own. Robin was teasing Nickie one day and told her that as much as she talks about having a baby, we may have to separate them until they turn eighteen. Nickie is a lot like her mothers in law, she didn't even look up when she asked Robin what makes her think it's not too late already. Poor Teddy just got redder.

I almost forgot to tell you what our precious little ladies names are. Since Becky named Lisa after her mother, she asked if any of us mind if she names them after my moms, Anne and Dianne. How could I mind that she wants to honor both my mother's by naming the girls after them. I think I may have been treading on thin ice with incurring the wrath of Ma Horton though. One evening when Anne was being particularly loud in letting me know she was not happy, with anything I had been doing on this particular night. I told her she reminded me of her namesake because it seemed like I could never do anything right for Ma either. That night all my parents came to me in a dream, and Ma smacked my behind for saying that, but then she smiled and thanked us for naming our lovely daughter after her. If that's what it's going to be like to die then I will have no problems with it at all.

I hope that won't be for a long while though, and until then I will enjoy living with our extended family and help any other families that may need our help along the way. The long winter nights allow us to catch up on our reading. We still stop at any and all libraries and stores that sold books to see if there are any that we haven't already found. I don't think we have ever come out empty handed from one of those places. It's a good thing we have so much help, because with the twins, Becky definitely needs it. Every time Sara, Jenna, or Morgan come over, which is pretty much every day, they tell me I have to start giving Dayna, Robin, Melissa, and Becky some rest from having babies. Sara told us it looks like we are starting our own personal daycare center. At least we can all laugh with each other because we know that we all depend on each other for our very lives, and I can't think of anyone, anywhere, I would rather trust with mine.

Tonight at dinner, Dayna and Robin told me that Sara, Jenna, Morgan, and Lindsay went to see Doc Betty today. Naturally I am concerned when four members of our family are not feeling well, until Melissa says that they will feel much better in about six months. All four of our friends, along with their husbands walk in at that moment, so Becky tells them it looks like someone else is working on their own day care center. There is some good natured bantering back and forth, but we are all very happy for them. They all say they will have to spend more time at our house now, especially at meal time, so that they can learn how to take care of babies. I knew that I would wind up getting the worst of it somehow. Now I will have to put up with even more cantankerous females. My sons come over to me when we are all laughing and harassing each other. They tell me we will do this like we do everything, together. None of us can argue with that logic, besides we are all looking forward to spending a lot of time together this winter, getting ready for spring. None of us would want it any other way.

Ten Years Later

Hello everyone, I've missed visiting with you, but the farm keeps us pretty busy. You should see this place now. We run like a well oiled machine, well almost. We have learned pretty much all that we need to know, to keep our little piece of this beautiful earth running, if not quite so smoothly sometimes. We seem to always have enough, even if there is a setback and we don't get the crops that we expected when we planted them. When you depend on the weather you have to expect that it will not always cooperate, but we have always planted more than we need, so in good years we have more than we need, and in bad years we use some of the excess from good years. I think the worst job we had to tackle was putting in a septic system, but even that wasn't all that bad. Like everything else we researched it and did it. We know without a doubt that there are people who could do the job faster and probably even better, but it works when the job is complete so what more can we ask for.

When last we talked, I told you about the other groups that were starting up in several states around us, the Midwest, and even farther out west. We stay in contact with several of the groups and so far they are all doing well. For a lot of the groups we kind of set the standard, because most of them have visited and took a lot of ideas home with them. Our groups have not been attacked in several years now, because we are very well prepared for anything like that. We make sure everyone knows that we are prepared to fight, and are more than willing to do whatever it takes to protect each other. About seven or eight years ago there was a pretty big threat from a large band, of what we call predators, riding around looking for settlements to take women and young girls from. We knew that they were listening in on the radio, whenever we would talk to the other groups around the country, so we made it clear that if any groups were attacked we would hunt down those responsible, and retribution would be swift and harsh.

As far as we know none of the groups that we communicate with regularly were ever attacked. In fact our group, as well as some of the others, had several men come and ask to join. They admitted that they had been riding with some other guys that wanted to cause trouble, but they had seen how we live, and decided it was easier and much safer to join us. We watched them closely and not one of them ever caused any trouble, or left because the work was too hard. We no longer have anywhere near as many single women as we did have. There are also only a few of us who are married to more than one woman. In our family it has worked out great, even if we have had to build an addition on the house, to accommodate the children we have been blessed with. Sara found a book just after we last visited that has something like 5,000 babies names in it. She gave it to us as a baby shower gift when Dayna was expecting our third child together. We all know it was meant as a joke, sort of, but that book has made the rounds through the entire group, and all the others as well. That beautiful young spirit we named Amanda, but we all call her Amy.

Amy is now eight and has learned how to be a little pain in the neck just like her older brothers and sisters. She is now helping them teach baby Billy, baby Gary, baby Sara, baby Morgan, baby Mindy, and baby Toni, how to wrap their daddy around their tiny little fingers, to get him to let them do anything they want. That will never happen, but me and their moms are pretty lenient, as long as what they want to do isn't dangerous or will hurt others. Dayna did not have all those babies, but they are all in the family. Teddy and Nickie are now married. They could not quite wait until they turned eighteen, but they were both seventeen and we all agreed that they have both been doing the work of an adult since they were twelve or thirteen, so what difference does a few months make.

They have made us all very proud grandparents, they have a very handsome son they named little Jon. Unlike Tim and Charity, they love the story of Robin Hood. Plus Nickie told us that being named after me; he can't help but be a handsome talented man. The ladies in the family, both young and not so young, told her that they are already married so she doesn't have to be nice to me anymore. Jerry married Paige. They are still waiting to have children. Jerry's sisters always tell Paige how sorry they are for her, because their brother is kind of slow. The biggest surprise when it comes to weddings is when Steve, who lived with us more than with his family, asked Lisa to be his wife. When she said yes, Becky said if she had known that Lisa liked him, she would never have let him stay at our house. Naturally she was kidding. We all love Steve like part of the family.

Kathy, Karen and Christy waited until just last year to get married. They dated several young men and wound up marrying young men from Doctor Dons group. Kathy's husband has been working with both Doctor Don and Doc Betty learning how to be a doctor. The twins, Tina and Tammy are not married yet. They say they want to make sure their little brothers and sisters get the maximum benefit of their knowledge, before they take the fatal plunge into matrimony. Zeus and Missy are still their constant companions, plus they look after the new children as well as they did the twins. There are two new puppies that tag along like Zeus did, when he was a puppy. The children named them Biscuit, and Cricket, and love them as much as the twins have always loved Zeus and Missy.

Little Timmy is not so little anymore. He reminds everybody of Teddy and seems to be following in his big brothers footsteps. At thirteen he is one of our best hunters, and always seems to know when he is needed, because he shows up like Teddy used to when he was needed most. He is as tall as I am, and weighs almost two hundred pounds. He is very popular with the girls his age, and even some a year or two older and younger. Billy's daughter Bobbi seems to be the young lady that he likes the most. I told him he can't marry her, because that would make Ramona and I related, so both Ramona and Bobbi, along with her Aunt Bobbi, smacked me and told me to leave young love alone.

Speaking of match making, okay I know we weren't exactly speaking about that, but you will get a kick out of this. You remember that Sara, Jenna, Morgan, and Lindsay were all expecting when we visited last. Well Sara and Jenna had beautiful little girls, who have personalities just like their mothers by the way, always picking on somebody. Morgan and Lindsay had bouncing baby boys that take after their parents as well. All four of those children can never seem to get enough reading, and they are always studying something. They are really great kids, and we are all sure they will help our community as much as their parents have. Anyway, where the match making comes in, is that whenever a baby is born into the family, no matter who it is, the women all get together and try to guess who they will marry when they get older.

When Sara's daughter Misty was born, all four of the women in our house, along with our daughters, said that she would marry my son Thomas some day. Ever since then I have been trying to brainwash Thomas by telling him that Misty would not be the girl for him. When he was four he just said that girls are yucky, so I had nothing to worry about. Now he's eleven and he says that she is pretty cute. Where did I go wrong? Sara keeps saying that she hopes at least one of our children get married, so that she would really be related to me. She always says you don't have to treat relatives as nicely as you do friends. Sara and I are like brother and sister, we tease each other constantly, but we would not hesitate one moment to defend the other in any and all situations. Heck, Sara brought the recipe for mayonnaise into this world. That alone makes her a saint in my eyes.

Doc Betty and Josh finally have a baby of their own. I say of their own, because they have taken in several children that lost their parents before joining us. They named their beautiful baby girl Faith, because Betty says, they never lost faith that Heavenly Father would bless them with a child of their own. Caroline was as happy as they were, Samantha and Samuel are now teenagers. Samantha is learning medicine from Doc Betty and Samuel is one of our best hunters and farmers. We have been keeping track of all the births since we moved here, and Faith was number one hundred. Listening to me you would think that all we have done for the past ten years is have people get married and have babies. Actually we have had some great progress in other areas as well.

You may recall that Mike, James, Ken, and many others, wanted to try to get the machinery in that factory running, to be able to finish the lids that had already been started, and to run the machine to make the rubber gasket like seals for the other style jars. I think it was only about a month or so after we last visited that we went back to try to get the process going again. Actually we got luckier than we could ever imagine when we ran into an older man and his wife that were living in that city. They had been in another city, but they said something told them to come back to that city, so they did. Anyway, to make a long story short, this man and his wife had worked at that factory before the war, and knew how to run all that equipment. Of course it took them a little while to remember how, but when they did they were very valuable to us.

We started out running the rubber gaskets, and that went better than any of us could have imagined. They even knew of a couple of steps in the process that we didn't. After the gaskets were cut, they have to go through a high pressure washer with this special chemical cleaner, then they are automatically boxed at the end of the cleaner. They also showed us an attachment that could be put on at the end that allowed us to package the rubber gaskets in plastic bags of one hundred each, and seal them until they are needed. Our new found friends, named Francis and Mary, had as much fun running those machines as we did, and they kept remembering stories about their friends that used to work with them. We ran all the rubber we knew about, but they showed us that the company used to keep most of their supplies in a warehouse behind the facility. When we checked that out there, we found about ten times the amount of sheet rubber than we already used, and that made over a hundred thousand gaskets.

When we started running the lids that get the rubber bonded to them, they also had some very good advice. They told us that the process specs are a little stingy with the rubber sealant on the lids, so everyone in the shop knew to turn up the settings for how much rubber to coat the lid with. They also told us that if you set them at an even higher level, if you are careful taking the lids off without bending them, you can get two uses off a lid. It was so much fun watching that machine spit out completed lids so fast we worked our butts off keeping up with it. We had so much fun we wish we could have been here to meet some of the people in the stories that Fran and Mary keep telling us about. Fran also knew where the company has the lids plated, so we took a ride over there to see if they had any more ready, before they were so rudely interrupted. When we got there, Fran explained that they usually brought a load back every

Monday, and picked up a load of lids needing processed. Sure enough the load that would have come back the day after the war, is sitting on the loading dock waiting for Monday morning. That's another million of the lids that we can run through the equipment.

I know you are probably thinking that there is no way we need that many canning lids. You are correct there, but there are many more groups than ours, and if we make them while we can, we should always have a ready supply for everyone needing them. Besides the materials will go to waste anyway, so we may as well use them. After running for a couple of hours, Mary remembered that on some occasions they would pack these lids in the plastic bags as well. It only takes a few minutes to convert the packaging, and we are back in business. We did have a couple of miscues, and the equipment had to be adjusted a couple of times while we were there, but aside from that everything went well and we had a great time. We found several more pallet loads of the completed lids that had been covered in plastic shrink wrap and are still usable. We have gone back a couple of times to run more of the lids and the rubber gaskets. We have never run out, but as I said, we feel we may as well use the material before it goes bad. It's a miracle that it hasn't already gone bad. That still fascinates James, Jenna, Mike, and Morgan.

The Arizona group found a factory similar to this one, so our resident experts of machinery, along with Fran and Mary, took a trip to help them. I guess they found out that the plant out there was a sister plant to the one we have been to, so they were able to help them with everything they needed. Representatives from Texas, Utah, Washington, California, and New Mexico also met them there, and they all went away with more rings, lids, and jars than they will need for several generations to come. We have made great steps in other areas as well. We found a bakery in one of the cities we visited. I know we have visited other bakeries, and were able to find some very usable items for our groups, but this was a bakery that made thousands of loaves of bread daily. We were able to bring back a couple of the smaller mixers that only hold about a hundred pounds of flour at a time, along with several thousand bread pans that were still in boxes, and had never been used.

It looked like the stuff we brought back was used for making specialty items, and not the main product of the company. Most of the ovens in the bakery were gas powered, but we did find a couple of smaller ovens that are electric. Now, you have to realize that smaller is a relative term, and compared to the large ovens these ovens are small, but they will still hold twenty five loaves of bread at a time. This allows the women in the groups to mix and bake enough bread for the entire group in just a few hours, instead of someone in every house having to spend at least that long just to make enough for their own family. We built what we call our bakery, to put the equipment in. The women and men take turns baking bread for the entire group a couple times a week. We found enough mixers and ovens for three bakeries like that, so when we make bread, we know we have to make it for some of the other groups as well. They take their turns just like we do, so it works out great for anyone.

We are also trying different types of seeds to grow our crops with. Frank, Dad, Eric, Rod, and Andrew, along with James and Jenna and several other members of our family, have been working with the seeds to make hybrid tomatoes, corn, beans, and many other crops to make them more resistant to conditions, and to make them grow more crops per acre. In the case of tomatoes, they have come up with some that we have grown in the smaller gardens that taste better than any tomato we have ever tasted. They have done some great work with strawberries and blackberries that have increased their yield by about thirty percent. They have done some experimentation with peanuts that has improved our peanut butter. I am always willing to sacrifice my taste buds in the interest of science. One crop that we have added to our smaller gardens is melons. We now grow cantaloupes, watermelons, and honeydew melons and they are a big hit with everyone. In fact we started growing them the last time we visited, and our teams of food experts have come up with some varieties of each that grow huge melons that are very tasty as well.

Of course we exchange information with all the other groups and settlements that we know of. In fact that's how we got some of the seeds to even get started on this project. In other parts of the country the growing season is shorter, and in some cases longer, so the seeds that they use to grow crops are specially developed to work in those climates and growing seasons. By mixing the characteristics of each individual group together, you can sometimes get a better crop. Sometimes it doesn't work quite like we thought it would, so that's why we keep trying whenever we find something that may work. We have also been trading goods with other groups as well.

Some of our family members developed a taste for sea food, either in the world we came from before this, or in visiting other groups. One such group is one that started in the panhandle portion of Florida. The group there has been very active in restoring boats and going out into the Gulf of Mexico. They have been to Cuba and to Puerto Rico, as well as many of the other islands in that area, and found that there are groups living on all of the islands. They also catch a lot of fish along with shell fish and mussels. We have made several trips down there to trade some of the seafood, mainly the shrimp, clams, and mussels that they are able to harvest from the sea, in return for some of our excess wheat, oats, and other crops that we have an excess of. We have taken some of our excess to other groups who didn't have anything to trade as well. Another activity that our young people have done is to go house to house in other cities to get any usable food out of the houses before it is no longer any good, and we have taken this food to groups in other states that perhaps the food didn't last as long as it has down south here.

That's the case with a group we found out about on the radio up in New York. They are settling in the lower portion of upstate New York, around the Pennsylvania border. Some of our people decided to leave our group and go back up there to help those people. They said they miss the snow and knowing what they do now, they will be able to enjoy it better. We have been able to go over to the coast and get soft shelled crabs for our seafood lovers. I have never really acquired a taste for seafood, but just about everyone in our house loves it except me. That's okay; I enjoy the trips over to the coast to get it. We owe being able to get the crabs to our scientific friends as usual. It seems that James, Jenna, Mike, and Morgan have been getting those soft shelled crabs since they were children. We had to get a couple of boats running and into the water as well, but after what we have accomplished, we feel that we can do anything and we did.

Our scientific people are always coming up with ways to make our lives, and the lives of those we share this existence with, better and even a little easier. They are also always looking for ways to take advantage of all the technology that we have around us, but just can't tap into it yet. They are working on being able to perhaps have all of the groups, at least in the United States, connected by phone lines. Sara asked them when we can expect to have cable TV connected to our groups. I was thinking that, but would never actually ask it. That will probably be a while, but one thing we did do is visit a couple of TV stations in major cities we were in, and found thousands of movies in their files along with the equipment to watch them. We now have a movie night usually on Saturday evening, where we all get together and pop some of the popcorn that we now grow, and watch movies together in the church building we found back when.

The journey has been long, but the love we all share has kept it from being any more difficult than it had to be. Actually it has been fun most of the way, and we look forward to whatever the future brings. If the scientific members of our family have their way, we will not wait for the future to bring us anything. We will go out and find out just what the boundaries are, and then change them as we go past them. No one can know for sure whether or not our new society will ever be like the one that almost destroyed itself. We all agree that instead of concentrating on ways to destroy each other, just in case we have to, we will continue to work on solutions that will allow us to live in peace as one big family, no matter where we are from or the color of our skin. I still have my lucky Indian head nickel, so how can we fail. It's been great visiting with you. I hope to see you again soon, but right now I hear a couple of little ladies that are pretty sure it's time for their daddy to pay some attention to them. May the good Lord bless you as he has all of us. If you hear of anyone looking for a place to settle, please send them to us, they as well as you will always be welcome.

Other Books by Ed & Eunice Vought

2nd Earth
Shortfall

When you fall asleep on the subway you can wake up to some out of this world experiences.

When we get to the surface it is not dark so now we are totally confused. We couldn't have slept all night and most of the day on that train. The crowds during the morning rush would definitely have woken us up. While we are looking around for Tim to recognize where we may be we hear what sounds like someone screaming for help. It sounds like it is coming from a couple of blocks over so we head in that direction. By the way there are cars all over the place but no people on the street. This is starting to get kind of spooky. When we turn the corner we see three young men running. They are being followed by a young lady who is apparently the one yelling for help because following her are four other young men who look like fugitives from a punk rock concert. I don't stop to analyze the situation because the punks are gaining steadily on the young lady who is yelling at the guys running in front of her.

When Jon and Tim boarded the subway to visit Tim's family they had no idea what kind of life changing adventure they were going on. They will need all the training that they have had as Navy SEALs to survive in a world that is familiar yet totally different.

2nd Earth
Adversary

When Jon, Tim, and some of the others go for a boating excursion they run into a situation they were not expecting.

We pretty much run out of stories to tell, so we all kind of sit around with our thoughts. We are all glad that we brought along jackets as well as rain gear, in case we ran into a squall of some kind. The fog is cold and very damp, but none of us want to go below deck, even if we are uncomfortable. I look at my watch and even that has quit working. Tim is looking at his, then he looks at me and says it can't be. LT starts to say that this is what the fog was like that night he and Kathy came into our world, but stops when he realizes what Tim and I were thinking. All of us came into this world in some kind of dense fog. I think I am speaking for all of us in this boat when I say a prayer to Heavenly Father, praying that he is not sending us back where we came from.

When the guys boarded the boat to explore the coastline they only expected to be gone for a day. When the fog rolls in they are not sure if they will even still be in the world they now love.

Best Friends: The Beginning (Published 2009)

Sometimes being in the wrong place at the right time can be a good thing.

Oh well, I will go in. I close my eyes as I get into the girls locker room though, I can live with bruises, I'm not sure I could explain a black eye to my mom's satisfaction. I am ready to call out when from inside I hear a voice that is plainly angry and plainly Mindy. I know that voice well, but now I hear boys' voices laughing. I shouldn't be hearing that in here. I follow the sound and wind up just outside the girls shower room. This is not good, what in the heck is going on? I hear Kathy's contemptuous voice.

"You will never get away with it and when Ed catches you, you'll be very sorry."

I hear a boy's voice answer.

"Well, he will never find out will he? Because if you tell anyone the next one we get will be your aunt or maybe your mom." Then he laughs a very evil laugh. I know that voice, I pinned him tonight. Now I am mad but I want to make sure I get as much information as I can before I go in to break this up.

Join Eddie, Mindy, Kathy, Ramona and Amy as they forge a friendship and share life's adventures together. This first book in the Best Friends series introduces you to Eddie Marlow and his ever increasing group of friends as they experience growing up in a world where true friendship is a very scarce commodity.

Best Friends 2: First Summer (Published 2010)

Sometimes when you love someone you may be asked to do things that make you uncomfortable.

I don't like the way Mindy is looking at me. She leans close and whispers in my ear.

"Do you want to sing a song with me? *Pleeeeeease?*"

"I don't know how to sing."

"What about that song you like that your dad plays sometimes, you know that Marie Osmond and Dan Seals song?"

"I don't know. How does that thing work anyway?"

"They show you the words to the song on a screen and you sing to the music."

Before I know what is happening she is out of her chair dragging me up to the stage. It's a good thing she knows how this thing works, wait a minute scratch that, no it's not. Anyway the music starts playing and I see the words coming up on the screen but I can't make any sound come out of my mouth.

Join Eddie, Mindy, Kathy and the gang as they encounter uncharted area's in their relationship and in life.

Best Friends 3: Sophomore Year (Fall 2010)

Best Friends 4: Sophomore Year (Fall 2010)

Sometimes being in love is a good way to expand our horizons and do things that we wouldn't normally do.

"Eddie, you love me don't you?"

"You know I do. What do you want me to do this time?" Now I know I am in trouble.

"It's nothing really, did you hear about the play the sophomore class is putting on in the spring?"

"Yes, each class is putting one on." I am sensing impending doom.

"This year the class sponsors got together and decided to do something different. Instead of doing traditional, well known plays they decided to allow each class to choose a theme and let them write their own play and put it on."

We are going in a circle so that everyone gets an opportunity to participate. It seems every time I think of something someone else has the same idea. Finally I have an idea that I think might be worth something and nobody else said it first.

"Maybe we could do something with a patriotic theme, everyone here is talented, except perhaps me, with either musical instruments, singing or dancing. I know a lot of you have been hoping our play would be a musical so you can show those talents off. What if we did something like a USO show, we could pretend we are holding auditions for acts to visit our troops and the people auditioning would do it for our audience. The grand finale could maybe be a song everyone knows and could include the audience." Everyone is looking at me like I just grew a second head. "Or not, sorry it was just a thought."

Eddie, Mindy and the rest of their ever expanding group of friends are now sophomores. Their experiences and challenges grow right along with them. Join them as they continue to learn about themselves and the world we live in.

Best Friends 5: A Time of Maturing (Coming soon)

When Mindy's mom asked Eddie to spend the night there was no way any of them could imagine how much and how quickly their lives could change.

Somewhere around midnight I must have dozed off but now I am completely awake. Did I hear something or is my imagination playing tricks on me? I have stayed here enough to know the night sounds the house makes, every house is different. There it is again, it sounds like someone at the back door. Not knocking, working the doorknob or something like that.

I get up and grab an aluminum baseball bat that is in the family room for some reason, I'm glad it is. I walk as quietly as I can into the kitchen staying close to the wall so I won't be highlighted by the light in the family room. Every sense in my body is alive and I have a very sick feeling in the pit of my stomach. What if someone breaks in and gets past me? I'm still just a teenager, and these may be men, mean vicious men. The mind has a tendency to over react at times like this.

I am almost right by the door now, there is definitely someone or more than one someone's outside that door, I can hear voices. I definitely hear one tell the other.

"The women are home, I saw them this morning, the old man isn't, his old lady says he's in Arizona." These guys are some nasty customers, they are not just interested in stealing, they want Mindy and her mom. If I have anything to say about it they will have to take them over my dead body. That sounds a bit dramatic but that's the way I feel.

In the next few seconds all heck breaks loose, I am getting better I don't even swear in times of stress now. They must have used a pry bar because the door breaks inward and the first guy is through into the kitchen in a step or two. He is followed by another one but I am not sure if there are more or not, can't worry about that now.

Join Eddie, Mindy and the rest of their ever expanding group of friends in their most challenging experiences and adventures yet.

They Call Me Nuisance (Published 2010)

With a name like Nuisance life can be challenging to say the least.

Dakota horse stops dead in front of the general store, there's a wagon out front and he stops right next to it. I am sitting here looking stupid, well stupider than usual. A few minutes after we stop here a very pretty young lady comes out of the store yelling at someone inside. She is dressed in a man's clothing which is strange for the west these days. She is talking like a man too, this lady can cuss with the best of them. She looks around and sees me staring at her. I've never seen a woman as pretty as her.

"What are you looking at? Maybe the question should be what are you?"

Now I'm embarrassed, I'm trying to get that horse to move but he ain't going nowhere.

When Nuisance, Dakota horse and the dog ambled into town they had no idea what they were getting into. Not that it would have changed anything, they are simply not the type to allow anyone to ride roughshod over a lady. Join them as they help Miss Emily and prove to the bad guys that he is only a nuisance to them.

Made in the USA
Monee, IL
08 April 2021